BLOOD & SCRIPTURE

Book One of The Hood & The Halo Trilogy

Lampert X Griffin Urban Universe

This is a work of fiction.

ISBN: 978-1-969709-27-2

First Edition

For everyone who prayed in the dark

and found their own light.

CHAPTER ONE

RUNES IN THE RUM

Guttersea don't sleep. It just closes one eye and watches you with the other.

Tonight the docks breathe their usual stink—brine, rotted fish, ether-smoke curling off the siphon dens. Rain slicks the cobblestones. Somewhere down the block a woman screams, then stops. Nobody runs to check. You don't run toward screams in Guttersea. You run from them, or you mind your business and thank whatever god still takes prayers from sinners.

I pour a splash of gutter shine into my tea—three fingers of ether-cut rum that burns blue going down. Call it medicine. You grow up down here, you learn that blessings need something stronger than faith to make them stick.

Mama used to pray for me every night before the coughing took her. Said God had plans. Said I was meant for something. Mama believed a lot of things that didn't save her.

"Clock says move."

Sable leans in the doorframe, arms crossed. Her dress is the color of a fresh bruise. Silver rings climb her left ear. She smells like clove smoke.

She hooks one finger under my chin, tilts my face toward the lamplight. Studies me.

"You look like hell, prophet."

"Hell ain't got nothing on Guttersea."

Her eyes narrow. Track the lines at the corners of my eyes, the gray threading through my temples that wasn't there six months ago. I'm twenty-three. I look thirty-five on a good day. The Relic Tongue takes payment in years, and I've been spending like a man who don't expect to see old age anyway.

Her thumb grazes my jaw. And then—so quick I almost miss it— her other hand twitches toward her collarbone. Toward the silver scars that web across her skin like lightning frozen mid-strike. The binding marks from Velvet House.

She catches herself. Drops her hand. But I saw it. The scars were moving. Crawling toward me like roots seeking water.

"Our man's at the Bone Dice up-alley." Her voice is steady, but her pulse isn't. I can see it jumping in her throat. "You got the shard money or just that prophet grin?"

I show her the roll. Tight. Stained with something that might be garden-sap, might be old blood. In this city, same thing.

"We pay clean," I say. "We get the chip. We go home."

"Cute." She almost smiles. Almost. "Let's go make some bad decisions."

• • •

The Silk Crypt pounds beneath us—Winter's temple-club. Bass thumps through the floorboards like a heartbeat too big for one chest. Through the gaps in the wood I see bodies moving slow, arms raised, mouths open. More worship than dancing. Priestesses in silver masks pour moon-milk into crystal skulls.

We cross the balcony, push through the service door, step into the alley. Rain hits my neck, slides down my spine. Cold. Dirty. The gutters are running brown.

The Bone Dice ain't much—plank walls, witch-chalk on the floor, a table scarred with numbers and what they call a sin tax. Old men throw bones in the corner, reading futures they don't want to hear. Young bloods post up along the walls, knives on their hips.

I keep my hood up. My rune itches beneath the skin at my wrist—that spider-smear of black ink that showed up the night my brother died. It's been quiet for months. Tonight it feels awake. Hungry.

I don't like when it wakes up.

The dealer's a slick piece of work named Thrix—thin face, oil-shine hair, smile like a floorboard about to give under your weight. He sits behind the scarred table with his fingers laced, every ring on his hands worth more than my whole block pays in rent.

"Rico Marrow." He tastes my street name like wine he ain't sure about. "Word says you got a hand in sermons and sin."

"Word says a lot of things. Most of it's wrong."

I lay the roll on the table between us.

"We said ten slivers and a bottle. That's ten slivers and a bottle. We square?"

Thrix weighs the roll without counting it. His eyes flick past my shoulder.

Sable's already clocked it—I can tell by how her weight shifts. She's mapped three exits, two gunhands, and one big problem: Pale Wardens hovering outside the front door. I catch their white masks through the gap in the shutters. Holy cops. Church enforcers. Their blades sing when they breathe—little hymns of judgment that make your bones want to kneel even when your mind says run.

"Shard's hot." Thrix's voice drops. "Bronze Syndicate's been sniffing around. Night Parliament sent feelers. Wardens want it melted into rosary nails so nobody can use it."

He opens his palm. Shows me nothing. Dealer talk for 'I'm about to raise the price.'

"And you? What do you want?"

"I want a future where my children can afford to bury me somewhere dry."

Sable leans in. Her voice goes quiet. With her, quiet is worse than loud.

"Take the money, eel. Before I decide your children need practice grieving early."

The door splinters inward.

• • •

Three Wardens pour through. White masks. Singing steel. The first one's already swinging for Thrix—execution stroke, no hesitation. They're not here to arrest.

Moe materializes from shadows I didn't know he was in. His blade catches the Warden's mid-swing, turns it aside. Metal screams. The whole room freezes. Moe's a mountain that learned to move—ex-Warden himself, they say, before something changed his mind about which side of the mask he wanted to be on.

"Out," he says. One word. That's Moe.

Sable's already moving, thin wire unspooling from her sleeve. She takes the second Warden low, across the tendons. He drops, hymns going sharp with pain.

The third one comes for me.

The rune at my wrist blazes hot. Not warning—recognition. Power surges up my arm, into my chest, behind my eyes. My mouth opens before I decide to speak.

The verse comes out guttural. Old. Shaped for a throat that ain't quite human:

"You who wear the mask of mercy—

Feel the weight of all you've taken—

Every prayer unanswered, every faith forsaken—"

The Warden's blade freezes mid-arc. His eyes behind the mask go wide. The hymns stuttering from his steel turn to whispers, then screams, then silence. He drops. Not dead—worse. He's feeling every sin the Church committed in his name, all at once.

I fall to my knees. The verse echoes in my skull like a bell that won't stop ringing.

Something warm slides down my upper lip. I touch it. Fingers come back red.

Moe catches my arm before I hit the floor.

"You're graying faster, kid."

I don't answer. Don't need to. Every time I speak the Tongue, it takes a little more. Months off the back end. Years, maybe, for the big verses. Mama always said I'd burn bright and burn quick.

Didn't know she meant it literal.

• • •

The Silk Crypt swallows us back. Heat and hunger and candle-smoke thick as secrets. Winter's office is up three flights, behind a door that looks like wood but feels like something else when you touch it.

She waits inside with her feet up on a desk older than Parliament, knife carving little stars into the mahogany. Her tattoos coil in the candlelight. Silver ink. Living ink. Wards and warnings etched into skin the color of good coffee.

She doesn't stand. Doesn't smile.

8

"You look like you crawled out a grave and stopped halfway. My shard. Now."

I set the pouch on her desk. Don't throw it. Don't slide it. You don't disrespect something that old, that powerful.

The room shifts. That weight again—the sense of everything pausing to pay attention.

Winter picks up the pouch with two fingers wrapped in fresh ward-ink—the black lines tightening around her skin, then loosening, like they're breathing—and peels back the velvet.

The shard inside is maybe three inches long. Jagged. Black as a hole in the world, but shot through with veins of gold that pulse in a rhythm too slow to be heartbeat, too steady to be random.

Everything in the room bows its head a fraction. The candles. The shadows. The smoke.

"This one's got a name." Winter whispers it, almost reverent. "Hunger."

She holds it up to the candlelight. The gold veins pulse faster.

"The Crown kept its sins separate. Like spices in a saint's kitchen. Each one a different flavor of damnation."

Sable unscrews a vial from her belt, taps out a line of angel salt on Winter's desk, and kisses it off the wood without breaking eye contact with me. Her pupils go wide.

Her hand drifts to her collarbone again. The scars there are faintly luminous—silver threads glowing like they're reflecting something that ain't in the room. She doesn't seem to notice.

"Fitting." She licks powder off her lip. "Ashy's always hungry. For money. For mercy. For me."

I pour rum and shine into the same cup until the cup forgets its purpose. Drink it without tasting.

"What's the play?"

Winter sets the shard on a cloth that curls away from it like it's afraid.

"Bronze Syndicate wants my docks. Wardens want my head on a pike. Parliament wants me bent over and begging. So we flip the table. We feed this to a spell. Make the whole city crave something new. Something only we supply."

Moe speaks from the corner. "You want to hook an entire district."

"They're already hooked. I just want better margins."

The door creaks open without anyone touching it.

A boy stumbles in. No—not a boy. A thing that used to be a boy. Glass eyes that don't blink. Skin the color of old paper. His breath smells like church candles and the dirt they bury you in when nobody can afford better.

Courier. Dead twice and hired once. The Parliament uses them for messages they don't want traced.

He drops a wax-sealed letter on Winter's desk, opens his mouth like he wants to say something, and collapses into powder that smells like apologies.

My rune burns like someone touched it with a live wire.

Winter breaks the seal. Her expression locks down.

"Night Parliament. They're calling an Accord. Every crew at the Glassbone Gardens, midnight. 'Bring your divines, bring your liars, bring the leader who bleeds the least.'"

"Trap," Sable says.

"Stage," Moe counters.

"Prophecy."

That last word comes from somewhere else. Somewhere inside me that I don't remember opening.

They all look at me. I look down at my wrist.

The rune—that spider-smear that's been quiet for months—is different now. The black lines have shifted. Spread. New shapes forming in the ink like a chrysalis remembering it's supposed to become something else.

Teeth of light. Little crown points. A halo designed for someone the angels gave up on.

My dead brother's voice whispers in my ear, clear as the day I killed him:

Five shards for hunger, four for the throne,

Three for the saint who sins alone,

Two for the traitor's pretty lie,

One for the boy who cannot die.

Winter's knife stops carving. Her eyes fix on my arm.

"How long?"

"Since the dock. It's louder now."

My cup is empty. I don't remember drinking it.

Sable's hand is on my wrist before mine is. Her fingers are warm.

"It's choosing you, Ash."

I laugh, but it comes out wrong. Too sharp. Too wet.

"Everything chooses me when it needs dying."

The shard on Winter's desk hums back at my skin. A call and response. A recognition.

Like it knows my mama's name. Like it remembers what she used to pray for.

Winter pockets the pouch.

"We attend the Accord. We take the room. We leave with more than we brought."

"And if the Wardens crash the garden?" Moe asks.

"Then we plant them."

• • •

The music climbs back up from below. The walls sweat with the heat of bodies and belief. Somewhere downstairs, priestesses are lifting cups to a ceiling pretending to be sky, praying to something that probably isn't listening but might be watching anyway.

Sable leans into me.

"You gonna drink, chosen?"

"I been drinking."

"Then drink me later."

She steps away before I can answer. That's Sable—only asks questions she already knows the answer to.

Winter stands, brushing ash from her coat.

"Two squads and a quiet one. Ash, you're my quiet. You speak when the room needs a miracle or a threat."

"Those sound the same."

"In this city, they are."

We move out into the night. Rain's eased to a shine on the cobbles. The ward drums from the Ivory Spires toll midnight closer.

My rune thrums beneath the skin. A bass note under everything.

12

I ain't your boy, I tell the mark under my skin.

But it laughs with my dead brother's voice. Laughs like patience. Like inevitability. Like a promise nobody remembers making that everybody's going to have to keep.

The city opens its mouth.

We walk inside.

CHAPTER TWO

THE ACCORD OF GLASSBONE GARDENS

The river runs black tonight. Thick enough to chew. Rain clings to us, won't let go.

Our skiff cuts through the murk slow, oars dipping in and out of water that glows faint ether-green in patches—runoff from the refineries. Winter sits at the bow in a white fur. She hasn't said ten words since we left the Crypt. Doesn't have to.

Moe rows without looking like he's rowing. His shoulders roll smooth, mechanical—the kind of motion you develop when you've been moving weight your whole life. Weight of oars. Weight of bodies. Weight of things you don't talk about at dinner.

Sable sits across from me, watching our wake. Her eyes track patterns only she can see. I want to ask what she's thinking, but with Sable, that's like asking a knife what it dreams about.

The Gardens rise out of the far bank like something that shouldn't exist in the same world as Guttersea. Glass towers grafted onto marble ribs. Balconies stacked like altar steps. Bridges stitched from crystal veins, catching moonlight.

I feel poor just looking at it.

The rune under my wrist warms. Not burning—not yet. Just warming.

Winter speaks without turning around. "Hands visible. Tongue invisible. Whatever happens inside, we don't start fires we can't finish."

"And if they start one?" Sable asks.

"Then we burn brighter."

Moe grunts.

"That thing getting loud again?" Sable nods at my wrist.

"It's been running me for months. I just learned to jog with it."

"That's not comforting."

"Wasn't meant to be."

· · ·

We dock under a ribbed arch where the river laps against stone. Wardens line the entrance like statues carved from bone and sermon. White masks beading with rain. Blades sheathed but singing anyway— you can hear them humming hymns of judgment even when they're sleeping.

The lead Warden steps forward. His voice comes out washed clean of accent, of warmth.

"The Accord welcomes the Dock Queen. Weapons to be peace-bound at the gate."

Moe unbuckles Mercyless slow. The blade hums protest as it leaves his hip. He hands it to a Warden who lifts it like it weighs nothing—which is a lie that sword tells everyone who ain't Moe.

Sable produces knives from places I didn't know she had places. Two from her thighs. One from her boot. A hairpin that could stitch a throat shut. A ring with a blade hidden in the setting. She sets them all on the collection tray with casual grace.

She's still got three more hidden somewhere nobody's checking.

Winter offers her wrists to a priestess in silver veils. The priestess spirals ward-ink across her skin—black lines that tighten, then loosen, like they're learning to breathe. Binding her magic. Collaring her power.

Winter doesn't flinch. Queens don't flinch where servants can see.

The priestess comes for me last. Her veil hides everything but her eyes, and those eyes are counting my sins before I can confess them. I show her my palms. Nothing to hide.

She touches my right wrist—And the rune kicks like a mule that just saw a snake. Her fingers jerk back. The veil trembles. Those counting eyes go wide.

"That is not authorized."

"Neither am I. We still going in?"

She looks to Winter. Winter gives her that soft-teacher smile—the one that promises expulsion for three generations if you don't do what she wants.

The priestess steps aside.

• • •

Inside the first garden, the air changes. Smells like rain and expensive perfume and old iron that learned to hide its rust. Orchids drip from chandeliers in cascades of purple and white. Statues of saints stand in shallow pools, bleeding color into the water—some enchantment that makes them weep dye instead of tears.

Nobles float paper prayers shaped like tiny crowns across the pools. The water eats them one by one.

This place runs on symbolism. Everything means something. Everything costs something else.

Sable leans close, breath warm on my ear, words cold. "Eyes up. Every reflection in this place got a blade on layaway."

Moe scans the balconies the way he always does.

Music drifts through the garden. Harp notes arranged like money, each one placed precisely where it'll do the most work. Drums soft as a heartbeat under a velvet pillow.

We pass under a second arch where angels are sealed into the glass itself. Wings spread wide. Faces smooth as forgiveness. They glow when you walk beneath them. Blue-white at first. Then gold. Then something I don't have a name for—a color that feels like being judged and found wanting.

The rune at my wrist hums the same frequency.

• • •

The Accord chamber is a circle with no corners to hide in. No shadows to slip into. No walls to put your back against. Just you and everyone who wants something from you.

Seven thrones stand on a raised platform. A chair carved from crystal so dark it eats its own reflection. A seat grown from bone-white branches that might still be alive. One made entirely of mirrors facing inward, so whoever sits there has to look at themselves forever.

The Night Parliament waits.

Speaker Vail in a coat that looks woven from melted starlight. Their face is beautiful the way a knife is beautiful—designed for one purpose and very good at it.

Cardinal Red robed to the floor in crimson so deep it's almost black, eyelids thread-sewn shut with blessed silk. Mouth thin as a paper cut. Somehow still watching everything despite having no eyes to watch with.

The Glass Duke with skin like a living window—you can see his organs working inside him, heart beating steady, lungs expanding slow. Everything on display like he's proud of what he's made of.

The others stay half-shadowed by design.

Vail lifts both hands. "The Accord welcomes our honored guests."

Winter dips her head a fraction of an inch. No more. "Honors are expensive. Spend them careful."

"Peace requires cooperation."

"Peace," I mutter, low. "Always sounds like a truce somebody pre-loaded with excuses."

Sable's shoulder brushes mine. Warning.

They seat us at a crescent table below the thrones. Each place has a cup that pulses with slow light—ether steeped in something floral, something sweet, something that whispers *drink me* while your survival instincts scream *don't*.

I don't touch mine.

Wardens ring the chamber, blades kissing their scabbards every time someone breathes wrong. Which, in this company, is everyone.

Cardinal Red unrolls a scroll that's definitely not inked in anything you'd find at a stationer's. The writing moves. Shifts. Rearranges itself like it's deciding what to say based on who's reading.

"The Accord acknowledges the escalation in ether commerce. The sacrilege of unsanctioned shard distribution. The rise of false saints and gutter miracles."

False saints. That one lands close.

"Henceforth, the Crown requires tithe: ten percent of purity, ten percent of soul. All who trade shall wear seals. All who refuse shall be made obedient."

18

Winter's face is the still pond nobles hope to drown in without messing their hair. Perfectly calm. Perfectly dangerous.

"Obedience don't scale across my docks, Cardinal. Fishermen drown in rules before they drown in storms."

"The Crown is not a storm. The Crown is law."

"Law gotta feed people before it feeds itself."

I didn't mean to say it. The words just walked out like they were tired of waiting for permission. The rune at my wrist flared warm, and suddenly my mouth was moving without my brain's approval.

The whole room shifts. Vail's smile cracks. Just a little. Just enough.

"And this is the prophet from the Rust Warrens. They say you pray in rhyme. Say you make miracles with your mouth and your blood." Vail's gaze settles on me. "Say a blessing now, perhaps. For humility."

Moe's knee hits mine under the table.

Sable's hand goes lazy over her cup.

Winter doesn't look at me.

I pick up my cup. Take a sip of the glowing ether-drink just to have something to do with my hands. It tastes like roses, lightning, and the thing I told myself I'd quit.

"Blessings cost. Got change for anyone got thanks. But we ain't blessing no tithe that robs the living to furnish dead men's closets."

A ripple runs through the chamber.

Vail's smile cracks wide enough to show teeth. "The Dock Queen's man is bold."

"My men speak because I let them." Winter's voice cuts clean. "My crews eat because we work, not because we pray. If Parliament wants ten percent of my soul, it gotta find where I keep it first."

Laughter ripples around the circle—honest and mean.

Then the door explodes inward.

• • •

Three Wardens pour through. White masks. Singing steel. The first one's already swinging for the Glass Duke—execution stroke, no hesitation.

Parliament didn't call this hit. Somebody else did.

Chaos erupts.

Sable's already moving. She doesn't run—she glides. Two shots crack the ceiling. Plaster rains down. She didn't surrender all her weapons. Of course she didn't.

A guard trying to circle us takes one clean shot through the knee. He drops. She's already past him, grabbing his blade on the way.

Vail raises a hand like he can bless this chaos back into order. He can't.

"We're leaving." Winter pulls the fur from her shoulders and folds it over the back of her chair like she just finished dinner at a restaurant that disappointed her. "Anybody disagree, step up and get famous."

Two Wardens do.

One lunges toward me.

I drop. Palm slapping the glass floor. The verse comes up from somewhere deeper than thought:

"Street saints lean in, hold air like a grip,

freeze blade and breath, let courage slip—

Crown hear my call, Crown grant my right,

stop this second, hold the fight."

The words hit and the world hiccups.

The Warden's swing freezes mid-arc. Raindrops pause in the air like beads on invisible strings. The harp's note stretches into a long, thin shriek that goes nowhere.

For exactly two heartbeats, everything's a painting. Everything except us.

My skull feels like somebody stuck a fork in a socket. The rune jerks, sending black fireworks up my arm.

Sable doesn't waste the seconds. She slides past the frozen Warden, palm on his mask, shoves him just enough that when time kicks back into gear his own momentum throws him into another man.

Moe uses the gifted seconds to close distance with a third guard. The stolen sword sings off glass and bone.

The chamber erupts. Parliament scribes scramble for exits. Nobles press back, robes bunching. Cardinal Red lifts his stitched eyelids toward the ceiling, chanting something old and sharp that makes the air taste like copper.

"Stand down!" Vail's voice tries to cut through. "They want a spectacle—don't give it."

Too late. We already took it.

Winter flicks her wrist. Two of her runners—kids I thought were servers—peel from the side doors. One tosses Sable a fresh mag. The other slams a smoke vial at the floor.

Violet fog blooms thick as perfume.

"Move."

We move.

We push through swirling fog, Wardens coughing behind us, glass singing underfoot as somebody's spell misfires against the ceiling.

We hit the side archway Winter clocked when we first walked in—because Winter always clocks the exits. Two more Wardens try to block it. Moe rams the first with his shoulder. Blade rises under the second's guard, punching clean through plated gut.

We spill into a corridor lined with orchids the size of dinner plates. The flowers turn toward us as we pass. Colors deepening. Mouths opening.

"Don't brush 'em," Sable snaps. "They drink more than water."

A guard stumbles after us, half-blind from the smoke. He swings wild. His blade kisses my bicep—heat blooms, wet follows.

An orchid leans in like it's been waiting for exactly this. My blood hits its petals and the damn thing shivers. Makes a soft, satisfied sound.

"Nasty ass plants."

Moe finishes the guard with bored efficiency.

We crash through a service door into an alley that smells like rain and old fear. The chaos of the Accord fades behind us.

Sable checks my arm. Her fingers are warm against the cut, professional and quick.

"You'll live."

"For how long?"

"Longer than tonight if you stop asking stupid questions."

Winter stands at the alley's edge, looking back at the Gardens—all that glass and beauty and corruption glittering in the rain.

"Ash. What you did in there. The time-freeze."

22

I know what she's asking. I don't have an answer.

"I don't know."

"That's what scares me."

The rune at my wrist pulses once. Warm. Full. Growing.

And somewhere inside my skull, my dead brother's voice laughs at a joke only he understands.

CHAPTER THREE

DEALS CUT IN VELVET

The city ain't quiet tonight. You can feel unrest humming under the pavement. After the Accord, after the Gardens, after we painted their pretty glass floors with blood that wasn't supposed to spill—the whole damn city feels like a held breath waiting to become a scream.

We cut through back alleys, Moe at rear guard, Sable navigating, Winter leading without seeming to lead. The rain finally stopped an hour ago, but the wet stays—clinging to stone, to skin, to the kind of air that makes your lungs feel borrowed. My arm throbs where the Warden's blade kissed it. Sable's quick field wrap keeps the bleeding down, but the cut ain't the problem. The problem is the rune. It's louder now. Hungrier. Every time I blink, I see gold flash at the edges.

"Where we going?" I ask.

Winter doesn't look back. "Somewhere Parliament won't think to look."

"The Velvet Quarter."

Sable's voice is flat. Professional. But something underneath cracks at the edges.

"We're going to the Velvet Quarter."

• • •

The Velvet Quarter lives like a rumor between districts—tucked between Ivory Spire money and Guttersea hunger, belonging fully to neither. Lanterns hang in shapes that mean things. Moons for discretion. Lips for pleasure. Crowns for power plays disguised as pillow talk.

We cut through side streets where the cobbles are cleaner than any in the Warrens, where the air smells like incense trying to cover sin and only half succeeding. Sable walks a step ahead now. Not leading—just knowing. This is familiar territory.

Too familiar.

She rolls her shoulders once—a small motion, like something itches beneath her skin. Her hand rises toward her collarbone, hovers over the silver scars hidden under her collar, then drops.

I notice. The deeper we go into the Velvet Quarter, the more Sable changes.

It's subtle at first. The way her shoulders drop. The way her steps become quieter, more controlled. The way she starts tracking every shadow, every doorway, every person who might be watching.

I've seen her work before—seen her move through Winter's territory with the confidence of someone who knows she belongs. This is different. This is a woman returning to a place that shaped her into something she doesn't want to be.

A group of Velvet attendants passes us, all silk and calculated smiles. One of them—a young man with silver paint on his eyelids—sees Sable and stops. His smile falters.

"Little shadow." The words come out like he's greeting a ghost. "You're back."

"Passing through."

"Does the Bishop know?"

"The Bishop knows everything." Sable keeps walking. "That's the problem."

The attendant watches us go. I catch his expression before we turn the corner—not hatred, not fear. Something closer to pity.

"Friend of yours?" I ask.

"We trained together." Her voice is flat. "Twelve years ago. He specialized in poison. I specialized in other things."

"What other things?"

She doesn't answer. Doesn't have to. The scars at her collarbone pulse faintly—silver light I'm learning to recognize as her binding marks responding to stress.

We pass a doorway hung with red silk. A woman's laugh floats out, musical and practiced. A man's voice answers, low and urgent. Business being conducted in the oldest currency.

"This is where they train you?" I ask. "The Velvet House?"

"This is where they break you." Sable's hand brushes the hidden knife at her hip. Habit. Comfort. "The training comes after. Once you understand that you belong to someone else and there's no way out."

Moe rumbles something behind us, too low to hear. Sable glances back at him, and something passes between them—one survivor recognizing another.

"Winter bought you out of here," I say. It's a guess. But it feels right.

"Winter bought my contract. There's a difference." Sable's jaw tightens. "The Velvet House doesn't sell people. It loans them. The original binding stays. The debts accumulate. Eventually, everyone comes back."

"But you didn't."

"I didn't have a choice. Winter needed an asset, and Symeon needed Winter's protection from Parliament. So they made a deal." She touches the sigil at her wrist—the golden mark that binds her to Winter now. "I'm still property. Just different property."

The words hit harder than they should. I think about the rune on my arm. The power I didn't ask for, the burden I can't escape. We're both carrying chains we didn't choose.

"It doesn't have to be that way."

"Yes, it does." Sable looks at me—really looks, for the first time since we entered the Quarter. Her eyes are darker than I've ever seen them. "That's what you don't understand yet, Ash. Power always has a source. Magic always has a cost. The only question is who pays."

"And who paid for you?"

"Everyone I ever loved." She turns away. "Come on. We're almost there."

"You been here before." It's not a question.

Winter answers, low enough only I hear. "Sable belongs to that world. Let her swim in it or claw out of it. Either way, I'll know where she stands by dawn."

"That's cold."

"That's business."

Sable leads us to a building with no sign out front. Just a door of dark wood banded in gold, and a curtain of beads carved like tiny eyes.

"House of the Second Veil," she says. "Speak soft in here. They got long memories and sharp ears."

She knocks a pattern I can't follow. The door opens without hands.

• • •

Warmth hits first. Then music—not the harp-money of the Gardens, but lutes and soft horns, a rhythm designed to slow your breathing, loosen your fists. The interior is all plush carpets and low couches, shadows draped in more shadows. Beautiful folk in beautiful clothes having beautiful conversations that probably cost someone their soul.

Velvet attendants move through the room like silk given purpose. Half-masks hide their faces.

None of them look surprised to see Winter.

A figure detaches from a column near the entrance. Tall, wrapped in a robe blacker than arguments, face hidden behind a mask shaped like a fox's grin. The mouth is cut out, revealing lips painted dark as dried blood.

"Dock Queen." The voice is rich as poured syrup. "You bring thunder to our doorstep."

"Bishop Symeon." Winter inclines her head—the smallest gesture of respect she can get away with. "I bring business. Thunder just follows me around."

"We'll need a private room. And a fast pour."

"For you, always."

Symeon's eyes slide across our group—over me, over Moe, finally settling on Sable. They linger there. Too long.

"Little shadow. Didn't expect you back so soon."

My stomach drops. Sable doesn't bow. Doesn't smile. Doesn't blink.

"Job ain't finished."

"Isn't it?" Symeon's head tilts like a curious predator.

"We'll see."

A Velvet attendant materializes at Moe's elbow, murmuring something about a side chamber with bandages. Moe looks at Winter. She nods. He lets himself be led away, glancing back with a look that says *don't get murdered without me.*

The rest of us follow Symeon up a curling staircase. Hidden rooms press close on either side. Voices bleed through the walls—low, breathy.

Symeon gestures us into a balcony room draped in burgundy and shadow. One wall is all lattice, looking down over the main floor like a confessional window—see everything, be seen by nothing.

"Drink. Speak."

Winter pours herself a glass but doesn't sit.

"Parliament just tried to collar my docks in front of angels. That ain't how you invite someone to choir practice."

Symeon laughs—soft, genuine, unsettling. "They overstep often. It's a habit we plan to cure."

"Then we have common ground. The city's about to go to war over the Crown. Velvet can stay under the table and eat scraps. Or you can get a seat."

Symeon tilts the fox mask.

"Brave. Or foolish."

"Same thing, first round," I mutter.

Symeon's gaze slides to me. Under the mask, I can feel them cataloging everything.

"And the prophet. We've heard your name sung in the siphon dens. They say you bend verse like other men bend truth."

"They sing loud when they high. Don't mean they on key."

"Perhaps."

29

Symeon passes a hand near my wrist—not touching, but close enough that the rune stirs.

"The Crown has eyes on you, little sermon. Eyes, and maybe teeth."

I pull my arm back. "I ain't on the market."

"Everyone is. Even those who swear they paid their last debt."

• • •

Winter negotiates like she fights—patient, precise, always three moves ahead. Symeon matches her step for step, parry for parry. They dance around terms like lovers who hate each other. I tune most of it out. Politics ain't my language.

Sable sits beside me on the couch, close but not touching. Her scars are hidden, but I can feel them anyway—like heat from a fire that's not supposed to be lit.

"You okay?"

She doesn't look at me. "Fine."

"That ain't what I asked."

"That's the answer you're getting."

Fair enough. We all got doors we don't open.

The rune at my wrist pulses—soft, steady, patient. Whatever's inside it is waiting for something. I just don't know what.

Winter and Symeon shake hands. Or close enough—Symeon extends two fingers, Winter touches them with her own. Some Velvet ritual I don't understand.

"We have terms," Winter announces. "Velvet stays neutral in public, supports us in shadow. In return, they get first cut of any Crown fragments we acquire."

"And Sable?" Symeon's lips curve beneath the mask. "Does she stay with us, or continue her... extended field work?"

Winter looks at Sable. Waiting.

Sable's jaw tightens. "I stay with the Dock Queen. Until the job's done."

"And after?"

"After is after."

Symeon laughs again. "Little shadow. Still trying to outrun what you are."

"We're done here."

Sable stands. Doesn't wait for permission. Walks toward the door like staying in this room one more second might kill her.

I follow. So does Winter.

Behind us, Symeon's voice floats through the curtains: "The Crown remembers, prophet. Even the parts it's forgotten."

The rune burns cold at my wrist. Cold like recognition. Cold like prophecy.

I don't look back.

• • •

We collect Moe from the side chamber. His head's wrapped in fresh bandages, his eyes sharper than before—whatever they gave him for the pain also seemed to clear something else.

"Trouble?" he asks.

"Always."

"Then let's move."

We cut back through the Velvet Quarter as dawn starts to pink the eastern sky. The lanterns are dimming. The beautiful people are stumbling home. The city's changing shifts—night workers giving way to day workers, sins giving way to survival.

Sable walks beside me now. Silent. Tense.

"Whatever happened back there—" I start.

"Don't."

"Sable—"

"I said don't." Her voice is sharp enough to cut. Then softer: "Please. Not now."

I let it go. Some doors only open from the inside.

We're halfway across the Merchant Bridge when Winter's runner catches up to us—a kid no older than twelve, breathing hard, eyes wide with the kind of fear you only see when the news is bad.

"The Warrens," he gasps. "Parliament's moving. Wardens everywhere. They're—"

He stops. Swallows.

"They're burning the Street of Prayers."

My street. My people. My home.

The rune at my wrist doesn't burn this time.

It screams.

I start running before my brain catches up to my feet. Behind me, I hear Winter curse, hear Moe's heavy footfalls, hear Sable calling my name. Doesn't matter. Nothing matters except getting there.

The Street of Prayers is where Mama taught me to pray. Where I spoke my first verse. Where the gutter monks first called me prophet.

If Parliament's burning it—If they're burning my people—The sun comes up red over the city. Red like warning. Red like blood. Red like the color my vision's turning at the edges.

I run faster.

CHAPTER FOUR

THE PRICE OF MIRACLES

The Street of Prayers ain't burning when we get there. Small mercies.

But the damage is done. Wardens came through like a storm with badges, tore up market stalls, dragged off anyone who looked like they might've said something prayerful without proper licensing. The gutter monks scattered. The street vendors are still picking up the pieces of their livelihoods.

An old woman sits in the rubble of her herb stall, crying without sound. A man holds his arm where it bends wrong. Children huddle in doorways, watching us with eyes that learned not to hope.

This is my neighborhood. These are my people.

And I wasn't here to protect them.

"Ash." Winter's voice cuts through. "We need to move. Standing still makes us targets."

She's right. I know she's right. But my feet won't listen.

Because there's a crowd gathered at the corner of Blessing Street and Third. And in the center of that crowd, someone's dying.

• • •

The boy is maybe twelve. Rust Warrens stamped on every bone—the way hunger writes itself in hunched shoulders and visible ribs. His chest is a mess of red. His breath rattles like broken glass.

Someone in the crowd mutters: "Warden raid up the block. Kid caught a blade trying to run."

Another voice: "Priest on the way?"

Bitter laughter. "Priests patch tithers, not nobodies."

The boy's mouth moves. No sound. Just the shape of *please* repeated over and over.

I see my brother's face overlaid on his. Same wide, terrified eyes. Same too-thin neck.

Moe glances at me. "Ash..."

"Don't." Winter's voice is soft razor.

Sable grabs my arm. Her grip trembles. She can feel what I'm about to do.

The crowd notices us. A woman whispers: "That's him. The one from the docks." Another: "Saint Ash."

The boy's fingers twitch. He grabs at empty air like he's reaching for a hand that ain't there.

I move before anybody can tell me not to.

• • •

I kneel in blood. It soaks my knees, crawls cold down my shins. The wound's deep, under his ribs, pulsing slow.

I ain't no healer. I'm a hustler with a curse and too many dead people already living rent-free in my head. But the rune at my wrist is burning, and if I walk away from this, it's gonna burn me from the inside out anyway.

"You from the Warrens?"

He nods. Barely.

"Got a name?"

"Dee." He breathes it more than says it.

I put my palm over the wound. Hot, sticky, smelling like iron and fear. I lean down close. So close we're sharing air.

And I let the verse come:

> *"Gutter gods, hear me, don't play dumb,*
>
> *take my years, not this boy's sum,*
>
> *stitch his breath, rewrite his fate,*
>
> *I'll pay the toll—just don't be late."*

The words drag something out of me like thread from a sweater. The rune goes nova. Pain spears up my arm, across my chest, behind my eyes.

I can smell my own skin cooking from the inside.

Light leaks from between my fingers. Not clean white church light—amber and smoky, full of dust motes. Light that's been living in the Warrens as long as the rest of us.

It pours into the boy's chest. His back arches. He gasps like someone yanked him up from underwater.

The wound knits under my hand. Flesh crawls back together. Leaves an ugly starburst scar where death almost won.

I feel something deep in me—years, days, I don't know which—get up, pack a bag, and walk out without saying goodbye.

When it's done, I'm hunched over him, sweat cold down my spine. The boy blinks up at me, chest rising and falling steady now.

"You okay?" I manage.

"I… yeah." Confusion becoming awe. "You an angel?"

"Hell no. I'm just late."

I try to stand. My legs vote against it. Moe's hands are there before I can fall, hauling me up. Sable presses a cloth to my forehead. It comes away damp with something gold and shimmering.

The crowd murmurs. "Saint Ash." "He healed him." "Miracle."

That word bounces around the room, gathers weight, comes back changed into something bigger than four syllables should hold.

Winter watches it all with that measuring look. No joy. No anger. Just math.

"What'd it cost you?" she asks, low enough only I hear.

I swallow. My heart feels slower. My bones feel older.

"Don't know yet. But the Crown took its cut."

She nods. Understanding. Worried. Hungry.

"You just made me richer and poorer at the same time."

"Welcome to the club."

• • •

Later, in the quiet of Winter's warehouse, the memory finds me.

It always does when I see dying children. When I see that particular shade of fear in young eyes—the one that knows death is coming and doesn't understand why.

Eli had that look. At the end.

• • •

We were seventeen and fifteen, the night it happened. Running a job for a fence named Callow who promised us thirty silvers for a simple handoff. Meet the buyer at the old mill. Exchange the package for coin. Walk away clean.

Eli didn't want to go. I remember that now—remember it every night when the guilt comes calling.

"Something feels wrong," he said, sitting on the edge of our shared mattress in the squat we called home. "Callow's never paid this much for a simple run. Why now?"

"Because we're good." I was already counting the money in my head. Thirty silvers could buy us three months of food. Could get Eli the medicine for his lungs—he'd had the cough since winter, and it wasn't getting better. "We're the best runners he's got. He's finally paying what we're worth."

"Or he's paying for something he doesn't want to do himself."

Eli always saw the angles I missed. He was the smart one. The careful one. The one who still prayed every night even though Mama was three years dead and God hadn't done a damn thing to save her.

"One more job," I told him. "One more, and we're out. I'll find us something legitimate. Something safe."

He looked at me with those eyes—brown like Mama's, soft like hers too. Eyes that wanted to believe me even when believing was stupid.

"You always say that."

"This time I mean it."

He laughed. Not because it was funny. Because what else could he do?

"Fine. One more job. But I'm coming with you."

"Eli—"

"I'm coming. You're not walking into something wrong alone."

I should have said no. Should have locked him in the squat and gone by myself. Should have done a hundred things different.

But I was seventeen, and I thought I was immortal, and I wanted my little brother to see me be the hero for once.

"Okay," I said. "Together."

He smiled. That crooked smile that made everyone trust him, even people who knew better.

"Together."

• • •

The old mill sat at the edge of the Warrens, where the city bled into marshland and nobody asked questions about screams in the night. The kind of place deals went wrong and bodies disappeared.

I should have known. The signs were all there.

The buyer was already waiting when we arrived. Three men in dark coats, faces shadowed by hoods. The leader had hands covered in silver rings—church rings, I realized too late. Warden rings.

"You're Callow's boys." Not a question.

"We've got the package." I held up the satchel. "You've got the coin?"

The leader smiled. I remember that smile. It's the last thing I see before the nightmares take me.

"We've got something better."

They moved fast. Faster than street thugs should move. One of them grabbed Eli before I could blink—arm around his throat, blade at his ribs.

"The package," the leader said. "And everything else Callow's been running through this district. Routes. Contacts. Safe houses. You're going to tell us all of it."

"I don't know—"

The blade pressed into Eli's side. He gasped. A line of red appeared, soaking through his shirt.

"Let's try again. You're going to tell us everything. Or we're going to open your brother from throat to groin and make you watch."

Eli's eyes found mine. Not panicked—that was the worst part. Calm. Accepting. Like he'd known this was coming all along.

Run, he mouthed.

I didn't run.

"Okay," I said. "Okay. I'll tell you. Just—don't hurt him. Please."

The leader nodded. Magnanimous. Like he was doing me a favor.

"Smart boy. Start talking."

So I talked. Gave them everything—every route I knew, every safe house, every name Callow had ever mentioned. Sold out every runner and fence and friend we had in the Warrens.

And the whole time, Eli watched me. Not with judgment. With something worse.

With love.

It's okay, his eyes said. *I understand. You're trying to save me.*

When I finished, the leader smiled again.

"Good. Very good. You've been helpful."

"So let him go. I told you everything. Let him go and we're done."

"Oh, we're done. But I'm afraid your brother's seen our faces. Heard our questions. He knows we're hunting Callow's network."

The blade moved before I could scream.

One stroke. Throat to chest. The way they'd promised to do it if I didn't talk.

Eli's eyes went wide. Then confused. Then—Then nothing.

He fell. Blood spreading across the mill floor, black in the moonlight. His hand reached toward me, fingers twitching, grasping for something he couldn't find.

I don't remember crossing the space between us. Don't remember dropping to my knees. Don't remember screaming his name until my throat tore.

I just remember holding him. Feeling the warmth leave his body. Watching the light go out of his eyes.

"Eli. Eli, stay with me. Stay—"

His mouth moved. Shaped words his lungs couldn't push out anymore.

I leaned close. Close enough to feel his last breath against my cheek.

"Not... your fault."

"Don't—Eli, please—"

"Pray... for me."

His hand found mine. Squeezed once. Weak. So weak.

"Love... you... big brother."

Then nothing. His grip went slack. His eyes stayed open, staring at something I couldn't see.

And the Wardens laughed.

"Touching," the leader said. "Really. You should write poetry."

Something broke in me. Something that had been holding together through the fear and the begging and the betrayal. Something that had kept me human.

I felt it snap.

And something else rushed in to fill the space.

• • •

I don't remember what happened next. Not clearly. There are flashes—the rune burning into existence on my wrist like a brand from nowhere. My voice speaking words I'd never learned. The leader's face melting into something that wasn't a face anymore.

Screaming. So much screaming. Not mine.

When I came back to myself, I was alone in the mill. Eli's body in my arms. Three piles of ash where three men used to be.

And a voice in my head that sounded like my brother, laughing softly at a joke only the dead could understand.

Well, the voice said. *That's new.*

I sat there until dawn. Holding Eli. Rocking back and forth. Praying—actually praying, for the first time since Mama died—that this was a nightmare I'd wake up from.

I never woke up.

• • •

I buried him in the potter's field next to Mama. Three copper coins in his mouth. A promise that I'd find him again, wherever he went.

The rune stayed. The power stayed. The guilt stayed longest of all.

"Not your fault," he'd said. His last words. His gift to me.

But he was wrong. I'd taken the job. I'd brought him along. I'd talked when I should have fought, and when the fighting finally came, it came too late.

Eli died because I was too slow to save him. Too weak. Too stupid.

And now I carry a piece of something divine in my flesh, and I still can't save everyone. Can't even save most of them. All I can do is what I did tonight—kneel in blood and beg the powers that killed my brother to spare someone else's.

It's not enough. It's never enough.

But I keep doing it anyway.

Because every dying child I save is Eli. Every miracle is a prayer he never got to finish. Every year the Crown takes from me is a year I should have given him instead.

That's the math. That's the deal.

And I'll keep paying until there's nothing left to pay.

• • •

The ether distribution runs smooth that night. Sable checks quality at each station while I try not to look too hard at the faces waiting to pay for their slow-motion suicides.

But I look anyway. Can't help it.

The woman with callused hands who used to be a seamstress before the factories moved in. The twin brothers, maybe sixteen, splitting a single vial because they can't afford two. The old man with dock-worker hands and sailor tattoos who probably hauled cargo for forty years before his back gave out.

The old man recognizes me.

43

"Saint Ash. Is it true? You can heal?"

My throat closes. The rune at my wrist pulses warm.

"I... sometimes."

He taps his chest. "My lungs. Forty years of dock dust. Priests won't waste healing on a sinner like me. But you—they say you heal the forgotten ones."

Sable's hand lands on my arm. Warning.

"He can't help everyone," she says, voice firm but not unkind. "The gift takes from him too."

The old man's face falls. Then hardens.

"Sure. Even saints got limits. Even miracles got price tags."

He takes his moon-milk and shuffles away, and I feel something crack in my chest that ain't the rune.

"I could have—"

"No." Sable cuts me off. "You couldn't. Not without killing yourself faster. And if you die, who helps the next hundred?"

She's right. I hate that she's right.

"When did you become the practical one?"

"When you became the martyr. Somebody's gotta balance the scales."

• • •

The call comes just before sunset.

A runner bursts into Winter's warehouse, pale as old bone.

"Tithe House. Something's wrong. Mara says you gotta come. Now."

44

The Tithe House sits three blocks from the docks, in a basement beneath a closed butcher shop. It's where the desperate go when they've got nothing left to sell but themselves—blood-tithes for power, pain-tithes for protection, memory-tithes for forgetting.

We move fast through the Warrens. The closer we get, the wronger the air feels.

By the time we reach the butcher shop, I can smell it. Copper and flowers and something burning that shouldn't burn. Something that smells like music, if music had a scent.

Mara waits outside, arms wrapped around herself. She's seventy if she's a day, but right now she looks like a scared child.

"I told him," she whispers. "I told him three tithes was too many. I told him the body can only pay so much before—"

She breaks off. Gestures at the door.

"See for yourself."

●　●　●

The basement stairs creak under our weight. The candles down here are burning colors they shouldn't—green and purple and a shade of red that hurts to look at.

And in the center of it all—A man. Or what used to be a man.

He's on his knees, shirtless, covered in fresh tattoo-work that's still wet with blood and ink. His mouth is open. His eyes are open. But nothing about him looks alive.

And his flesh is moving.

Not breathing. Not twitching. *Moving.* Like something underneath his skin is trying to rearrange the furniture.

"What did he ask for?" Winter's voice is steady, but her knuckles are white.

Mara shakes. "Strength. Protection. And… and the ear of something old."

"Three tithes in one night?"

"I told him no. But he paid triple my rate. Said something was coming and he needed to be ready."

The man in the circle makes a sound. Not a scream. Not a moan.

A note.

A single, perfect musical note that hangs in the air like it's waiting for accompaniment.

I step closer. The rune at my wrist flares hot.

The man's mouth opens wider. Too wide. His jaw unhinges like a snake's, and from his throat comes another note. Then another. Then a chord.

And then—He begins to sing.

Not words. Not any language I know. Just sound shaped like prayer, like prophecy, like a hundred voices braided into one throat.

His body shudders with each note. The tattoos on his skin start to glow—first red, then gold, then white-hot.

"Can you help him?" Winter asks.

I reach for the verse. For the power. The rune at my wrist screams—not with power, but with warning. The magic inside me recoils from whatever magic is eating him.

"No. Whatever's eating him… it already owns him. The tithes opened a door. Something walked through."

The man's song hits a pitch that makes my teeth ache. His body starts to unfold—there's no other word for it. Flesh peeling back like petals, revealing layers beneath that aren't flesh at all.

They're music. They're scripture. They're the price of asking for too much from things that don't count cost the way humans do.

His mouth opens one last time. The final note hangs in the air, shimmering, solid as stone.

And then he's gone.

Not dead. *Gone.*

His body collapses inward and outward at the same time— becoming the song that was eating him.

Where the man knelt, there's nothing left but a burn pattern on the stone floor.

It's shaped like a crown.

• • •

We stand in the alley behind the butcher shop. Winter's already giving orders—seal the room, question Mara, find out who the man was.

I lean against the wall and try to remember how to breathe.

Sable finds me there. Doesn't say anything at first. Just stands close.

"You okay?"

"No."

"Want to talk about it?"

"No."

She nods. Leans against the wall beside me.

"Then I'll just stand here and not talk about it with you."

We stay like that for a while. Not touching. Just breathing the same air. Sharing the silence.

Finally, I ask: "What's happening to me?"

"I don't know." Her voice is quiet. Honest. "But whatever it is… you're not alone in it."

Her hand finds mine. Squeezes once.

The rune pulses warm. The burn pattern on the basement floor flashes behind my eyes—that crown shape, that warning, that promise of something bigger than street miracles and gutter prayers.

Something's coming.

And I'm starting to think I'm part of it whether I want to be or not.

CHAPTER FIVE

SABLE'S SHADOW ERRAND

The sigil on my wrist burned cold at three in the morning.

I lay in the narrow bed of Winter's safehouse, staring at the water-stained ceiling, feeling the summons pulse through my blood. Third time this week. Symeon was getting impatient.

Beside me—not touching, never quite touching when we slept—Ash breathed the slow rhythm of exhaustion. Three days since he'd given years of his life to save a boy he didn't know.

He looked younger when he slept. Softer.

I watched him and felt something twist in my chest. Something that wasn't supposed to be there.

The mission had been simple: infiltrate Winter's operation, get close to the Dock Queen's assets, report back to Symeon. Standard shadow work.

But nobody had told me about Ash.

Nobody had warned me that Winter's new acquisition would be a half-broken prophet with sad eyes and a voice that made me forget, sometimes, that I was supposed to be lying to him.

The sigil pulsed again. Colder. More insistent.

I slipped out of bed without waking him—years of practice made my footsteps silent—and dressed in the dark. Black on black. Knives in their sheaths. The face I wore for Symeon carefully arranged over the one I'd started showing Ash.

As I buckled my belt, something warm pulsed at my collarbone.

Not the sigil—that burned cold. This was different.

The silver scars from years of binding contracts. They were glowing. Faintly. A soft silver luminescence that painted the dark room in ghost-light.

I pressed my palm against them, willing them to quiet. They'd been doing this more often lately—ever since I started sleeping beside Ash. Ever since I started getting close to whatever power lived inside him.

Binding scars weren't supposed to do this. They were dead marks, ownership records written in flesh. They weren't supposed to wake up.

I pushed the thought away and finished dressing.

At the door, I paused. Looked back.

Ash had shifted in his sleep, one arm reaching across the empty space where I'd been. His brow furrowed, like even unconscious he was searching for something.

I wanted to leave a note. Something that would explain, or apologize.

But notes were evidence. Notes were weakness.

I slipped through the door and let the night swallow me.

• • •

The Velvet Quarter at night was a different beast than its daytime face.

During the day, it wore respectability—pleasure houses disguised as tea rooms, the whole district pretending to be nothing more than a place where wealthy folk spent money on art and conversation.

At night, the pretense melted away. The houses breathed.

I moved through it all like a knife through water. This was my territory. Had been since Symeon first found me—a half-starved orphan with quick hands—and offered me a choice between the gutter and the silk.

I'd chosen silk.

Hadn't understood, then, that silk came with chains. That the name Symeon took from me—my true name, the one my mother whispered when I was born—would become a leash no knife could cut.

By the time I understood, it was too late. The binding was complete. The sigil was burned into my wrist.

And Sable Korran became property disguised as partnership.

• • •

The House of the Silver Throat sat at the end of a street that most maps forgot to include. No sign. No windows. Just a door of dark wood banded in silver, and a curtain of beads carved like closed eyes.

I knocked the pattern Symeon had taught me years ago. Three sharp, two soft, one sharp.

The door opened without hands.

Inside, the air was thick with smoke that smelled like burning roses. Candles burned in alcoves, their flames a color between blue and purple.

This wasn't the public face of Velvet. This was where Symeon actually lived.

Bishop Symeon emerged from shadow like they'd been born there. The fox mask gleamed—that grinning, sharp-toothed face I'd learned to fear before I learned to read.

"Little shadow." The voice was rich enough to drown in. "You kept me waiting."

I dropped to one knee. Not from respect—from survival.

"The prophet was restless. I couldn't slip away until—"

"The prophet." Symeon's tone curled around the word. "Yes. I've heard so much about your prophet. 'Saint Ash.' 'The Dock Queen's Miracle.' Such devotion in your voice when you speak of him. Such... warmth."

My stomach clenched. This was the trap.

"I report what I observe. The prophet is—"

Symeon's hand caught my chin, tilting my face up.

"The prophet is making you forget yourself. I can smell it on you, little shadow. The stink of genuine feeling."

"I'm doing my job. Getting close was the assignment."

"Does the target believe your affection is real?"

"Yes."

"And is the target correct?"

The question hung in the air like a blade waiting to fall.

"No."

As the word left my mouth, heat bloomed at my collarbone. The binding scars flared silver beneath my clothes.

Lying. The scars knew I was lying. They responded to the truth my mouth wouldn't say.

52

I kept my face stone. Kept my breathing even.

Symeon's smile stretched beneath the mask.

"Liar. I own your name, little shadow. I feel your pulse in my palm. And your pulse says 'yes' even when your mouth shapes 'no.'"

They released me.

"But lies can be useful. Let the prophet believe. Love makes people stupid. Stupid people make mistakes. And mistakes create opportunities."

• • •

Symeon led me through a curtain of black silk into a chamber I'd never seen before.

Maps covered every wall. Not the maps merchants used—these showed the city's true geography. Power lines. Influence flows. The invisible architecture of who owned what and who owed whom.

"You've been busy," I murmured.

"I've been prepared. The Accord wasn't just a negotiation. It was a declaration. The Night Parliament has chosen its moment."

"Their moment for what?"

Symeon moved to the largest map—the one that showed the whole city with the Crown shards marked in golden pins.

"The Crown was shattered centuries ago. Seven shards for seven sins. But shattered isn't destroyed, little shadow. Shattered is just… waiting to be reassembled."

Ice crawled down my spine.

"They want to reforge it."

"They've wanted to for generations. But they needed the right catalyst." Symeon's finger tapped one of the golden pins. "The prophet.

Your prophet carries a piece of the Crown inside him. Didn't you know?"

My heart stuttered.

The rune. The power that kept growing. The burn pattern shaped like a crown in the Tithe House.

It all made horrible sense now.

And at my collarbone, the scars blazed. Silver fire, bright enough that I had to clamp my hand over them to hide the glow.

"He doesn't know," I whispered. "He doesn't know what he is."

"How delightful. A vessel who doesn't recognize his own contents. Parliament will enjoy unwrapping him."

"'Unwrapping'?"

"The shard must be extracted. The methods are… unpleasant. But effective."

I thought of the man in the Tithe House. The way his flesh had folded.

"They'll kill him."

"They'll use him. His death will simply be a byproduct."

Something cold settled in my chest. Not fear—decision.

"What do you want me to do?"

"Continue as you are. Stay close. Report his movements, his power, his weaknesses. When Parliament moves, I want to know first. Information is currency, and I intend to be rich when the market crashes."

"And Ash?"

Symeon tilted their head.

"Does it matter? He's a vessel. A tool. Tools get used and discarded. Surely you've learned that by now."

I had learned it. Had lived it. Had been the tool, the vessel, the thing that got used.

"I understand."

"Good." Symeon produced a small vial from their robe. Clear liquid that glowed faintly purple. "A gift. For the Dock Queen's next shipment. It will make the ether... more effective. More addictive. More profitable."

I took the vial. My hand didn't shake.

"Anything else?"

"Just this." Symeon leaned close. The fox mask filled my vision. "Remember who owns you, little shadow. The prophet may warm your bed, but I hold your name. Cross me, and you'll discover how many ways a person can hurt without dying."

"I remember."

"See that you do."

• • •

I walked back through the Velvet Quarter as dawn started to gray the eastern sky.

The vial sat heavy in my pocket. Poison disguised as profit. Another weapon for Winter's arsenal, another chain around my throat.

And underneath it all, the scars at my collarbone hummed.

They'd never done that before tonight. Never responded to my lies, never glowed when I felt things I wasn't supposed to feel.

Something was changing.

I didn't know if it was the Crown's influence bleeding through Ash. Didn't know if it was the binding magic finally breaking down after years of strain. Didn't know if it was a different creature altogether—something that had been sleeping inside me, waiting for the right spark to wake it up.

All I knew was that I couldn't serve two masters forever.

Ash or Symeon. Truth or survival. Love or chains.

Eventually, I would have to choose.

• • •

When I slipped back into the safehouse, Ash was awake.

He sat on the edge of the bed, watching the door like he'd been waiting. His eyes found mine in the gray pre-dawn light.

"You left."

Not an accusation. Just a fact.

"I needed air."

"At three in the morning?"

"I don't sleep well. You know that."

He studied me for a long moment. I kept my face neutral, my breathing steady, my hands relaxed at my sides.

The lies came easy. They always did.

But the scars at my collarbone pulsed warm, and I wondered how long I could keep telling them.

"Come back to bed," Ash said finally.

Not a demand. An invitation. The kind of gentleness that made me hate myself for deserving none of it.

I crossed the room. Sat beside him. Let him take my hand.

56

"I'm sorry," I said.

"For what?"

For everything. For the lies. For the vial in my pocket. For the betrayal I haven't committed yet but probably will.

"For leaving without saying anything."

He squeezed my hand.

"When you're ready to tell me, I'll be here."

Something cracked inside my chest. A small break in a wall I'd spent years building.

I didn't deserve him. Didn't deserve his patience or his trust.

But maybe—just maybe—I could find a way to earn it.

The sigil burned cold against my wrist. Ash's hand stayed warm on mine.

Two masters. Two loyalties. Two versions of myself fighting for control.

Eventually, I would have to choose.

But not today.

Today, I let him hold my hand, and pretended that was enough.

• • •

Sleep doesn't come.

Hours later, with Ash's breathing steady beside me, I slip from the bed again. Not to run errands—just to think. Just to sit in the dark and be alone with the war inside my head.

The night streets of Ashvein have their own language. I learned it young—the way shadows deepen near safe houses, the patterns of lamplight that mark territory, the silence that falls when Wardens patrol. Symeon taught me to read the city like a book, and I've been fluent for fifteen years.

I climb to the roof. The view from up here stretches across half the Warrens—a patchwork of tenements and temples, all of them sleeping the restless sleep of people who know tomorrow might be worse.

The binding marks on my body pulse warm. Symeon tracking me even now. Even in these quiet hours when I should be invisible.

Some cages you carry inside your skin.

I think about the girl I was before Symeon found me. Twelve years old. Motherless. Starving on the streets because the orphanages were worse than hunger. I remember the moment they appeared— silver-masked, silent, offering me everything I thought I wanted.

Training. Purpose. Belonging.

I didn't understand the price. Didn't understand that belonging meant being owned. That purpose meant obedience. That training meant becoming a weapon that someone else would aim.

By the time I understood, it was too late. The marks were in my flesh. The contracts were signed. The girl I'd been was gone, and Sable had taken her place.

Now there's Ash.

Ash, who looks at me like I'm a person instead of a tool. Who touches my scars like they're something to be honored, not hidden. Who asked me what I wanted—actually asked—and waited for an answer.

I don't know what I want. That's the truth I can't tell him. Fifteen years of having every choice made for me has left me hollow in places I'm only now beginning to map.

But when I'm with him, when we're working together or talking or just sitting in comfortable silence, I feel something stirring in that hollowness. Something that might be hope. Something that might be freedom.

Something that terrifies me more than Symeon ever could.

Because if I let myself want this—if I let myself believe I can have something other than service—what happens when it's taken away? What happens when Symeon calls in their debts and I have to choose between the life I'm building and the life I've always lived?

The scars at my collar pulse again. A reminder. A warning.

You belong to us, they say. *Everything else is borrowed time.*

I stay on the roof until dawn breaks. Watch the city wake up. Count the faces of people who've never had a master, never had their choices taken, never known what it's like to be property instead of person.

Then I go back inside. Back to Ash. Back to the lie I'm living and the truth I'm too afraid to tell.

Tomorrow, I'll do my duty. Run Symeon's errands. Report what I'm supposed to report.

But tonight—for just a few more hours—I let myself pretend I'm free.

CHAPTER SIX

WINTER'S FEAST

The Silk Crypt breathes tonight.

The Silk Crypt at full power is something I've never seen.

Every surface gleams. The chandeliers cast light in patterns that seem to tell stories if you watch long enough. The music doesn't come from any visible source—it just exists, filling the space like perfume.

And the people.

Lords in masks worth more than everything I've ever owned. Ladies with tattoos that move across their skin, shifting to match their moods. Bodyguards whose eyes never stop scanning. Servants who might be slaves, moving with the too-perfect grace of people who've learned not to make mistakes.

Winter walks among them like she was born here. Maybe she was. Her past remains a mystery to me—none of us do, not really. She's the Dock Queen, the woman who built an empire from nothing, but the girl she used to be is locked somewhere even she doesn't visit.

I follow a few steps behind, trying not to look like I'm drowning.

"You're doing fine." Sable materializes at my elbow. She does that—appears without warning, like she's been there all along. "Just keep breathing. Don't accept any drinks you didn't pour yourself. And if someone offers you a contract, walk away."

"A contract?"

"The Silk Crypt isn't just a club. It's neutral ground for deals." She nods toward a corner where two men are signing something that glows faintly purple. "Blood contracts. Soul bonds. Arrangements that outlast death. Winter facilitates them for a percentage."

"And the Church allows this?"

Sable almost smiles. "The Church has a private booth in the back. Cardinal Red himself was here last month."

I want to be surprised. I'm not.

The music shifts—something slower, more deliberate. Couples drift toward the dance floor. The light dims to something intimate.

"You know," Sable says quietly, "in another life, this could have been normal. Parties. Dancing. People who smile because they're happy, not because they're calculating."

"You've been to parties where people are actually happy?"

"I've heard they exist." She looks at me sideways. "Somewhere that isn't Ashvein."

Bass throbs through the walls. Bodies press together on the dance floor—silhouettes in colored lantern-light, moving to rhythms that feel older than the city itself.

We're celebrating. That's what Winter called it. A victory party for surviving the Accord, for expanding the territory.

I'm not sure what I'm celebrating. The miracle I performed? The years I lost? The way people keep whispering my name like it belongs to someone better than me?

But the rum is good. And Sable's beside me. And for one night, I'm trying to pretend the world isn't closing in.

Winter holds court near the back, seated on a velvet throne that probably belonged to some dead bishop. People come to her all night. Lieutenants with reports. Merchants with bribes. Desperate folk with desperate requests.

She handles each one with the same measured calm.

Moe leans against the bar with his arm freshly wrapped and a drink that's definitely not his first.

"You gonna mope all night or actually enjoy yourself?" he asks when I wander over.

"I'm not moping."

He gestures at my face. "You got that look. The 'I'm thinking about something heavy' look. This is a party, prophet. Heavy thinking is for mornings."

Sable appears at my elbow, two drinks in hand. She passes one to me without asking if I want it.

"He's always thinking," she says. "It's his tragic flaw."

"I thought my tragic flaw was the glowing curse eating my lifespan."

She smirks. "That's your second tragic flaw. You're collecting them."

But something's different about Sable tonight. I can't name it exactly. She's here, she's smiling, she's saying all the right things—but there's a distance in her eyes. A calculation behind the warmth.

I catch her hand. "Hey. You okay?"

Her smile doesn't waver. "I'm here. That's all that matters."

It's not an answer. We both know it's not an answer. But the music's loud and the rum is warm in my chest and I let it go.

Just for tonight.

• • •

There's a moment, between courses, when Winter finds me alone by the window.

The party continues behind us—the music, the laughter, the careful dance of power and want. But here, in this pocket of quiet, it's just the two of us.

"You're not eating," she says.

"Not hungry."

"Everyone's hungry. They just lie about what for." She leans against the wall beside me, close enough that I can smell her perfume—something dark and floral, like funeral flowers. "You're not what I expected."

"What did you expect?"

"Someone desperate. Someone willing to trade anything for protection." Her eyes meet mine, and for a moment the queenpin mask slips. "Someone I could control."

"Is that what you want? To control me?"

"It's what I do. It's how I survive." She looks out at the city—her city, the empire she's built from nothing and blood. "Everyone in that room is a tool or a threat. I've spent twenty years learning to tell the difference. But you…"

"I'm neither?"

"You're something else entirely. A street prophet who heals without charging. A hustler who gives more than he takes. A man who walked into my club without a single thing to bargain with except his own strange power." She shakes her head. "You defy my usual categories."

"You could let me help."

"Help with what?"

"Whatever you're planning. I can feel it—the tension in this room, the way everyone's watching everyone else. Something's happening. Something big."

Winter is quiet for a long moment.

"Parliament's moving against me," she says finally. "They've been squeezing my territory for months. Buying off my suppliers. Threatening my clients. Bit by bit, they're trying to strangle everything I've built."

"Why?"

"Because I'm not one of them. Because I rose from the streets instead of the spires. Because they're afraid of what happens when someone like me accumulates too much power." Her smile is bitter. "They're not wrong to be afraid."

"What are you going to do?"

"Whatever I have to." She turns to face me fully. "That's where you come in, prophet. Your healings have made you popular. People trust you. Believe in you. That kind of faith is valuable—maybe more valuable than gold."

"I'm not going to be used."

"Everyone's used. The only question is whether you get to choose how." She puts her hand on my arm—light, casual, but I feel the steel underneath. "I'm offering you a choice. Help me fight Parliament, and I'll protect your people. I'll give them territory, resources, safety. I'll make sure no Warden ever touches them again."

"And if I refuse?"

"Then you keep healing in the Warrens until Parliament decides you're too dangerous to leave alone. They'll come for you eventually, Ash. The only question is whether you face them with allies or alone."

I look at her. At the calculation in her eyes, yes—but something else too. Something almost like hope.

"You really believe you can beat them?"

"I believe I'd rather die trying than live on my knees." She squeezes my arm, then releases it. "Think about it. Take whatever time you need. But don't take too long. The game is moving faster than either of us likes."

She returns to the party. The queenpin mask slides back into place—all smiles and charm and lethal hospitality.

I stay by the window.

The city sprawls beneath me, a maze of lights and shadows. Somewhere out there, people are praying in gutter temples with my name on their lips. Somewhere out there, Wardens are hunting and faithful are hiding and the whole sick system keeps grinding on.

Winter's right about one thing. The game is moving.

The only question is whether I'm ready to play.

$$\bullet \ \bullet \ \bullet$$

The mood shifts when Lira Nine walks in.

You can feel it—a ripple moving through the crowd. Even the violin seems to miss a note.

Lira looks like someone who lived inside a fever dream too long and forgot how to wake up. Hair wild. Pupils blown wide. She walks barefoot across the dance floor, humming something discordant, and people part around her.

"The oracle's here," Moe mutters. "This ought to be fun."

"Since when does Winter invite her to parties?"

Sable's voice is carefully neutral. "Since Winter started thinking about the future. Oracles see futures. Winter collects them."

Lira stops in front of me. Just… stops. Her eyes find mine and something in them sharpens.

"Prophet." Her voice is like sand and broken glass. "You spark like a bargain gone bad."

"Hi, Lira. You look… vertical."

She grins, showing three teeth. "Barely. The Crown keeps trying to knock me over. I keep standing up. We're in negotiations."

She reaches toward my wrist—toward the rune—and I pull back.

"Don't."

"I'm not trying to take it. I'm trying to hear it. It's singing, prophet. Can't you hear the song?"

Winter appears beside us. "Lira. Thank you for coming."

"Did I have a choice?"

"Everyone has choices. Some are just more expensive than others."

Winter gestures to the crowd. "Prophet hour. The oracle reads for the house."

The club goes quiet. Even the music dims.

Lira smiles wide enough to crack her face. "Gimme a hit."

A runner steps forward with a vial of angel salt. Lira snorts half of it in one drag. Her neck twitches. A wind that isn't wind moves across the room.

• • •

Lira's head snaps back. Her eyes roll up, showing whites shot through with tiny veins of gold.

When she speaks, her voice is different. Lower. Older. A hundred voices braided into one throat.

"One of you will wear the Crown.

One of you will break it.

And one of you will burn."

The entire club goes silent.

Lira's head jerks sideways. She points at me.

"Saint Ash. You think you ain't chosen, but choice ain't never been the point. The Crown chose you before you were born. Now it waits to see if you're worth the investment."

Cold slides down my spine.

Her finger swings to Sable.

"Knife-girl. You'll love someone too much to keep breathing right. Your heart and your hands want different futures. One of them is going to win."

Sable's jaw locks. Her hand tightens on mine—not seeking comfort. Bracing.

Then Lira points at Winter.

"Queen of the docks. You gonna build a crown so heavy it breaks your own spine. Every empire you make becomes a prison."

Moe steps forward, half-laughing. "What about me? I don't get a prophecy?"

Lira doesn't look at him.

"You? You already dead in every way that counts."

Moe goes still.

"What's that supposed to mean?"

Lira ignores him. She staggers toward me, hand reaching for my wrist again.

This time I don't pull away.

Her fingers touch the rune.

And the world tears open.

• • •

Pain hits like a hammer made of light.

I see—Shards pulling together. Fire that glows gold. Someone crying over a body. A smile that doesn't reach her eyes. Me, power pouring out of my skin, becoming something that doesn't have a name anymore.

Then it's over.

I'm on my knees on the dance floor. Sable's got my head in her hands. Moe's standing over us like a guard dog. Winter watches from three steps back, face unreadable.

Lira lies crumpled beside me, laughing and crying at the same time.

The crowd murmurs. "Prophecy." "One of them gonna wear the Crown." "One of them gonna burn."

Winter claps once. The sound cuts through the chaos.

"Enough. The oracle has spoken. The party continues."

But nobody moves. Because everyone heard what Lira said. And everyone's wondering which of us gets which fate.

• • •

Then I hear it.

A sound that doesn't belong. Distant at first—could be nothing. Could be a fight in the street.

But Winter's head turns. Sharp. Alert.

Moe straightens from his lean against the bar.

And the sound gets louder.

Boots. Marching. Dozens of them.

"Wardens," Winter whispers.

The word ripples through the club. Conversations die. Drinks freeze mid-lift. The music stops.

Then the doors explode inward.

• • •

Pale Wardens flood through the entrance. White masks. Blades already singing—that eerie hymn-hum that means they're charged with holy fury.

The lead Warden points directly at me.

"RELIC SORCERER! BY ORDER OF THE IVORY SAINT, YOU ARE TO BE DETAINED FOR CRIMES AGAINST THE CROWN!"

Sable's knives are in her hands before I can blink.

Moe's already moving toward the nearest Warden.

Winter's voice cuts through the chaos: "POSITIONS!"

The Silk Crypt becomes a battlefield.

Winter's guards pour out from hidden doors, armed with blades and street magic. They crash into the Warden line.

Sable disappears into shadow, knives flashing. She's everywhere and nowhere.

69

Moe meets the lead Warden head-on, catching a blade swing on his forearm and headbutting the mask hard enough to crack it.

And me?

The rune blazes. I don't think—I react.

A Warden charges toward me and I throw out my hand:

"Air bend, bone break—

Holy wrath, mistake—"

The Warden hits an invisible wall and flies backward.

But the cost hits immediately. My vision swims. The rune burns hot enough to cook my wrist from the inside.

More Wardens pour through the doors. Too many. This wasn't a raid—it was an invasion.

Someone told them we'd be here.

• • •

"ASH!" Sable appears beside me, blood on her cheek that isn't hers. "We need to move!"

"I can fight—"

"You can barely stand! This place is lost. We need to go."

Winter's voice rings out: "BACK EXIT! NOW!"

We run. Through the back corridors, past storage rooms and hidden vaults.

The sounds of fighting fade behind us, replaced by something worse.

Fire.

Somewhere in the battle, something ignited. Maybe a spell gone wrong. Maybe intentional—a purging flame to cleanse the sin from Winter's unholy ground.

Either way, the Silk Crypt is burning.

We burst through the back door into a rain-slick alley. Moe's right behind us, half-carrying a wounded runner. Winter comes last.

Behind us, glass shatters. Flames lick through broken windows.

We stand in the alley, breathing hard, watching Winter's empire burn.

The Silk Crypt. Her temple. Her palace. Her proof that the streets could build something beautiful.

Gone.

Winter's voice breaks. Just a hair.

"They touched my home."

Sable's hand finds mine. "We're still breathing. That's what matters."

Winter closes her eyes. Inhales. And when she opens them again, the break is gone.

"This means war."

"We were already in it," Moe spits blood on the cobblestones.

"No. We were playing at it. Now it's real."

She looks at me. At the rune still glowing faintly at my wrist.

"One of us wears the Crown. One of us breaks it. One of us burns. Tonight, we find out who's who."

The fire reaches the ceiling. The church bells across the city start to ring.

And everything that comes next is going to hurt.

CHAPTER SEVEN

WARDENS' WRATH

Three days since the fire. Three days since Winter's empire turned to ash.

I sit by a cracked shutter in a safehouse that smells like mildew and old prayer, watching the streets through a gap barely wide enough for one eye.

The city looks different now. Pale Wardens patrol in groups of six, stopping anyone who looks poor, anyone who looks scared. I've seen three arrests in the last hour. Two beatings. One body left in the gutter because nobody dared drag it inside.

Martial law. That's what Winter called it.

I call it war.

Sable sleeps on a pallet in the corner—or pretends to. I can tell the difference now. When she's really asleep, her breathing goes deep and slow. When she's faking, there's a tension in her shoulders that never quite releases.

She's been faking a lot lately.

Moe paces the narrow strip of floor between the window and the door. His arm's healing wrong—the wound from the Silk Crypt didn't get proper treatment.

"Sit down," I tell him for the fifth time.

"Can't. Sitting makes me think. Thinking makes me want to kill something."

"We're hiding. Killing things would draw attention."

He punches the wall softly. "I know. That's why I'm pacing."

A knock at the door—three soft, two hard, one soft. Winter's code.

Moe's at the door before I can move. A runner slips through—kid maybe fourteen, face smeared with ash.

"Message from the Queen. She's at the old cannery. Wants you there by nightfall."

"All of us?"

The runner's eyes flick to me. There's something in them—not fear exactly. Awe. "Especially him. The Wardens put out a bounty. His face is on every prayer board in the city."

Sable sits up from her pallet. "How much?"

"Five hundred silver. And a pardon for any crimes committed in service of his capture."

Moe whistles low. "They really want you dead, prophet."

"They want me quiet. Dead's just the easiest way to get there."

• • •

We move after dark, hoods up, keeping to alleys the Wardens haven't learned to patrol yet.

The city I grew up in has become a foreign country. Shops I remember as busy and bright are shuttered. Street vendors who used to hawk everything from fish to fortunes have vanished. Even the beggars are gone—rounded up in the first wave of "cleansing."

74

What's left is silence. Fear. The occasional sob leaking through a window.

"This ain't sustainable," Moe mutters as we duck past a patrol. "They can't keep this pressure up forever."

"They don't need forever," Sable answers. "They just need long enough to break the resistance. After that, the people police themselves."

She sounds like she's speaking from experience.

We round a corner and freeze.

Checkpoint. Three Wardens with a family stopped in front of them—father, mother, two kids young enough that they're still holding hands.

The father's papers are out, his voice pleading about market permits, about just trying to feed his children.

The lead Warden doesn't like the answer. His gauntleted fist catches the father across the jaw. The man goes down. The mother screams.

The children don't make a sound. They've already learned that sound draws attention.

Moe's hand goes to his blade. I grab his wrist.

"Don't."

"They're beating an innocent man."

"And if we intervene, we get caught. Then we can't help anyone."

It's the right call. I know it's the right call.

Doesn't make it hurt less.

We slip past while the Wardens are distracted. The father's groans follow us down the alley like accusations.

Two blocks later, Sable stops walking.

"Ash. Look."

Someone's painted a face on the wall beside us. Crude strokes, probably done fast and in the dark, but recognizable. A man with tired eyes and a glowing mark at his wrist.

Words beneath it in dripping red: SAINT ASH WILL SAVE US.

I stare at my own face staring back at me.

"When did this happen?"

"The harder they crack down, the louder the people pray." Sable's voice is quiet. "You're becoming a symbol, Ash. Whether you want to be or not."

Moe snorts. "Symbol's just a word for 'target that inspires people.'"

"Thanks, Moe. Real comforting."

"I'm here to keep you alive, not comfortable."

• • •

The old cannery sits on the edge of Guttersea, a hulking skeleton of rust and memory.

Winter's people have converted the main floor into something between a barracks and a hospital. Cots line the walls. Cook fires burn in metal drums. It's less than the Silk Crypt. So much less.

But it's something.

Winter finds us at the entrance. Her fur coat exchanged for practical wool. Her hair tied back for function rather than style.

She looks smaller without her throne. More human. More dangerous.

"You made it. I was starting to worry."

"The streets are thick with Wardens."

Her jaw tightens. "I know. They've arrested forty of my people in the last three days. Killed six. The rest are either hiding or running."

"What about the docks?"

"Seized. Parliament claimed them for 'public safety.' They're running the ether trade through Church channels now."

We gather in what used to be the foreman's office. Maps cover every surface. The air smells like ink and desperation.

"Options," Winter says. "Give me options."

Sable speaks first. "We go underground. Full shadow protocol. Let the heat die down, rebuild slowly."

"That could take months. By then, Parliament will have consolidated everything."

Moe cracks his knuckles. "We hit back. Hard. Show them the Dock Queen doesn't bow."

"With what army? Half my people are in cells."

Winter looks at me. "And you, prophet? What does the saint of the gutters suggest?"

I stare at the map. At the streets I grew up in, now marked with Warden patrol routes. At the graffiti reports—my face appearing on walls across three districts.

"The people want a miracle. So we give them one."

• • •

"Explain."

"The Wardens are winning because people are afraid. They feel alone. They think nobody's fighting back."

I tap the map where my face has been painted.

"But they're painting my face on walls. They're whispering my name in the dark. They want to believe someone's on their side. So I give them proof. Public healings. In the open. Where the Wardens can see but can't stop me."

Moe laughs—sharp and surprised. "You want to walk into occupied territory and perform miracles in front of the people trying to kill you."

"Yes."

"That's insane."

Sable murmurs, understanding dawning. "That's theater. He makes himself untouchable. Every healing becomes a story. Every story becomes faith. Every faith becomes a soldier."

Winter studies me. "It'll cost you. The healings. You know that."

"I know."

"And you're willing to pay?"

I think about the boy in the Velvet House. The years I lost. The rune that keeps growing stronger even as it eats me alive.

"I've been paying since the day my brother died. Might as well get something for it."

• • •

We're interrupted by another runner—older than the first, with the scarred hands of someone who's done more than carry messages.

"Queen. Got word on the Warden operations. They've assigned a special commander to the prophet hunt. Name's Captain Theron. Ex-Pale Guard. They say he's never lost a target."

Moe goes rigid beside me.

I notice because Moe is never rigid. Moe is loose, easy, always ready to move. Tension is foreign to him.

But at that name—Theron—every muscle in his body turns to stone.

Sable's watching him too. "Moe? You know that name?"

Moe doesn't answer for a long moment. When he does, his voice is flat. Dead.

"He trained me."

Winter straightens. "Trained you?"

"I was a Warden once. Before. Theron was my mentor. My father, in all the ways that matter. He taught me everything I know about fighting."

"And now he's hunting us," I say quietly.

"Now he's hunting you. I'm just the blade that got away."

The room waits. Even Winter doesn't push. This is Moe's truth to share or keep.

He chooses to share.

"I was good. Really good. Youngest to make Pale Guard in a generation. Theron was proud. Called me his legacy."

"What changed?"

His voice goes bitter. "I found out what the Guard actually does. Not the public stuff—protecting pilgrims, enforcing holy law. The other stuff. The secret contracts. The political assassinations dressed up as divine justice."

He finally looks at me.

"They had me kill a family once. Parents and three kids. The father had spoken against Parliament at a public gathering. Nothing violent. Just words. And they sent me to make sure he never spoke again."

Sable's breath catches. "Did you do it?"

Moe's eyes are empty. "I did the father. Couldn't do the rest. Theron finished the job while I watched. Then he told me I was weak. That mercy was a sin. That the Crown demanded obedience, not conscience."

"So you left."

"I killed six Wardens on my way out. Would've killed more if they hadn't stopped chasing. Theron let me go. Said he wanted me to live with the shame of being a traitor."

Winter exhales slowly. "And now he's been assigned to hunt Ash."

"He'll do it right. Theron doesn't fail. Doesn't hesitate. Doesn't stop."

• • •

We leave the cannery at midnight, planning to scout locations for the first public healing.

We don't make it three blocks.

They come out of the shadows like they were born there—a dozen Wardens in full armor. At their head, a man in captain's insignia, his mask removed to show a face carved from stone and discipline.

Theron.

He looks at Moe. Just looks. And something passes between them—decades of history compressed into a single glance.

80

"Son."

Moe draws his blade. "Don't call me that."

"I trained you to be better than this. A street thug. A heretic's bodyguard."

"You trained me to kill children."

"I trained you to serve the Crown. You chose to betray it."

Sable pulls me toward a side alley. "Ash. We need to move."

But Moe's already stepping forward, putting himself between us and Theron's squad.

"Go," he says without looking back. "I'll hold them."

"Moe—"

"GO!"

Sable drags me into the alley. The last thing I see before we round the corner is Moe launching himself at Theron, blade meeting blade.

• • •

We run. Behind us, the sounds of fighting—grunts, screams, the wet thunk of metal finding flesh.

I want to go back. Every instinct screams at me to go back.

But Sable doesn't let me stop.

We're halfway through a drainage tunnel when I hear footsteps behind us. Heavy. Uneven. Dragging.

I spin, verse already forming on my lips—It's Moe.

He's covered in blood. Most of it isn't his. His sword hangs loose in his grip. His face is blank in a way that scares me more than any wound.

"Moe? Is he—"

"Dead. They're all dead."

He staggers past us, not waiting to see if we follow.

"Theron?"

Moe stops. Doesn't turn.

"I put the blade through his heart. Same way he taught me. Same way I killed those Wardens when I left."

His shoulders shake once. Could be a laugh. Could be a sob.

"He was proud of me. At the end. Said I finally became what he trained me to be."

He keeps walking. We follow.

Nobody speaks for the rest of the night.

• • •

Dawn finds us back at the cannery, hollow-eyed and haunted.

Moe sits alone in a corner, cleaning his blade with mechanical precision. He hasn't said a word since the tunnel.

Winter receives our report with her usual controlled calm, but I see something flicker in her eyes when we describe the fight.

"Theron's death will buy us time. They'll need to regroup, assign a new commander. That gives us a window."

"A window for what?"

"For your miracle, prophet. The first public healing. Tomorrow night. The old marketplace in Rust Warrens."

Sable stiffens. "That's deep in occupied territory."

"That's the point. We show them we can reach anywhere. That no checkpoint can stop us. That Saint Ash protects his people no matter what the Wardens do."

I look at Moe—at the blood still crusted under his fingernails, at the emptiness in his eyes.

I think about what this is costing. What it's going to cost.

And I nod.

"Tomorrow night."

The rune at my wrist pulses. Agreement or warning—these days, I can't tell the difference.

CHAPTER EIGHT

THE PRICE OF ETHER

The old marketplace in Rust Warrens used to be the heart of the district—vendors shoulder to shoulder, voices competing for attention. My mother bought me my first pair of boots here, haggling with a cobbler until he threw in extra laces just to make her stop.

Tonight it's a cathedral.

Hundreds of people pack the square. They've come despite the patrols, despite the checkpoints, despite the risk. Word spread through the whisper network—Saint Ash heals at midnight. Bring your sick. Bring your wounded. Bring your faith.

I stand on an overturned cart at the center of the crowd, rune blazing at my wrist. Sable guards my left. Moe—still silent, still hollow—guards my right. Winter's runners ring the perimeter, watching for Wardens.

The Wardens are watching back. I can see them at the edges of the square, masks catching torchlight. They don't move. Don't interfere.

"Why aren't they stopping us?" Sable murmurs.

"Because they want to see what I do. They're taking notes for next time."

• • •

The first woman in line carries a child—maybe six years old, skin gray with fever, breath rattling. Ether withdrawal. I've seen it a hundred times. The body forgets how to function without the drug.

I place my hand on the child's forehead. The rune flares. Heat pours through me—down my arm, into my palm, into the child.

The verse rises without thought:

"Fever break, breath return—Let the innocent unlearn The habit forced upon the weak. Heal the flesh. Still the shriek."

Light pulses between us. The child gasps—then breathes deep and clean for the first time in days. Her mother weeps. The crowd murmurs. Someone shouts "Saint Ash!" and others take up the cry.

I stagger. Just slightly.

"Ash—"

"Next."

There are so many. Too many.

I heal a man with a blade wound gone septic. A grandmother whose lungs are filling with fluid. A teenager with withdrawal shakes so bad he can't stand.

Each healing takes something from me—a piece of my time, my strength, my self. The rune grows brighter even as I grow dimmer.

By the twentieth healing, I can barely stand. By the thirtieth, Sable has to hold me upright.

But I keep going. Because the line keeps growing. Because this is the only weapon I have that actually works.

• • •

Then something changes.

A woman pushes to the front of the line—the same woman from an hour ago. The one whose husband I healed from withdrawal. She's dragging him behind her.

He's seizing.

"Saint Ash! He was fine! He was healed! Then he took just one hit to calm his nerves and he—he started—"

Her husband convulses on the ground. His veins glow faintly gold—the color of bad ether, of product cut with something that shouldn't exist. Foam bubbles at his lips.

I drop to my knees beside him. The rune screams as it makes contact—a warning, a recognition.

This isn't withdrawal. This is poison.

"It's in the ether," I gasp. "Something's in the ether."

"What do you mean?"

"The product. It's been tampered with. Something divine. Something—"

The man screams. His back arches so high only his heels and head touch the ground. The gold in his veins brightens, spreads, begins to crawl across his skin like living scripture.

"Hold him down!"

Moe moves. Two of Winter's runners move. They pin his limbs as I press both palms to his chest:

"Poison purge, blood run clean—Burn the curse the Crown has seen—"

The light intensifies. The man's screams become something not quite human, not quite divine.

Then, suddenly, silence. He goes limp. Breathing. Alive.

But the gold doesn't leave his veins. It fades to a dull glow, hidden beneath the skin. Waiting.

"I can't heal this," I whisper. "I can only hold it back."

• • •

The healing ends early.

We carry the man—and three others who collapsed the same way—back to the cannery. By the time we arrive, Winter's runners have brought news from every district.

The same thing is happening everywhere.

"Two hundred cases in Guttersea alone," a runner reports, barely able to stand. "At least a hundred in the Warrens. More coming in every hour."

"Symptoms?"

"Seizures. Gold veins. Some of them are speaking in tongues—scripture, they're saying. Holy words in unholy mouths."

Winter stands at the center of the chaos, coordinating runners, dispatching medical teams. Even she looks shaken.

"Parliament," she says flatly. "They've weaponized the supply."

"How?"

"They took my docks three days ago. They've been running the ether trade through Church channels since then. Plenty of time to contaminate every batch in the city."

"But why? These are their people too. Their workers. Their taxpayers."

Winter laughs—bitter and short. "These aren't people to Parliament. They're addicts. Sinners. If they die, Parliament calls it divine judgment. If they survive, they're dependent on the Church for treatment."

"They're creating a plague to justify their cure."

"Welcome to politics, prophet."

• • •

Winter's alchemist is a woman named Vera—hunched, ancient, fingers stained permanently yellow from decades of dangerous work. She examines a sample of the contaminated ether under a magnifying glass etched with runes.

"Well?" Winter presses.

Vera holds up the vial. The liquid inside glows faintly gold.

"Crown shard dust. Ground fragments of divine relics. Mixed with standard ether."

My blood goes cold. "Shard dust. You're sure?"

"I've been working with ether for forty years, boy. I know what Crown contamination looks like." She squints at me. "You carry a piece yourself, don't you? I can smell it on you. That rune of yours isn't just magic—it's a shard embedded in flesh."

Sable stiffens beside me.

"What does the contamination do?" Winter demands.

"In small doses? Heightened effects. Better high. The users would've thought they were getting premium product."

"And in large doses?"

Vera sets the vial down carefully. "It tries to make them vessels. Forces divine energy into mortal flesh. The body can't contain it, so it burns. The mind can't process it, so it breaks."

"Is there a cure?"

A long silence.

"No. Once the shard dust takes root, it's permanent. You can slow the progression. Manage the symptoms. But you can't remove it."

"So everyone who used contaminated ether—"

"Is infected for life. Yes."

• • •

The numbers come in through the night. Each report worse than the last.

By dawn, we're counting in thousands.

"It's spreading," a runner gasps. "Not just the users. Their families. Their neighbors. The people who touched them, breathed near them—"

"Divine plague," Winter whispers. "They made a divine plague."

Sable grabs my arm. "Ash. Can you heal this? Any of it?"

I think about the man in the marketplace. The way the gold faded but didn't disappear. The way the shard dust settled into his veins like it belonged there.

"I can slow it. Maybe stop it from killing them. But cure it? This is Crown-level contamination. It's not disease—it's transformation. They're being turned into something else."

"Turned into what?"

Vera answers from her workbench. "Vessels. Broken vessels. Their bodies are trying to become Conduits, but without proper binding, proper training—they're just fracturing."

I think about Devon at the Tithe House. About the way Parliament uses people as raw material.

"They're making an army."

"What?"

"The infected. If Parliament can control the transformation—find a way to finish what the shard dust started—they'd have thousands of half-vessels. Weapons. Bombs made of people."

Winter's face goes pale. "They wouldn't."

"They already did. They just haven't deployed them yet."

• • •

I stand at the entrance to the cannery's main floor, looking out over the rows of cots. The infected lie in various stages of collapse— some seizing, some catatonic, some screaming verses they don't understand. Gold light flickers beneath their skin.

"I have to try."

Sable steps in front of me. "No."

"They're dying—"

"And if you burn yourself out healing them, we lose you. We lose the only person in this city who can actually fight Parliament."

"What good is fighting if I let people die when I could save them?"

"What good is saving a hundred if you could save a thousand by staying alive?"

She's right. I know she's right. But the math of sacrifice has never felt right in my chest.

"Sable—"

"No." Her voice cracks. "I watched you nearly die last night. I felt your heartbeat getting weaker through—" She stops herself. Looks away. "You can't save everyone, Ash. And some of us need you to save yourself."

The words hang between us. More than anger. More than fear. Something she's been carrying that she's finally letting me see.

90

I reach for her hand. She lets me take it.

"Okay," I say. "I'll be careful."

"You're a terrible liar."

"I know."

• • •

I heal fifty more that night. Not enough. Never enough. But enough to stabilize the worst cases, to give them time, to prove that divine power can heal as well as harm.

I wake up in the same cot twelve hours later. Sable sits beside me, holding my hand. Her eyes are red.

"You stopped breathing twice. Winter's alchemist had to shock your heart back into rhythm."

"The infected—"

"Stable. For now. You bought them time." She doesn't look at me. "But you almost killed yourself doing it."

"It was worth it."

Now she looks at me. And her eyes are burning.

"Was it? Because I had to sit here for six hours not knowing if you were going to wake up. I had to feel your heartbeat getting weaker and weaker and wonder if this was the moment I lost you forever."

"Sable—"

She pulls her hand away.

"Don't. Don't tell me it was worth it. Don't tell me the people you saved matter more than you do. Don't make me watch you die in pieces because you think suffering is the same as helping."

As she speaks, I notice something strange. The silver scars at her collarbone—the binding marks—are glowing. Faintly at first, then brighter as her anger builds. Silver light bleeding through her shirt like something trying to escape.

A voice from the doorway interrupts. Vera stands there, watching with eyes that miss nothing.

"Girl. Those scars on your chest. They're moving."

Sable freezes. Her hand goes to her collarbone.

Vera steps closer. "Moving. Glowing. Like they're alive. I've worked with binding magic for forty years. I've never seen contract scars do that."

"It's nothing. Just—"

"Don't lie to me. I can smell Crown energy from across a room." She gestures at me. "He reeks of it. And now you're starting to smell the same way. Something's waking up in those scars. Something that's been sleeping for a long time."

Sable looks at me. I look back. Neither of us knows what to say.

Vera shrugs, turning away. "Not my business. Just thought you'd want to know. When things start stirring, they usually want to be fed."

She shuffles out, leaving us in heavy silence.

• • •

I reach for Sable. She doesn't move away, but she doesn't move closer either.

"I don't know how to stop," I admit. "When I see them hurting and I know I can fix it—"

"You can't fix everything, Ash. You can't save everyone. And if you keep trying, you won't be around to save anyone."

She touches her collarbone. The scars have dimmed, but we both know they're still there. Still changing.

"And apparently I'm changing too. Into what, I don't know."

"We'll figure it out."

"Will we? Because I've been trying to figure out what's happening to me for weeks, and all I know is that it started when I got close to you."

The words hang between us. Accusation and confession all at once.

Winter appears in the doorway.

"She's right. You're more valuable as a symbol than a sacrifice. Dead prophets make good martyrs, but living ones make better generals."

"I'm not a general."

"You will be. Because that's what this city needs. Not a saint who dies for them—a leader who fights with them."

• • •

The runner arrives near midnight—one of Symeon's, marked with the fox-and-chains tattoo of the Velvet Order. She passes a sealed note to Sable, then vanishes.

Sable reads it. Her face goes pale.

"Parliament's announcing a cure. Tomorrow. Public ceremony at the Cathedral steps. Cardinal Red presiding."

Winter takes the note. "They're fast. Too fast."

"They planned this," I realize. "The contamination. The plague. The cure. It's all one operation."

93

"Make the people sick, then save them. The oldest game in the scripture."

"But if they actually have a cure—"

"They don't." Sable's voice is flat. "Symeon's contacts in the Cathedral say there's no cure. The ceremony is a purification ritual."

My blood runs cold. "What kind of purification?"

"The kind that burns the infected from the inside out. They're going to kill them and call it mercy. Frame it as divine judgment on the sinful."

Moe speaks for the first time in days. His voice is rust and gravel. "How many infected are they expecting at the ceremony?"

Sable checks the note again. Stops. Swallows.

"They've been rounding them up. Promising healing. The estimate is five thousand."

The number lands like a body hitting the ground.

"They're going to murder five thousand people," I whisper. "In public. On holy ground. And the city will applaud them for it."

• • •

The war council convenes in Winter's office. Maps covered with patrol routes. Reports stacked in piles.

"Options," Winter says.

Sable speaks first. "We expose them. Get word to the people that the 'cure' is a death sentence. Cause a panic. Stop the ceremony before it happens."

"And the infected?"

"They scatter. Go into hiding. We smuggle out as many as we can before Parliament rounds them up again."

Moe shakes his head. "Won't work. Most of them can barely walk. And Parliament controls the streets. They'd catch ninety percent before they made it three blocks."

"Then we attack," I say. "Hit the ceremony. Disrupt it. Save who we can."

Winter raises an eyebrow. "Against the entire Cathedral guard? Against Cardinal Red and however many Prelates he brings? We'd be slaughtered."

"Then what? We just let them die?"

Silence. The weight of five thousand lives pressing down.

Winter speaks slowly. "There's a third option."

"Which is?"

She looks at me. "You. You walk into that ceremony. In front of everyone. In front of Parliament, the Cardinal, the whole city. And you heal them."

"I can't heal five thousand people. I nearly died healing a hundred."

"You don't heal them all. You heal enough. Publicly. Undeniably. Show the city that Parliament's cure is murder and your miracles are real. Turn their propaganda into proof of their lies."

Sable's hand finds mine under the table. Squeezes tight.

"It'll kill you," she whispers.

"It might."

"Then don't do it."

I look at her. At the fear. At the love she's not quite hiding anymore.

Then I look at the reports. At the numbers. At the names of five thousand people who will burn tomorrow if someone doesn't stop it.

"I have to try."

Sable doesn't argue. She just holds my hand tighter.

Under the table, I feel her grip tremble. And against my fingers, I feel something else—a faint warmth where my skin touches hers. Like her scars are radiating heat.

Whatever's waking up in her—whatever Vera saw—it responds to me. To my power. To my presence.

I don't know what that means yet.

But I file it away, like I file everything that might matter later.

And we start planning how to storm a Cathedral.

CHAPTER NINE

BROKEN SAINTS

The gutter temple exists in the basement of what used to be a tannery, hidden beneath floorboards that creak with every footstep overhead. The smell of old leather clings to the walls, mixed now with incense that can't quite mask the desperation.

Sable leads me down the stairs, her hand never leaving her knife. She's been even more protective since the mass healing—watching me like I might collapse at any moment.

I can't tell her she's not wrong to worry.

What I find at the bottom stops me cold.

They've built a shrine.

Candles arranged in patterns I don't recognize. Offerings of bread and shine and coins worn thin from too much hoping. Drawings of my face tacked to the walls—some crude, some surprisingly skilled, all showing me with light pouring from my hands.

And kneeling in front of it all: thirty people, maybe more, heads bowed in silent prayer.

"What is this?" I whisper.

An old woman rises from the front row. Her face is weathered, kind, desperate.

"Saint Ash." She breathes, reaching for my hand. "You came. You actually came."

"I'm not—I'm not a saint."

"You heal the sick. You stand against Parliament. You gave my grandson back his life." Her voice breaks. "What else would you call it?"

• • •

The old woman leads me deeper into the basement. Behind the shrine, cots have been arranged in rows—makeshift hospital beds holding people too sick to move, too weak to reach the public healings, too poor to hope for anything else.

A man with lungs that rattle when he breathes. A child with the gold veins of shard-dust contamination spreading across her arms. A teenager whose hands shake so badly from withdrawal that she can't feed herself.

Sable grabs my arm. "Ash. Don't."

"There are only a dozen."

"You said that about the hundred. And the hundred before that."

"What am I supposed to do, Sable? Walk away?"

She looks at the dying. At the shrine. At faith pressing down from every angle.

"I don't know," she admits. "But I know what happens if you keep giving pieces of yourself away. Eventually there's nothing left."

I kneel beside the first cot—the child with gold veins. Her mother hovers nearby, tears streaming.

"Please," the mother whispers. "Please, Saint Ash. She's all I have."

I place my hand on the child's forehead. The rune ignites.

98

And I begin.

• • •

By the fifth healing, I'm shaking. By the tenth, Sable has to steady me between patients. By the twelfth—the last—I can barely stand.

The old woman tries to give me water. I drink without tasting. Someone pushes bread into my hands. I eat without feeling. The world has gone soft at the edges.

"Ash." Sable's voice cuts through. "Look at me."

I look. Her face goes pale.

"Your hair."

I reach up. Touch the strands above my temple. They feel different. Coarser. Wrong.

Sable produces a small mirror. She holds it up.

Gray. A streak of gray running through my hair that wasn't there this morning. And beneath my eyes, shadows so dark they look like bruises. Cheekbones sharper than I remember. Skin stretched tight.

I look five years older than I did a week ago.

"The rune takes more than magic," I whisper. "It takes time."

"How much?"

I think about the months. The healings. The cumulative drain.

"I don't know. Years, maybe. A lot of years."

Sable doesn't say anything. She just takes my hand and holds it so tight I can feel her pulse racing against my palm.

• • •

Winter's war room has grown crowded. Maps layer maps. Reports stack in corners. The core group gathers around the central table: Winter, Sable, Moe, and two of Winter's lieutenants.

I stand at the edge, trying to hide how heavily I'm leaning on the wall.

"The ceremony begins at noon," Winter says, pointing to a diagram of the Cathedral. "Cardinal Red will conduct the 'purification' from the main altar. The infected will be gathered in the courtyard— approximately five thousand."

"Security?"

"Heavy. Wardens at every entrance. Prelates at the altar. They're expecting trouble."

Moe studies the diagram. "So we don't go through the entrances."

Winter nods. "The Cathedral has maintenance tunnels beneath it. Old, supposedly sealed, but my people have found a way in. We send a small team underground while the ceremony's starting. Emerge in the courtyard. Disrupt before they can begin the ritual."

"Disrupt how?"

All eyes turn to me.

"By giving them something else to look at," I say. "A miracle they can't ignore. Proof that Parliament's cure is a lie and my healings are real."

"You'll be on their ground," Sable says. "Surrounded by Wardens. With nowhere to run if things go wrong."

"That's why it'll work. Because no one expects a prophet to walk into the lion's den."

• • •

Winter's jaw tightens. "If you're going to take that kind of risk, you need to commit fully."

"Meaning?"

"Meaning you don't just heal. You fight. You take out the Prelates. You show Parliament that the Saint of the Gutters isn't just a symbol—he's a weapon."

"No."

"Ash—"

"I'm not killing them, Winter. Not the Wardens, not the Prelates, not even Cardinal Red if I could."

Moe snorts. "Why the hell not? They're going to murder five thousand people."

I meet Winter's eyes. "And if I kill them, what does that make me? Just another weapon. Just another monster in religious clothing. The people don't follow me because I'm powerful. They follow me because I heal instead of hurt. The moment I become just another killer, I lose everything that makes me dangerous."

"Dangerous isn't the same as effective."

"In this war it is. Parliament has all the swords. All the Wardens. All the scripture. The only thing we have is faith—and faith has to mean something different than more blood."

Sable speaks quietly. "He's right."

Winter raises an eyebrow. "The one time you agree with his suicidal plans?"

"He's not wrong about this. The people paint his face on walls because he heals them. Because he's different. The moment he picks up a sword, he's just another warlord with better marketing."

Winter is silent for a long moment.

"Fine. No killing. But if they corner you—if it's your life or theirs—"

"Then I trust Sable and Moe to do what I can't."

Moe cracks his knuckles. "Finally, a job I'm qualified for."

• • •

Later that night, Sable touches my shoulder as I study maps by candlelight.

"I need to check on the tunnel entrance. Make sure our scouts have the route right."

"I'll come with you."

"No." Too quickly. "You need to rest. Conserve your strength for tomorrow."

There's something in her voice. Something she's hiding.

"Sable—"

"Trust me. Please."

I should push. Should demand answers. But I'm so tired, and she's asking so sincerely.

"Be careful."

She leans in. Presses her lips to my forehead. The gesture is so gentle, so unexpected, that I feel tears prick behind my eyes.

"Always," she whispers.

Then she's gone, slipping into the dark like she was born from it.

• • •

The House of the Silver Throat doesn't change, even when the city burns around it.

Sable moves through familiar corridors, past attendants who don't acknowledge her, through doors that shouldn't open but do.

Symeon waits in their private chamber. Fox mask gleaming. Robes flowing like smoke.

"Little shadow. You've been busy."

"I want out."

The words hang in the perfumed air.

Symeon tilts their head. "Out? Of our arrangement? After all we've shared?"

"You own my name. You feel my pulse. You control whether I can even speak the truth to the people I care about. I want out."

"And why would I release my most valuable asset?"

Sable steps closer. The sigil on her wrist flares—warning, danger—but she ignores it.

"Because I know what's happening tomorrow. I know about Parliament's fake cure. I know about the Cathedral ceremony. And I know that Velvet has been playing both sides—feeding information to Winter while taking coin from the Night Parliament."

Symeon goes very still. "Careful, little shadow."

"I'm done being careful. If I'm going to die at that Cathedral tomorrow, I'm going to die free. Not with your leash around my throat."

"And if I refuse?"

"Then I tell Parliament exactly which Velvet bishop has been sabotaging their operations. I have names. Dates. Enough evidence to burn your entire network."

The silence stretches. Then Symeon laughs. Low, delighted, almost impressed.

"You've learned well. Perhaps too well."

• • •

Symeon circles her slowly, robes whispering against stone.

"I cannot simply release your name. That's not how binding works—the magic itself would shatter us both."

"Then find another way."

"There is... one possibility. A transfer. Your debt passed to another holder. Someone who might be willing to trade your freedom for something else."

"Who?"

Symeon's voice goes silky. "The prophet, of course. His power grows by the day. A binding to a name like that... it would be quite valuable."

Sable's blood runs cold. "You want me to bind Ash?"

"I want you to offer him the choice. Your freedom for his binding. His name for yours. A fair trade, by any magical standard."

"He would never agree."

"Then perhaps you don't know him as well as you think. Or perhaps you underestimate how much he loves you."

The words hit like a blow. Because Symeon isn't wrong. Ash would do it. He would trade himself for her without hesitation, without complaint, without counting the cost to himself.

That's exactly why she can't ask.

"No. Find another way."

"There is no other way."

She steps close enough to feel the power radiating from the mask.

"Then our arrangement continues. But hear me, Symeon—if you use that binding to hurt him. If you force me to betray him. I will find a way to destroy you even if it destroys me."

Symeon studies her for a long moment.

"You really do love him. How... inconvenient."

Sable turns to leave.

"One more thing." Symeon calls after her. "Velvet will help with tomorrow. Not for you—for our own interests. But you'll have backup at the Cathedral. Consider it a gesture of good faith."

Sable doesn't answer. She just walks into the night, the sigil burning cold against her wrist.

• • •

Sable finds me on the cannery roof, watching the city lights flicker through the haze.

She doesn't say where she's been. I don't ask. Some truths are too heavy for the night before battle.

She sits beside me, close enough that our shoulders touch. The warmth of her feels precious. Fragile.

"You should sleep," she says.

"Can't. Head's too full."

"What's in there?"

"Faces. The people I couldn't save. The ones I might not save tomorrow. The ones who'll die because I'm not fast enough or strong enough or—"

She takes my hand. "Stop."

"I'm just—"

105

"I know what you're doing. You're counting your failures like prayer beads. Telling yourself you deserve to hurt because somewhere, someone is hurting worse."

She turns to face me.

"You don't get to punish yourself for being human, Ash. You don't get to carry every death in this city on your back."

"Someone has to."

"Why? Why you?"

I don't have an answer. Just the rune at my wrist, glowing faintly in the dark. Just the weight of a shard of something divine embedded in my flesh, choosing me for reasons I'll never understand.

"Because it's all I'm good at," I finally say. "Carrying things."

• • •

Sable is quiet for a long moment. When she speaks, her voice is softer than I've ever heard it.

"There are things I haven't told you."

"I know."

"You don't know what they are."

"Does it change anything?"

She looks at me—really looks, like she's searching for something in my face.

"It might."

"Then tell me. Or don't. Either way, it doesn't change how I feel."

"You don't even know how you feel."

"I know that you're the first person who makes me want to survive instead of just sacrifice. I know that when you're next to me, the rune hurts less. I know that if I die tomorrow, the thing I'll regret most is not telling you—"

I stop.

She's watching me. Waiting.

"Telling me what?"

The words stick in my throat. Too big for the air between us. Too heavy for the night before we might not have another night.

So I show her instead.

I lean in. Slowly. Giving her time to pull away.

She doesn't.

The kiss is gentle. Terrified. Honest in a way words can't be.

Her lips are warm, slightly chapped. Her hand comes up to cup my jaw, and I feel her pulse racing against my skin.

When we break apart, her eyes are bright with something I don't have a name for.

"I'm more tangled up than you know," she whispers. "Debts. Bindings. Things I can't explain and you shouldn't forgive."

"I don't care."

"You should."

I pull her closer. "I don't. Whatever you're carrying, we carry it together. That's what this is, isn't it? That's what we are."

• • •

The vigil candles burn low as midnight passes.

I'm supposed to be sleeping—Winter's orders, for once I agree with—but my mind won't quiet. Every time I close my eyes, I see them.

107

The people I've healed. The ones I couldn't save. The faces blending together into a single expression of need.

The rune on my wrist pulses warm. Not painful tonight. Almost comforting. Like a hand held against fever-hot skin.

Eli's ghost stirs.

Can't sleep?

"Never could. Not since you died."

I remember. His voice is soft, careful. *I used to hear you at night, in the squat. Pacing. Muttering. Praying.*

"I stopped praying after the mill."

Did you?

I don't answer. He knows—he's in my head, after all. He knows about the desperate bargains I make when no one's watching. The deals offered to powers I don't name because naming them would make them real.

You're not as godless as you pretend.

"I'm godless enough. What happened to you—what they did— that proved there's no one listening."

Or it proved that what's listening doesn't work the way you expected. I feel him thinking, sorting through my memories like old letters. *The rune appeared that night. The power came. Something answered, Ash. Just not in the way you wanted.*

"Something answered by making me a weapon."

Something answered by making you able to protect people. Different framing. Same truth.

I stare at the ceiling. The cracks make patterns that almost look like scripture—the old kind, from before Parliament standardized divinity.

"Do you remember Mama's prayers?"

The ones she said over our beds?

"Yeah. Those."

"May the broken road find purpose. May the hungry heart find peace. May the child I raised remember: mercy multiplies, and cruelty eats its own."

The words settle into me like stones into water.

"She knew. Somehow she knew what the world would try to make us."

Mama knew a lot of things. Eli's presence shifts—warmer, closer. *She knew the streets would try to break us. She knew Parliament would never care about people like us. And she knew that the only way to survive was to become something they couldn't predict.*

"Like what?"

Kind.

The word hangs in the darkness.

They expect us to be hard, Ash. Bitter. Broken in the ways they want us broken. But Mama taught us different. She taught us that kindness is resistance. That every gentle act in an unkind world is a revolution.

"That's naive."

Is it? You've been healing people for free. Giving away power that could make you rich. Building something that has nothing to do with control and everything to do with care. His laugh is sad and proud. *You're Mama's son. Even when you don't want to be.*

I feel tears on my face. Don't remember starting to cry.

"I miss her."

I know.

"I miss you."

I know that too. His presence wraps around me—not physical, but present. Real in a way that matters. *But I'm still here. Different form. Same love. And I'm going to stay with you, Ash. Whatever comes next.*

"Even if the Crown consumes me?"

Even then. Especially then. His voice firms. *You're not going to face it alone. None of us are alone anymore. That's what the rune means. That's what the power's for. Connection. Even across death. Even across the gap between what is and what should be.*

I lie there for a long time. The candles gutter and die, one by one, and the room fills with darkness.

But not emptiness.

Not anymore.

· · ·

We stay on the roof until the cold drives us inside.

The small room Winter gave us has one bed, narrow and hard. We've slept in it separately every night—one taking the floor, trading off, maintaining a careful distance that neither of us acknowledged.

Tonight, neither of us mentions the floor.

We lie side by side, fully clothed, breath mingling in the dark. Her head rests on my shoulder. My arm wraps around her waist.

We fit together like two broken pieces of the same thing.

Neither of us sleeps. But we talk. Quiet, careful words. Things we've never said to anyone.

She tells me about Symeon finding her. About the cold of the streets and the price of a warm bed. About watching her mother die slow from sickness no healer would cure because they didn't have coin.

I tell her about Eli. About the guilt that wakes me every night. About the way his voice still echoes in my head, whispering that I should have saved him, should have been faster, should have been better.

We tell each other the ugly truths. The secret shames. The fears we've never spoken aloud.

And somewhere before dawn, holding her in the dark, I realize something.

This is what the rune can't give me. This is what miracles can't buy. This is the thing that makes sacrifice worth something—not the people I save, but the person I save them for.

I press my lips to her hair.

"I'm going to survive tomorrow," I whisper. "Because I have something to come back to."

She squeezes my hand in the dark.

"You better. Or I'll drag you back from whatever afterlife and kill you myself."

I laugh. Quiet. Broken. Real.

And we wait for the dawn together.

CHAPTER TEN

THE BLOOD-MARKET

• • •

The Blood-Market's entrance is a hole in the world.

Not literally. But standing here, watching the twisted ether-light spill from that doorway, I can feel reality bending around the edges. The air tastes wrong. The shadows move when they shouldn't. Even Mercyless hums differently—not hungry, but wary.

"You feel that?" Moe asks. His hand hasn't left his sword since we entered the undercity.

"The wrongness? Yeah."

"It's old magic." Sable's voice is soft. Respectful, almost. "Older than Parliament. Older than the Crown, maybe. This place was sacred once."

"Sacred to what?"

She shakes her head. "Does it matter? Whatever was worshipped here is gone. Now it's just a market where desperate people trade pieces of themselves for power."

Winter stands apart from us, conferring with one of her contacts—a withered woman whose eyes are entirely white. Blind, but seeing things the rest of us can't.

I watch them talk. Watch Winter's face shift through expressions I can't read.

"What's she learning?" I ask Sable.

"The layout. The security. Where they keep the valuable merchandise." Sable's jaw tightens. "Where they keep the spirits."

"Spirits?"

"The Blood-Market doesn't just trade blood and bone. It trades souls. Ghosts bound to objects. Memories extracted and bottled. Anything that used to be part of a person can be bought and sold here."

My stomach turns. I think about Eli. About where his spirit might have gone when he died.

"The Church allows this?"

"The Church funds this." Sable's voice is bitter. "Where do you think they get their Executioners? Their bound weapons? Their scripture that actually works?" She gestures at the entrance. "Parliament preaches against blood magic in their cathedrals and buys its products in their basements."

"That's…"

"Hypocrisy? Power? Both?" She shrugs. "Welcome to Ashvein. The rules only apply to people who can't afford exceptions."

Winter finishes her conversation. The blind woman vanishes into the shadows, and our queen approaches with new lines around her eyes.

"We have a problem."

"Just one?"

"The auction tonight includes something unusual." Winter's voice is flat. Controlled. "A ghost bound in chains of divine scripture. Fresh capture. Strong enough that they're advertising it as the centerpiece of the evening."

"So?"

"So the description matches." Winter looks at me. "Teenage male. Rust Warrens accent. Connected to a shard-bearer who's still walking around."

The world stops.

Eli. They have Eli.

"That's not possible." My voice sounds far away. "He died two years ago. His spirit should have moved on."

"Spirits connected to Crown shards don't move on." Sable's hand finds my arm. Steadying. "They get stuck. Trapped in the space between. And eventually, someone finds them and sells them to the highest bidder."

I want to scream. Want to burn this whole market to the ground and salt the earth where it stood.

But that won't help Eli. That won't free him.

"We're going in," I say. "Tonight."

"That was always the plan."

"The plan was reconnaissance. Information gathering." I meet Winter's eyes. "Now the plan is a rescue."

She doesn't argue. Just nods once—understanding, calculating, already adjusting her strategy.

"Then let's go get your brother."

• • •

The stairs spiral down into a darkness that predates the Cathedral above, carved into stone so old the steps have worn smooth as prayer beads.

Every footfall echoes twice—once when your boot hits, once when something below answers.

I count the steps. Lose count after two hundred. Keep descending.

The smell changes as we go deeper. Incense fades. Rot rises. Something beneath the rot that's worse—metallic sweetness like blood left too long in the sun, mixed with ozone and something I can only call despair.

It has a scent, despair.

Sable moves ahead of me, silent as thought, her knives already drawn. Behind us, Moe fills the stairwell, his breathing steady despite the climb.

Winter stayed above—too recognizable, she said. Too valuable to risk.

What she meant was: too smart to walk into Hell's basement.

• • •

The tunnel opens into a cavern that steals my breath.

It's massive. Impossible. A space that couldn't fit beneath the Cathedral, that seems to bend the rules of stone and sky. The ceiling arches up into darkness studded with what look like stars but aren't—they pulse, they watch, they remember.

And below that false heaven: the Blood-Market.

Imagine a cathedral turned inside out. Pews become cages. The altar becomes an auction block. Where you'd find candles, there are braziers burning something that makes the air shimmer. Where you'd

115

find hymns, there's a sound like music played backward through broken glass.

Hundreds of buyers fill the space. Maybe thousands.

They wear masks like ours—weeping, laughing, screaming, sleeping. Robes in colors that hurt to look at. Jewelry that moves.

Some of them might be human. Some of them definitely aren't.

I see nobles whose signet rings I recognize from court portraits. Merchants whose shops I've passed in the Ivory Spires. Priests whose sermons I've heard echo through the Warrens on holy days.

They're all here. Shopping for souls.

Sable's hand finds mine in the crowd. Squeezes once.

"Steady," she breathes behind her laughing mask. "We're here to observe. That's all."

But I can already feel the rune at my wrist stirring. Warming. Recognizing something in this place that calls to it.

• • •

The auction is already in progress.

A figure on the central platform—face hidden behind a mask of pure gold—gestures toward a cage being wheeled into the light.

"Lot forty-seven. Soul-chattel, female, mid-twenties. Bound with iron gospel, intact memories, minimal wear. Previous owner deceased. Starting bid: five sins and a promise."

The cage holds a woman. Living. Breathing. Eyes that see nothing because she's been taught that seeing leads to suffering.

Paddles rise. Voices call out bids in currencies I don't fully understand. Sins. Favors. Years. Secrets.

One bidder offers "the name of a child not yet conceived."

Another counters with "the memory of his mother's face."

The woman is sold for three sins, a secret, and the echo of a firstborn's scream.

They wheel her away. Bring in the next cage.

Moe's hand lands on my shoulder. Heavy. Warning.

"Breathe," he rumbles through his blank mask. "Just breathe."

I'm not sure I remember how.

• • •

Twelve more lots. Twelve more souls sold to the highest bidder.

A child with the gift of prophecy, bought by a merchant who wanted to know if his ships would survive the season.

A soldier whose memories of battle strategy were extracted and bottled for resale.

An old woman whose capacity for love was auctioned piece by piece—her love for her husband going to a lonely noble, her love for her children divided among three separate buyers, her love for herself discarded as worthless.

Each sale chips away at something inside me.

Then the auctioneer's voice changes. Drops a register. Takes on a tone of reverence.

"And now, honored buyers, a rare offering. Lot sixty-three."

"Crown-touched merchandise. Spirit-class chattel. Partially untethered. Extremely volatile. Extremely valuable."

The cage they wheel out is different from the others. Iron bars inscribed with so much scripture they glow. Chains that seem to be made of frozen hymns.

And inside—The rune at my wrist doesn't warm. It screams.

· · ·

My brother stands in the cage.

No. Not stands. Floats. Drifts. Exists in a way that hurts to look at because it's not quite real and not quite false.

He's made of light and absence, of memory and pain, of everything I lost the night he died and everything the world took from him after.

Eli. My brother. My blood. My ghost.

He wears the same face he had the last time I saw him alive—thin, sharp, hungry in a way that food couldn't fix. Same crooked smile he had at twelve when we'd steal bread from the temple kitchens. Same eyes that always seemed to be looking at something just past the edge of the world.

But there are chains wrapped around that light. Scripture branded into that absence.

Someone has taken my brother's spirit—my brother's soul—and turned it into property.

Sable's hand tightens on mine.

"Ash." Her voice is distant. Muffled. "Ash, that's not—"

"It is."

"Your mask. The rune. Ash, you have to—"

I can't hear her anymore. I can only hear my brother's voice, whispering across the years, across the barrier between living and dead:

Hey, big brother. Took you long enough.

· · ·

The auctioneer's voice slides over my brother like oil on water.

"Crown-touched, as stated. This spirit was bound at the moment of death during a relic transaction. Unique resonance patterns. Previous owners report prophetic capabilities, minor reality manipulation, and—"

The rune at your wrist—that's from the night I died, isn't it? The shard. The deal gone wrong.

Eli's voice in my head. Not in my ears. In the place where the rune lives. In the space where his death carved a hole that never healed.

I can't speak. Can't move. Can't do anything but stare at my brother's ghost while buyers around me raise paddles to purchase him.

Easy, Ash. These vultures smell weakness.

"Starting bid," the auctioneer announces, "seven sins, a decade of healthy life, or equivalent trade."

Paddles rise.

Ash—whatever you're thinking about doing, don't. These people don't play fair. They'll—

"Sixty sins and a mother's last words."

"Seventy sins and the sound of a child learning to hate."

"One hundred sins."

The crowd murmurs. A hundred sins is a fortune. A hundred sins could buy a district, topple a guild, start a war.

My brother looks at me through the bars of his cage. Through the chains that bind his light. Through the years and the death and the distance between living and not.

Don't do something stupid, Ash. I've got nothing left to lose. You've still got something to hold onto.

119

I can't.

I won't.

The rune at my wrist doesn't warm this time. It ignites.

• • •

The pain is immediate and absolute. White fire racing up my arm, into my chest, behind my eyes.

My mask cracks down the middle. My vision splits into layers—the Market as it is, the Market as it was, the Market as it will be when I'm done with it.

Sable's voice, distant: "Ash, NO—"

Moe's hands, grabbing, missing.

Thrix, already running.

And my brother's ghost, laughing in his chains:

There's that temper.

The first verse tears out of me like a wound finally allowed to bleed.

• • •

The words aren't mine. They're older. Deeper. Spoken in a language I've never learned but somehow know:

"Release the soul the flesh left behind—Crack the cage, burn the price—Let the dead reclaim their sacrifice—"

The first death is the auctioneer. His golden mask doesn't just melt—it fuses with his face, becomes his face, transforms him into something that can only scream in frequencies no human throat should produce. He claws at the metal that was his skin. Falls. Doesn't get up.

The second death is a noble who tries to flee. My hand—not my hand, the Crown's hand wearing my flesh—gestures. The man's shadow detaches from his feet, wraps around his throat, squeezes until his eyes burst.

I'm watching this happen. I'm making this happen. I'm trying to stop and I can't because the rune doesn't want to stop, the Crown fragment doesn't want to stop, my brother's ghost is laughing and crying and begging me to run but I CAN'T—"Ash!" Sable's voice, close now, hands on my face, trying to force me to see her through the golden haze. "Come back! This isn't you!"

Isn't it? This is the you that watched your brother die. The you that survived when he didn't. The you that's been waiting for permission to burn it all down.

· · ·

The Blood-Market had defenses.

Wards carved into the stone, activated by the first verse. Guardians summoned from the space between prayers. A fail-safe that should have collapsed the cavern rather than let power like this escape.

None of it matters.

The wards shatter like glass against the Crown's authority. The guardians bow—actually bow—before the fragment in my flesh. The fail-safe tries to trigger and finds itself rewritten, its purpose inverted, its power added to mine.

Buyers die in waves.

A merchant who bought children's laughter chokes on the sound of their screaming. A noble who collected memories of love discovers he can no longer remember what love meant, and the void where the knowledge was drives him to claw out his own eyes. A priest who traded in broken faith finds his faith restored—violently, apocalyptically, in a revelation so pure it burns him from the inside out.

I can't look away. I can't stop.

Sable is still holding me, still screaming my name, but her voice is getting fainter, the golden haze is getting thicker, and somewhere in the distance I can hear my brother—*Ash, you're gonna*—

I can't hear him anymore.

I can only hear the Crown.

* * *

I don't know what stops it.

Maybe the rune runs out of power. Maybe the Crown gets bored. Maybe some part of me, buried beneath the gold and the fury and the endless screaming, remembers what it feels like to be human.

Or maybe it's Sable.

She doesn't cast a verse. Doesn't invoke a ward. Doesn't try to match power with power.

She just holds me.

Wraps her arms around my burning body and refuses to let go, even as the heat blackens her sleeves, even as the light sears marks into her skin, even as every instinct must be screaming at her to run.

"I've got you," she says. Whispers. Screams. I can't tell anymore. "I've got you. Come back. Come back to me."

Her lips find mine.

The kiss tastes like blood and smoke and desperation. Like someone drowning and not caring, as long as they drown with you.

Something inside me cracks. Not the rune. Something else. Something that was holding all that rage together, keeping it fed, keeping it burning.

The gold recedes. The power drains.

I collapse in Sable's arms, shaking, broken, hollowed out.

122

The Blood-Market is silent. Everyone is dead.

• • •

The cavern looks like the aftermath of a war between gods and men.

Bodies everywhere. Some recognizable. Some not. Some twisted into shapes that suggest they died experiencing things no living mind should comprehend.

I did this.

The thought moves through me like ice water.

I killed these people. Hundreds of them. Without trial. Without mercy. Without control.

They were monsters, sure. Buyers and sellers of souls. But I didn't judge them—the rune did. The Crown did. I was just the weapon.

Does that make it better? Does that make it worse?

Moe steps over corpses to reach us. His blank mask is cracked, his coat torn, his knuckles bloody from fighting his way through the chaos.

But he's alive. Sable's alive. Somehow, impossibly, we're all still breathing.

"Eli," I croak. My throat is raw. "My brother. The cage—"

Sable looks where I'm pointing.

The cage is empty. The chains that held my brother's spirit are broken, scattered across the ground like shed snakeskin.

But there's no sign of Eli. No ghost. No light. No whisper in my head.

"He's gone," Sable says softly.

"Freed?"

She doesn't answer. Neither does Moe.

We all know what "freed" might mean for a spirit that's been sold, resold, and chained for years.

Liberation. Oblivion. Something in between that none of us have words for.

I want to scream. I want to cry. I want to burn this whole city to the ground until someone tells me where my brother went.

But the rune is cold now. Empty.

And so am I.

• • •

Thrix finds us. Of course he does.

The Broker Eel didn't survive this long by being anywhere near danger when it exploded. He emerges from a shadow that's too small to hold him, adjusting his three-eyed mask like he's just arrived for tea.

"Well," he says, surveying the carnage. "That was certainly... memorable."

Moe grabs him by the throat. Lifts him off the ground.

"You knew." The words come out low. Dangerous. "You knew his brother was here."

Thrix's feet kick uselessly. "I knew—there was—Crown-touched merchandise—I didn't—"

"Put him down." My voice. Barely recognizable. "He gets us out. Then we talk."

Moe holds him a moment longer. Makes sure Thrix understands exactly what that talk will involve. Then drops him.

Thrix leads us through passages that don't appear on any map, through doors that open only to specific kinds of fear, through a space between spaces that smells like forgotten prayers.

At the exit—a grate in a sewer that spills into Guttersea—he turns.

"What you did back there," he says. "The things you killed. They had allies. Had clients. Had debts that other people will collect."

"Is that a threat?"

"It's information. I trade in information. And the information is this: The Night Parliament just lost their most profitable operation. They're going to want to know who's responsible."

He slips away before I can respond. Disappears into the shadows like he was never there at all.

Sable helps me climb through the grate. The night air hits my face, cold and clean compared to the tomb we just left.

Behind us, somewhere deep in the earth, the Blood-Market smolders.

And somewhere even deeper, in the space where my brother used to be, there's only silence.

CHAPTER ELEVEN

THE VELVET BETRAYAL

The night before everything changed, I dreamed of home.

Not the squat Eli and I shared before he died. Not the streets where I learned to hustle. Something older—a house I don't remember living in, with a door painted blue and a window box full of flowers.

My mother was there. Young. Smiling. Not the wasted woman who died coughing blood when I was nine.

She took my hand. Said something I couldn't hear.

Then the house caught fire, and I woke up.

Sable was already awake beside me, watching the ceiling, her binding scars glowing faintly silver in the pre-dawn dark.

"Bad dream?" she asked.

"My mother." I rubbed my eyes. "Haven't dreamed about her in years."

"Maybe she's trying to tell you something."

"Like what?"

Sable was quiet for a long moment. Then: "When I was young, my mother used to say that the dead visit us when we're about to make important choices. That they come to remind us who we were before the world made us what we are."

"You believe that?"

"I believe the dead don't leave us alone." Her hand found mine in the dark. "I believe they stay, whether we want them to or not. And I believe they show up when we need them most."

I thought about Eli. About his voice in my head. About the ghost that might or might not be real, whispering guidance I couldn't trust.

"Maybe you're right."

"Maybe." She squeezed my hand. "Or maybe it was just a dream."

But the feeling stayed with me all day. The sense that something was coming. That my mother's ghost—or whatever it was—had appeared to warn me about something I couldn't yet name.

I should have listened.

• • •

Two days since the Blood-Market.

Two days since I killed three hundred people without meaning to, without stopping, without mercy. Two days since my brother's ghost vanished into whatever comes after chains.

The safehouse Winter moved us to sits in the belly of an abandoned tannery, surrounded by the ghosts of leather and chemicals. It smells like rot trying to become something else.

Like me, maybe.

I haven't slept. Can't. Every time I close my eyes, I see the auctioneer's face melting into gold. See the noble's shadow strangling him. See my own hands making gestures I didn't choose, speaking words I didn't know.

The city remembers what I did. Even if Parliament managed to bury the evidence, the whisper network carries the story faster than any cover-up.

Saint Ash descended into Hell and unmade it. Saint Ash is no longer just a healer. Saint Ash is a weapon.

Some people say it with reverence. Some people say it with fear.

I can't tell which one scares me more.

• • •

"They've tripled the patrols." Winter's voice cuts through my brooding. She stands at the single window, peering through a crack in the boards. "Checkpoints at every major intersection. Random searches. They arrested forty of our runners yesterday alone."

"Looking for me."

"Looking for anyone connected to you. To us. To what happened."

Moe sits in the corner, cleaning Mercyless with movements that are too precise, too controlled. He hasn't spoken more than ten words since we escaped the Market. Something broke in him down there.

Sable is across the room, pretending to sharpen her knives. I can feel her watching me when she thinks I'm not looking. Feel the distance she's put between us since that night—not physical distance, but something worse.

"They needed an excuse to declare martial law," I say flatly. "I gave them one."

Winter turns. "You destroyed their soul-trafficking operation. Their most profitable venture. You didn't just hurt them—you humiliated them."

"And killed three hundred people in the process."

128

"People who bought and sold human souls for profit."

"Without trial. Without judgment. Without control."

Winter's jaw tightens. "You're not the only one who's killed for this crew, Ash. You're just the only one beating yourself bloody about it."

She doesn't understand. None of them do.

It wasn't me doing the killing. It was the Crown, wearing my skin like a puppet wears strings.

And the worst part—the part I can't say out loud—is that some part of me enjoyed it.

• • •

The runner comes just after sunset—a kid, maybe fourteen, with scared eyes and a sealed tube clutched to her chest.

"From the Wharf Quarter. Intercepted. Our people grabbed it off a dead courier. Parliament cipher."

Winter takes the tube. Cracks the seal. Unrolls the paper inside.

Her face doesn't change. That's how I know something's wrong. Winter's face only goes blank when she's processing information she doesn't want to believe.

"What is it?"

Winter doesn't answer. She reads the message again. Then a third time.

Then she looks at Sable.

Just looks.

Sable's knife stops mid-stroke against the whetstone. The silence stretches.

"Sable." Winter's voice is soft. Dangerous. "Would you like to explain why your name appears in a Parliament intelligence report?"

The temperature in the room drops ten degrees.

Sable sets down her knife. Her hands are steady—of course they are—but something shifts behind her eyes.

"What kind of report?"

"Asset management. Velvet Order liaison. Monthly updates on my operations, my alliances, my weaknesses." Winter's voice hasn't risen, but it cuts like a razor. "Signed by someone called 'Whisper.' Countersigned by Bishop Symeon."

Moe is on his feet, Mercyless drawn, before anyone can blink.

"I knew it," he growls. "I knew something was wrong with her."

"Moe—" I start.

"Don't. Don't defend her. Not now."

He points the blade at Sable.

Sable doesn't move. Doesn't reach for her weapons. Just sits there, cornered, caught, waiting for the blow to fall.

And when she speaks, her voice breaks something in me:

"It's true."

• • •

"Sit down, Moe." Winter's command carries the weight of someone who's killed for less than raising a blade in her presence.

Moe hesitates, jaw working, but he sits. Doesn't sheath the sword.

Sable stands. Slowly. Like someone approaching the gallows.

"When I was twelve, my mother died. Lung-rot from the refineries. No healer would touch her because we couldn't pay. I watched her drown in her own blood over three days."

Her voice is flat. Practiced. Like she's told this story before, to herself, in the dark.

"The Velvet Order found me. Symeon found me. They offered food, shelter, training. All I had to do was give them my name."

"Your name," Winter repeats.

"My true name. The one my mother gave me before she died. The one nobody else knows."

I feel something cold wrap around my chest. In Ashvein, names have power. True names can be used to bind, control, compel. Giving someone your true name is giving them the key to your soul.

"They wrote it into a contract. Blood-signed. Soul-sealed. As long as they hold my name, they can feel what I feel. Know when I lie. Punish me if I betray them."

She pulls up her sleeve. The sigil I've seen a hundred times—the one I thought was just a tattoo—pulses faintly with light that shouldn't be there.

"This is the leash. It connects me to Symeon. If I try to warn someone about my mission, they know. If I try to run, they know. If I try to lie to them about anything important..." She laughs, bitter and broken. "The pain starts in my spine and doesn't stop until I tell the truth."

• • •

"How long?" Winter asks. "How long have you been reporting on us?"

"Since the beginning. Since you took me in."

131

"And everything—the loyalty, the jobs, the midnight conversations—"

"Real." Sable's voice cracks. "All of it was real. I just... couldn't tell you about the rest."

She looks at me.

I want to look away. Can't.

"Ash. I never reported anything that would get you killed. I swear on whatever's left of my soul. I fed them information about Winter's operations, yes. Schedules, shipments, alliances. But when they asked about you—about your power, your rune, your plans—I lied. I lied and I took the pain and I lied."

The sigil on her wrist flares bright. She gasps, doubles over, and I realize she's telling the truth because the binding is punishing her for admitting she betrayed it.

But that's not all.

At her collarbone, where the silver binding scars have lived for years, something else happens.

Light. Silver light, bleeding through her shirt. Not faint like before. Not the soft glow I've glimpsed in quiet moments. This is burning— bright enough to cast shadows, hot enough that she cries out from two kinds of pain at once.

"What—" Moe takes a step back.

Winter's eyes narrow. "Her binding scars. They're... active."

Sable presses both hands to her collarbone, trying to smother the light. Her face is twisted between the sigil's cold punishment and whatever fire is crawling through those old marks.

"It's been happening," she gasps. "For weeks. The echoes—all the old contracts—they're waking up. I don't know why. The meaning escapes me."

She looks at me through the pain, and I see something in her eyes that might be terror or might be hope.

"It started when I got close to you."

. . .

The emotions tangle inside me.

There's anger, sure. Hot and sharp and justified. She lied to me. Every kiss, every whispered confession, every moment I thought we were building something real—all of it shadowed by secrets she couldn't share.

But underneath the anger, there's something else.

Something that looks at her doubled over in pain and wants to hold her. Something that remembers how she pulled me back from the golden fire, how she burned herself to anchor me.

"Ash." Her voice is raw. "I know you hate me. I know you should. But please understand—I never had a choice. Not until you."

"How do I trust anything that came from those lips?"

She flinches like I've slapped her.

"You can't. I'm not asking you to trust me. I'm asking you to understand that I tried. I tried to protect you the only way I knew how."

"By spying on us."

"By lying to Symeon. By taking their punishments. By telling them you were weaker than you are, less dangerous than you are, less worth hunting than you are."

She straightens.

"Every month for two years, I've written reports that make you sound like a street corner preacher with delusions. I've hidden your real power. Hidden what the rune can do. Hidden how much the people love you."

"Why?"

"Because—" The sigil flares. She gasps, fighting through the pain. "Because I knew what they'd do to you if they understood. And I couldn't let that happen. Even if it meant everything else."

• • •

Winter watches us. Calculating.

"Symeon owns her name," she says finally. "That's not something we can break. Not without killing her."

"There has to be a way," I say.

"There isn't. Not unless someone else takes the binding. Not unless she's transferred to a new holder." Winter's eyes land on me with weight I can feel. "Someone powerful enough to contest Velvet's claim."

Sable's head snaps up. "No."

"It's an option."

"I won't let him—"

"It's not your choice." Winter's voice is flat. "You're compromised, Sable. You're a liability. Either we find a way to neutralize that liability, or—"

"Or what?"

Winter doesn't answer. She doesn't have to.

"I'll take the binding," I hear myself say.

"Ash, no—" Sable starts.

"If it keeps you alive. If it keeps you with us. I'll take it."

"You don't understand what that means. You'd feel everything I feel. Know everything I know. Every lie I've ever told, every secret I've ever kept—"

"I don't care."

The words hang in the air. True. Terrifying.

• • •

The transfer happens at midnight.

Winter knows a binding-broker—someone who works outside the usual channels, someone who owes her enough to do this quiet. The ritual takes place in a cellar that smells like old blood and older promises.

The broker explains what will happen. The sigil will be rewritten. Symeon's claim will be severed. My name will replace theirs in the contract.

"Are you sure?" Sable asks me one last time. Her face is pale. Scared.

"Yes."

"Ash—"

"I'm sure."

The broker begins to chant. The sigil on Sable's wrist flares—not gold this time, but white. Pure. Hungry.

I feel it reach for me. Feel it searching for my true name, the one Mama whispered over my cradle, the one that lives in the space between heartbeats.

I let it find me.

The pain is—I don't have words for what the pain is. It's every nerve in my body screaming at once. It's my soul being read like a book, every page turned, every secret exposed.

And then it's over.

The sigil on Sable's wrist dims. Fades. Disappears entirely, leaving only smooth skin where the mark used to be.

She gasps. Touches her wrist. Stares at the absence like she's seeing a limb that's been cut away.

"I can't feel them," she whispers. "I can't feel Symeon anymore."

She looks at me. And I see everything.

Not memories—nothing that concrete. Just the shape of her. The truth of her. Every loyalty, every fear, every love she's ever tried to hide.

She's been carrying so much. For so long.

"Ash?"

"I'm okay," I manage. "I just…"

I can feel her. In my chest, like a second heartbeat. In my head, like a voice that's always been there but only now has permission to speak.

I'm sorry, she thinks. *I'm so sorry.*

I cross the room. Take her hand.

I know, I think back. *I know.*

She collapses into my arms. We hold each other in the blood-stinking cellar while Winter watches and Moe guards the door and somewhere above us the city burns.

It's not forgiveness. Not yet.

But it's a start.

• • •

Later that night, I find Moe on watch.

136

He doesn't look at me when I sit beside him. Just keeps his eyes on the dark street outside, hand resting on Mercyless.

"You should sleep," I say.

"So should you."

"Can't. Dreams are bad."

"Yeah." He's quiet for a moment. "They stay bad for a while."

"How long?"

"Depends on the person. Some people, the dreams fade. They learn to live with what they did, or they forget. And the others carry it. Every day. Every night. Until carrying it becomes just another thing they do, like breathing or bleeding."

"Which kind are you?"

"The carrying kind. Always have been."

I look at him—at the weight in his shoulders, the lines around his eyes.

"Is that why you protect people? To balance it out?"

He shrugs. "Maybe. Or maybe I just can't stop. Can't look at someone in trouble and walk away. It's a weakness, really."

"That's not a weakness."

"No?"

"That's what makes you worth protecting."

He's quiet for a long moment. Then he speaks.

"I had someone once. Woman named Grace. Met her before the Wardens, back when I thought I could be something other than what I am. She made me want to be better. Made me think maybe I could leave the blood behind."

137

His voice is steady. Old pain, well-worn.

"Then the church came. Offered her a way out. Safety. Coin. All she had to do was give them my unit's location. She took the deal. My brothers died in their beds."

"Moe…"

"I'm not telling you this for sympathy." He cuts me off. "I'm telling you because you asked why I do what I do. Why I can't stop protecting people even when it's stupid, even when it's hopeless."

He meets my eyes.

"Because I failed once. I was soft when I should've been hard, trusting when I should've been suspicious. And everyone I cared about died for it. I can't undo that. Can't bring them back. But I can make sure it doesn't happen again."

"Even Sable?"

He glances across the room at her hunched figure.

"Even Sable. She betrayed us, yeah. But she's crew now. And crew means I protect her too, even if I don't trust her, even if I'm watching her every second for the knife in the back."

"That's complicated."

"Everything worth doing is."

We sit in silence after that. The comfortable kind.

Somewhere outside, a bird starts singing. First light's coming.

"Moe?"

"Yeah?"

"Thank you. For not lying about the dreams."

"Lying doesn't help anyone." He stands, joints creaking. "Get some rest if you can. Tomorrow's going to be worse than today."

"You don't know that."

"Yeah, I do. It always is."

He heads for the door. At the threshold, he pauses. Looks back at the room—Winter with her papers, Sable in her corner, me watching him go.

Four people. That's what we're down to.

He nods once. Then the door closes behind him.

The night goes on.

CHAPTER TWELVE

THE QUEEN'S HUNGER

I don't sleep anymore. Haven't since the Crypt burned.

The others think I'm planning. Strategizing. Being the queen they need me to be. And I am—I'm always that. But in the hours between midnight and dawn, when even Moe's vigilance wavers and Ash finally stops pacing, I lie on my cot in this rotting safehouse and I count.

I count what I've lost.

The Silk Crypt. Twelve years of work. Every bribe, every murder, every compromise that built those walls—gone in one night of holy fire. The docks. My distribution network. The web of alliances and debts that made me untouchable. Seized, scattered, sold to Parliament for pennies on the gold piece.

My people. Forty-seven dead in the Fall. Another thirty arrested, probably tortured, certainly broken. The rest hiding in holes across the city, waiting for a signal I can't send because I don't know what to tell them anymore.

I had an empire. Now I have a tannery that smells like death and three broken people who look at me like I'm supposed to know what comes next.

Four. Four broken people.

I keep forgetting to count myself.

• • •

Sable sleeps in the corner. Or pretends to—I can never tell with her. Even now, after her confession, after Ash took her binding, I watch the way her breathing changes when someone moves. The way her hand drifts toward her knife even in dreams.

She was mine for two years. My best shadow. My sharpest blade. Every secret I whispered in her presence went straight to Symeon's ear, and I never knew.

I should hate her for it. Part of me does—the part that remembers every vulnerability I showed her, every moment of weakness she witnessed and reported. That part wants to cut her throat and dump her body in the river.

But another part—the part I try not to listen to—understands.

I would have done the same thing. If someone held my name in a contract, if every breath I took belonged to them, I would have spied and lied and betrayed to survive. That's not weakness. That's arithmetic. The same arithmetic I've been doing my whole life.

Survival isn't pretty. Anyone who says otherwise has never been hungry enough to know what they're really capable of.

• • •

Moe sits by the window. He hasn't slept either—I can see the weight of it in his shoulders, the way he holds Mercyless like he's forgotten how to put it down.

He loved a woman once. Grace. He told me about her years ago, drunk on moon-milk and mourning. She sold his unit to the Church for safety and coin. He found the bodies of his brothers in their beds.

I remember thinking: that's useful information. I remember filing it away—another lever, another pressure point, another way to ensure his loyalty if charm and payment ever failed.

I'm not proud of that. But I'm not ashamed either. That's what queens do. We collect secrets like merchants collect debts. We learn who people are so we can become whatever they need us to be.

Moe needs a cause worth dying for. So I give him one.

Ash needs someone to believe in him. So I do—or I perform belief so well that neither of us can tell the difference.

Sable needed a family that wouldn't sell her. So I became that family, and she loved me for it, even while she was betraying me to the people who actually owned her soul.

Three levers. Three pressure points. Three people who would die for me because I made myself indispensable to their survival.

That's not love. That's strategy.

But in the dark, counting my losses, I wonder if the distinction matters anymore.

• • •

Ash is the one I can't figure out.

He sleeps on the floor near the door—always near the exit, always ready to run. The rune on his wrist glows faintly even in rest, pulsing with a rhythm that doesn't match his heartbeat. Something else's heartbeat. Something older.

I've seen what he can do. The Blood-Market. Three hundred people unmade in seconds, their souls scattered like ash in wind. Power that Parliament's Prelates can only dream of, erupting from a street prophet who doesn't know how to control it.

He's terrified of himself. I saw it in his eyes when he came back from the Market, shaking, sick, asking if anyone had survived. He doesn't want this power. Doesn't understand it. Would give it away if he could.

That's what makes him dangerous.

Not the power itself—I've seen power before. Cardinals with scripture that could level buildings. Blood-mages who could stop hearts with a word. The Prelates with their masks and their judgment and their singing steel.

Power is just a tool. Tools can be controlled.

But Ash isn't trying to control his power. He's trying to reject it. And a weapon that doesn't want to be wielded is a weapon that fires in every direction at once.

I need to change that. Need to help him accept what he's becoming—or find a way to take it from him before it destroys everything I'm trying to rebuild.

The taking would be cleaner. Faster. Parliament wants the shard in his arm; maybe there's a deal to be made there. Ash for amnesty. Ash for territory. Ash for enough power to start rebuilding before the last of my people die in hiding.

I run the numbers. Calculate the odds. Feel the familiar comfort of strategy replacing emotion.

Then I remember the way he looked at me after Sable's confession. Not calculating. Not strategic. Just tired and sad and somehow still hoping I'd know what to do.

He trusts me.

The fool actually trusts me.

• • •

I think about my mother sometimes. Not often—she's been dead longer than she was alive for me. But in moments like this, when the dark is too heavy and the counting won't stop, I remember her hands.

She had beautiful hands. Long fingers, callused from the loom, always moving. She'd weave stories while she worked—tales of queens and kingdoms, of women who took what they wanted and made the world bow.

143

"You'll be a queen someday," she'd tell me. "Not by birth. By will. By hunger. The world gives nothing to girls like us, Winter. So we take. And we keep taking until there's nothing left to take."

She died when I was twelve. Lung-rot from the refineries, same as Sable's mother. Same as a thousand mothers in the Warrens, coughing up black until there was nothing left to cough.

I buried her in a potter's field with three copper coins in her mouth—a bribe for the ferryman, a promise that her spirit wouldn't linger. Then I walked to the nearest gang boss and offered myself for service.

I was tall for twelve. Strong for my age. And I had something the other street kids didn't have: hunger that wouldn't stop. Hunger that looked at every obstacle and asked not "how do I survive this?" but "how do I own this?"

That hunger built the Silk Crypt. Built the docks. Built everything I am and everything I've lost.

And now, lying in the dark, I feel it stirring again. Not satisfied. Never satisfied. Looking at the ruins of my empire and asking the only question that matters:

What's next?

• • •

The answer comes to me around the fourth bell. Not as revelation—I don't believe in those. As arithmetic.

Parliament wants Ash. They want the shard in his arm, the power that could complete their Crown. They'll send an offer soon—they always do, before the killing starts. Diplomacy first, violence second. That's how empires operate.

When the offer comes, they'll want me to hand him over. They'll promise amnesty, territory, maybe even my docks back. They'll make it sound reasonable. Inevitable. The pragmatic choice.

The old Winter would have considered it. Run the numbers. Calculated whether Ash's value as an ally outweighed his value as a bargaining chip.

The old Winter was weak.

I see that now, in the dark, with my empire in ashes and my people scattered. I see all the times I compromised, negotiated, accepted less than I deserved because taking more seemed too dangerous.

I built the Silk Crypt by taking. By refusing to accept the world's verdict on what a street girl could become. I took territory from gangs that had held it for generations. Took loyalty from people who'd sworn to other masters. Took respect from nobles who'd never looked twice at someone with dirt under their nails.

Then I stopped. Got comfortable. Started protecting what I had instead of reaching for what I wanted.

That's why I lost. Not because Parliament was stronger—because I'd forgotten how to be hungry.

Well.

I remember now.

• • •

I sit up on my cot. The movement is quiet—I've been quiet all my life, learned it in alleys where sound meant death—but Moe's head turns anyway.

"Can't sleep?" he asks.

"Thinking."

"That's dangerous."

"The alternative is worse."

He almost smiles. "What's the plan, then? You've got that look. The one that usually means someone's about to have a very bad day."

I swing my legs off the cot. Stand. Cross to the window where he's been keeping watch.

The city spreads below us—Ashvein's twisted sprawl, Parliament's spires in the distance, the dark stain of the Warrens where I was born. All of it hostile now. All of it waiting to see if Winter Vale will break.

"Parliament will send an envoy soon," I say. "They'll offer terms. Probably generous ones—they can afford to be generous when they think they've won."

"And?"

"And I'm going to tell them no."

Moe's quiet for a moment. Processing.

"That's suicide."

"Maybe."

"They'll throw everything at us. We don't have the numbers, the weapons, the allies—"

"I know what we don't have." I turn to face him. "What I need to know is: can I count on you when I tell them to go to hell?"

He stares at me. I watch him calculate—watch him weigh the odds, assess the risks, measure my certainty against his own survival instinct.

Then he laughs.

It's not a happy sound. But it's real, and it's his, and when he meets my eyes there's something in them I haven't seen in weeks.

Hope, maybe. Or madness.

With Moe, they look the same.

"You know I'm in," he says. "Till the end."

"It might be soon."

"Then it'll be a good end." He rolls his shoulders, settles Merciless more comfortably against his back. "Better than dying in my sleep."

I nod. Feel something loosen in my chest—not relief, exactly. More like recognition. I'm not alone in this. Not completely.

"Get some rest," I tell him. "Tomorrow starts the real war."

"And you?"

I look back at the window. At the city that tried to kill me and failed. At everything I've lost and everything I'm going to take back.

"I'm going to make a list."

• • •

I don't make a list. I don't need to—the targets have been living in my head for years. Every noble who looked through me. Every merchant who cheated my people. Every Warden who thought their mask made them untouchable.

Parliament at the top. Always Parliament.

But underneath the planning, underneath the strategy, there's something else. Something I don't want to examine too closely.

I look at Ash. At the glow of his rune in the darkness. At the power sleeping in his flesh.

The shard in his arm is a fragment of divinity. A piece of the Crown that ruled this world before Parliament learned to hoard it. With that shard, with what it could become, I could—No.

I push the thought away. Too far. Too fast. That's not who I am.

But the hunger doesn't listen to should and shouldn't. The hunger just calculates. And the calculation is simple:

147

Ash has power he can't control. Power he doesn't want. Power that could reshape everything, if someone who understood power were guiding it.

I've spent my life guiding power. Taking it from people who had it and using it better than they ever could. That's what made me a queen—not birth, not luck, but the willingness to see opportunity where others saw only risk.

And Ash is the biggest opportunity I've ever seen.

I don't want to think this way about him. He trusts me. He looks at me like I'm the answer to something, like I can fix what's broken in his world.

But trust is a tool like any other. And I've never let sentiment stop me from using the tools at hand.

Not yet, I tell myself. Not yet. He's still useful as an ally. Still more valuable fighting beside me than under me.

But if that changes…

If the arithmetic shifts…

I'll do what I've always done.

Whatever it takes.

• • •

Dawn comes eventually. It always does, no matter how much the dark feels permanent.

Ash stirs first—always does, like his body never quite trusts safety enough to stay asleep. He sits up, rubs his face, looks around with the disoriented expression of someone who keeps expecting to wake up somewhere else.

His eyes find mine. I'm still by the window, still counting, still planning.

"You didn't sleep," he says.

"Neither did you."

"Dreams are bad."

"I know." I cross toward him. Sit on the edge of his pallet. Let my voice soften the way I've learned makes people trust me. "The Blood-Market?"

He flinches. Just a little—most people wouldn't notice. But I notice everything.

"I keep seeing their faces," he whispers. "The ones at the edge. The ones who were just... there. They weren't slavers. They were merchants, servants, people who happened to be in the wrong place when I—"

"When the Crown used you."

"Does that matter? They're still dead."

I take his hand. Feel the warmth of his skin, the pulse of power beneath. The gesture is calculated—human contact builds trust—but something in me responds anyway. Something that isn't strategy.

"It matters," I tell him. "You didn't choose to kill them. The Crown did. Holding yourself responsible for what you couldn't control isn't justice. It's just another way to hurt yourself."

"And what if I could have controlled it? What if I'd been stronger, faster, better—"

"Then you'd find another reason to blame yourself. That's how guilt works, Ash. It's hungry. It takes whatever you feed it and asks for more."

He looks at me. Really looks. And I see something in his eyes that makes the calculation feel like cruelty.

"How do you do it?" he asks. "How do you keep going after everything you've lost?"

The honest answer would break something between us. The honest answer is: because losing makes me angry, and anger makes me effective, and I'd rather burn the world than admit I've been beaten.

But he doesn't need honesty. He needs hope.

"Because the people who hurt us want us to stop," I say. "Every time we give up, they win. And I refuse—I absolutely refuse—to let them win."

He nods. Slowly. Like he's trying to make himself believe it.

"Stay close to me," I tell him. "When Parliament's envoy comes—and they will come—stay close. Let me handle the talking. And when they make their offer..."

"Yeah?"

I squeeze his hand.

"Watch how a queen says no."

• • •

Sable is awake by the time I stand. She's been awake the whole time—I could tell by the tension in her shoulders—but she waited for the conversation to end before she moved.

Smart. Loyal. Dangerous.

The gold sigil on her wrist glows faintly—Ash's mark now, not Symeon's. She belongs to my prophet instead of my enemy. That should make me feel safer.

It doesn't.

"Winter." Her voice is careful. Testing. "What you said to Ash—"

"I meant it."

"All of it?"

I hold her gaze. Let her see whatever she needs to see.

"I've never lied to any of you. Not once. I've chosen what truths to share, yes. Kept my own counsel. But every word I've spoken has been real."

"And when Parliament comes?"

"We reject them. We fight. We take back what's ours."

"With what army? What weapons? What—"

"With hunger." I step closer. "The same thing that built the Silk Crypt from nothing. The same thing that made you survive two years of slavery to masters you hated. The same thing that keeps Ash standing when the guilt should have broken him by now."

I touch her face. Gentle. Almost tender.

"We're all hungry, Sable. Parliament thinks that makes us weak. They think empty bellies mean broken spirits. But they've never starved the way we have. Never wanted the way we want."

My fingers trace the line of her jaw.

"That's going to be their mistake."

• • •

The knock comes an hour later.

Three beats. Pause. Two more. Pause. One.

My code. Which means someone I trust. Which means the message is real.

Moe is at the door before I can signal, Mercyless drawn. "Who?"

"A friend," comes the voice from beyond. Smooth. Practiced. "Or perhaps an opportunity. Depending on how this conversation goes."

151

I know that voice. Know it the way you know a knife that's been at your throat—intimately, unwillingly, permanently.

Caius.

Parliament's favorite messenger. The Glass Duke's voice and will. A man who's survived three regime changes and two assassination attempts because he always knows which way the wind is blowing.

If he's here, the offer has come.

I look at Ash. At Sable. At Moe with his blade drawn and his eyes steady.

My people. Whatever else has changed, whatever else I've lost, I still have this. Three broken souls who've chosen to stand with me against an empire.

I straighten my spine. Lift my chin. Let Winter Vale settle over me like armor.

"Let him in," I say.

And I prepare to teach Parliament what it costs to underestimate a hungry queen.

CHAPTER THIRTEEN

PARLIAMENT'S OFFER

Dawn crawls over Ashvein like a wounded animal dragging itself toward a hole to die in. None of us have slept. The revelations of last night—Sable's betrayal, Winter's claim, Parliament's accelerated timeline—sit in the room like uninvited guests refusing to leave. Every time someone moves, the silence flinches. Winter sits at the small table, papers spread before her, making calculations I don't want to understand. Sable haunts the far corner, her new sigil pulsing soft gold against her wrist. She hasn't spoken since Winter's ritual. Hasn't looked at me either. Moe sharpens Mercyless with movements too precise for comfort. The blade sings a low note with each stroke, hungry and patient. And me? I sit by the cracked window, watching the city wake up to another day of fear. The rune on my arm throbs with a pulse that isn't mine, counting down to something I can't name.

You're in over your head, brother. Eli's voice, faint but present. *These people are playing games you don't understand.*

I don't answer. Don't need to. He's right. He's always right. Then the knock comes. Three beats. Pause. Two more. Pause. One. Winter's code. Known only to her innermost circle. Moe is on his feet before the last knock fades, Mercyless aimed at the door. "Who?" he growls. "A friend," comes the voice from beyond. Smooth. Practiced. Terrifyingly familiar. "Or perhaps an opportunity. Depending on how this conversation goes." Winter's expression goes flat. "Let them in."

The man who enters is neither soldier nor saint. He's dressed in Parliament colors—deep purple trimmed with silver thread that catches light wrong, like it's embarrassed to be noticed. His face is pleasant in a way that feels calculated, each smile-line placed with architectural precision. Middle-aged, maybe older, with eyes that have seen things they'll never tell. He bows precisely two inches. No more. No less. "Lady Winter. An honor, as always."

"Caius." Winter's voice could frost glass. "I thought you died at the Salt Rebellion."

"Reports of my demise were tactically convenient." His smile doesn't reach his eyes. "I serve the Glass Duke now. His voice. His will. His... offers." Sable shifts in her corner. I can feel her calculating angles, escape routes, kill points. Caius notices. Of course he does. "Miss Korran. I see you've changed allegiances. How delightfully flexible of you." Sable doesn't respond. Her new sigil flares once— warning or acknowledgment, I can't tell. "State your business," Winter says. "I have a war to plan."

"That's precisely why I'm here." Caius produces a scroll from his sleeve—sealed with wax the color of dried blood, stamped with the seven-pointed star of the Night Parliament. "My masters have authorized me to make an offer. One time. Non-negotiable. Expiring at sunset." He extends the scroll. Winter doesn't take it. "Read it aloud," she says. "I want witnesses."

Caius's smile tightens, but he unrolls the scroll. "'To Winter Vale, self-styled Dock Queen, Mistress of the Silk Crypt, and Holder of the Shard called Hunger.'" He reads with practiced neutrality. "'The Night Parliament, in its wisdom and mercy, extends the following terms for your immediate consideration.'" He pauses. Waits for reaction. Gets none. "'First: Full integration of your commercial networks into Parliament oversight. Your docks, your distribution channels, your client lists—all transferred to joint authority.'" Moe makes a sound like a dog hearing a threat. "'Second: Dissolution of your personal guard and military assets. Your people will be reassigned to Parliament command structures, retrained according to Church doctrine.'" Sable's hand drifts toward her knives. "'Third: Surrender of any Crown-touched materials or individuals currently in your possession.'" Caius's eyes flick to me. Just for a moment. "'This includes the prophet known as Ash Marrow and the shard embedded in his flesh.'" My rune ignites. Not warming—burning. I clench my fist to hide the light. "'In exchange,'" Caius continues, voice unchanged, "'the Night Parliament offers: Full amnesty for past transgressions. Protection under Church law. A permanent seat on the Parliament's advisory council. And—'" He pauses for effect. "'—the title of Duchess of the Western Docks, with all attendant privileges and revenues.'" He lowers the scroll. "They're offering you legitimacy, Lady Winter. Power without the constant war. Wealth without the blood. A throne you don't have to defend every day of your life." Winter hasn't moved. "And all I have to do," she says slowly, "is hand over my people. My autonomy. My prophet."

"A small price for immortality in the city's ledgers." Winter laughs. It's not a pleasant sound.

Winter stands. She walks to the window. Looks out at the city she's spent her life climbing, clawing, conquering. "Tell me something, Caius." Her voice is thoughtful. Almost gentle. "How many queens has Parliament made offers like this?"

"I'm not at liberty to discuss—" "How many queens accepted?" Silence. "And how many of those queens are still alive?" Caius's pleasant mask cracks. Just a fraction. "The Parliament honors its agreements."

"The Parliament honors its interests." Winter turns. "I've seen what happens to people who merge with your machine. They disappear. Not killed—that would be wasteful. They're absorbed. Their networks become Parliament networks. Their people become Parliament people. And eventually, their names become footnotes in ledgers nobody reads." She looks at me. At Sable. At Moe. I can see her calculating. Weighing the offer against the costs. Measuring survival against freedom. This is the woman who bargained away her fertility for power. Who keeps her ex-lover's heart in a jar for advice. Who built an empire from nothing and held it against all comers through cunning and blood. If anyone would take this deal, it would be Winter. The silence stretches. Then she smiles. "Caius. Do you know why I named my club the Silk Crypt?"

"I... no."

"Because silk is beautiful. Soft. Comfortable." Her smile sharpens. "But a crypt is where you put things that are already dead." She takes the scroll from his hands. Her fingers tremble—not with fear. With something else. Anticipation, maybe. Or greed.

She tears it in half. "Tell your masters I decline."

Caius's pleasant facade crumbles like paint off rotted wood. "You understand what this means."

"I understand Parliament expected me to grovel. To take their leash and call it a crown." Winter tosses the torn scroll at his feet. "They miscalculated."

"Lady Winter—" "I am no lady. I am the Dock Queen. I earned that title in blood and fire and buried bodies. And I will not give it up to become some council's pet." Caius's voice drops. The diplomatic smoothness replaced by something colder. "Then you will be destroyed. Your docks seized. Your people hunted. Everything you've built will burn."

"Let them try."

"They don't try, Lady Winter. They succeed. They have always succeeded." He steps closer. "The Blood-Market massacre bought you attention. The prophet's rampage earned you enemies. And now you've rejected their mercy. There will be no second offer." Moe rises. Mercyless hums in his grip. "You threatening us in our own house?"

"I'm stating facts. The Parliament has more soldiers than you have people. More gold than you have debts. More shards than your prophet carries in his arm." Caius's eyes find mine. "They will take him, Lady Winter. Whether you offer him or not. The only question is how many die before they do." Winter moves fast. One moment she's by the window. The next, she has Caius by the throat, pressed against the wall, her tattooed fingers glowing with something that makes the air taste like copper. "Run back to your masters," she whispers. "Tell them Winter Vale said no. Tell them the Dock Queen chooses war. And tell them—" Her grip tightens. "—if they want the prophet, they can come take him from my corpse." She releases him. Caius staggers, coughing, hand at his throat. "This is a declaration," he rasps. "You understand? Parliament will respond in kind."

"I'm counting on it." She opens the door. "Get out. Before I change my mind about letting you leave alive."

Caius straightens his coat with trembling hands. "The Glass Duke will hear of this. Cardinal Red will hear of this. The entire Parliament will know what you've done."

"Good." Winter's smile is pure predator. "Make sure they spell my name right." He leaves. The door closes. The silence that follows is different from before. Heavier. More real. Winter turns to face us. "Questions?" Moe speaks first. "You know what you just did?"

"Yes."

"They'll throw everything at us. Wardens. Executioners. Maybe Prelates."

"Yes."

"We don't have the numbers. Don't have the resources. Don't have—" "Moe." Winter's voice is steel. "I know what we don't have. What I need to know is: are you with me?" Moe stares at her for a long moment. Then he laughs. A real laugh. Something I haven't heard from him since before the martial law started. "Shit, Winter. I been waiting for someone to finally tell those silk-robed bastards to go to hell." He sheathes Mercyless with a flourish. "I'm in. Till the end." Winter's eyes move to Sable. Sable lifts her wrist. The gold sigil pulses. "You own my name," she says quietly. "You own my service. But for what it's worth... I would have chosen this anyway." Winter nods. Something that might be gratitude flickers across her face. Then she looks at me. "Ash."

157

"Yeah."

"This is your war now too. The prophet at the center of it. The catalyst for the Crown's reforging." She steps closer. "If we lose, they take you. Cut that shard out of your arm. Use you as fuel for their ritual. Everything you are, everything you could be—gone."

"I know."

"And you still want to fight?" I think about the Blood-Market. About my brother's ghost in chains. About the hundreds of people I killed without meaning to, without stopping, without control. I think about Sable's confession. About Winter's pragmatic cruelty. About Moe's steady violence and all the things none of us say out loud. I think about the rune spreading up my arm. About the Crown's hunger. About what I'm becoming and what it costs. "I was fighting before you named it war," I say. "The only difference now is the rest of the city knows."

• • •

Sable finds me on the roof an hour later.

The sun is setting, painting the city in shades of blood and gold. From up here, I can see the Rust Warrens spreading out like a wound—the district where I was born, where Eli died, where everything that made me started.

"You're scared." Not a question.

"Terrified."

She sits beside me. Close enough that our shoulders touch. The contact shouldn't mean as much as it does, but it does anyway.

"When I was twelve," she says quietly, "Symeon made me watch a man die. One of their informants who'd been feeding information to the wrong people. They didn't kill him fast. They made it educational."

"Sable—"

"I'm not telling you this for sympathy." She cuts me off. "I'm telling you because afterward, I was scared too. Scared of Symeon, scared of what they'd do to me if I ever failed, scared of everything."

"How did you survive it?"

"I stopped thinking about the fear. Started thinking about what I could control." Her hand finds mine. Squeezes. "You can't save everyone, Ash. You know that. But you can give them a choice. A chance to fight for something instead of just dying for nothing."

"And if they die anyway?"

"Then they die fighting. They die free." Her eyes meet mine. "That's more than most people get."

I think about Eli. About his last words: *Not your fault. Pray for me. Love you, big brother.*

He didn't get to fight. Didn't get to choose. The Wardens took that from him.

Maybe Sable's right. Maybe giving people a choice is the most I can offer.

"Stay with me," I say. "Tonight. At the Market."

"You don't have to ask."

"I'm asking anyway."

She leans her head against my shoulder. We watch the sun die together, and somewhere in the city below, thousands of people are waiting to hear their prophet speak.

I hope I have something worth saying.

• • •

"We have three days." Winter spreads new maps across the table. "Maybe less, depending on how fast Cardinal Red moves."

"Three days for what?" Moe asks. "To crash their ceremony. Stop the reforging. Free the hostages." Winter marks positions on the map with quick, decisive strokes. "And to build an army capable of doing it."

"With what?" Sable leans forward. "Your docks are seized. Your gold is frozen. Half your people are dead or arrested."

"I have something Parliament can't freeze." Winter's finger taps a district on the map. The Rust Warrens. My district. "I have ether." The word hangs in the air. "The contaminated supply destroyed Parliament's distribution network," Winter continues. "They poisoned their own product trying to destabilize us. Now half the city is in withdrawal and the other half is desperate for clean product."

"You're going to sell drugs to fund a war," I say flatly. "I'm going to trade the only currency that matters in Ashvein right now. The only thing people need more than food, more than shelter, more than safety." Her eyes meet mine. "Ether is pain relief. It's escape. It's the thing that makes this city bearable for people who have nothing else. And I control the only clean supply left."

"Parliament controls the official facilities. But I've spent years building shadow refineries. Hidden labs." Winter's smile is thin and sharp. "They thought they were being clever, poisoning my supply. They just created a monopoly."

For just a moment, I see something flicker across her face—hunger, maybe. The kind that doesn't know when to stop. Then it's gone, replaced by the calculating mask she always wears. Moe whistles low. "You're going to make every crew, every gang, every desperate hustler in the city dependent on you."

"I'm going to make them allies. Ether for soldiers. Ether for information. Ether for weapons and wagons and bodies willing to stand against the church." Winter leans back. "War is expensive. But addiction is cheaper."

"There's a gathering tonight at the Old Market. Your people. The ones who've been calling you Saint Ash." Winter hands me a piece of paper. "Two thousand expected. Maybe more."

160

"And you want me to what? Tell them to take up arms?"

"I want you to tell them the truth. That Parliament is coming for everyone they love. That the Crown they're trying to reforge will enslave every magic user in the city. That the only way to protect their families is to stand together."

"That's propaganda."

"That's survival. There's a difference?" I look at the paper. It's a list of names. People who've come to my healings. People who've prayed at the gutter temples built in my name. People who've trusted me with their children, their sick, their dying. "If I do this," I say slowly, "if I turn them into soldiers... some of them will die."

"Some of them will die anyway." Winter's voice is gentle. Almost kind. "The question isn't whether people die, Ash. The question is whether they die for something." Sable speaks up. "She's not wrong." I look at her. She's been quiet since the meeting started, processing everything through the filter of her new loyalty. "Parliament doesn't take prisoners from the street faith," she continues. "They take examples. Anyone connected to you is already marked. The only question is whether they're marked as victims or warriors."

"You sound like her now."

"I sound like someone who's seen what the church does to people who don't fight back." Her eyes meet mine. "You gave them hope, Ash. Now give them a chance to defend it." I fold the paper. Slip it into my pocket. "Fine. I'll speak tonight." I look at Winter. "But I do it my way. No scripts. No propaganda. Just the truth." Winter's smile is satisfied. "The truth will be enough."

The Old Market used to be the heart of the Rust Warrens. Before the refineries poisoned the ground. Before the nobles built walls to keep us contained. Before hope became something you had to buy by the vial. Tonight, it's a cathedral. Torches ring the square, casting shadows that dance and writhe against the crumbling walls. Two thousand people—maybe more—pack the space, standing shoulder to shoulder, breath fogging in the cold air. They wear the rags of

Guttersea and the worn clothes of honest labor. They carry children on their shoulders and elders by the arm. They came because word spread that Saint Ash would speak, and in these dark days, any promise of light draws a crowd. I stand on a makeshift platform built from crates and boards. Sable guards my left. Moe guards my right. Winter watches from the shadows, calculating the value of every face in the crowd. The rune at my arm pulses with each heartbeat. The crowd's faith presses against me like a tide—expectation, desperation, need. They want a miracle. I'm about to give them something else. "You know me," I begin. My voice carries further than it should—the rune's doing, or maybe just the acoustics of hope. "You've come to my healings. You've prayed in the temples built in my name. You've called me Saint Ash." Murmurs ripple through the crowd. Affirmation. Reverence. "I'm not a saint." The murmurs stop. "Saints are perfect. Pure. Chosen by divine will to guide the faithful toward paradise." I let the words settle. "I'm not that. I'm a man who got lucky with a bad rune and worse choices. I've killed. I've failed. I've watched people I love die because I wasn't fast enough, strong enough, holy enough to save them." Silence now. Complete and heavy. "But I'm not here to confess. I'm here to warn you."

"Three days from now, the Night Parliament plans to execute three hundred of our people at the Grand Cathedral. A public purification, they'll call it. A cleansing of heresy." Gasps. Cries. Someone in the crowd starts weeping. "But that's not all. The executions are a distraction. A sacrifice to power something bigger." I let the rune flare—just a little, just enough for them to see the light beneath my skin. "They're going to reforge the Crown. A divine artifact that will give them control over every magic user in Ashvein. Control over me. Over your healers and protection-workers and fortune-tellers. Over everyone who's ever used verse or rune or prayer to make this city a little more bearable." The crowd shifts. Fear becoming anger. Despair becoming defiance. "They mean to make themselves gods," I say. "And they mean to make slaves of everyone else." A man's voice rises from the crowd. "What do we do? We can't fight the Parliament!"

"No. Alone, we can't." I step to the edge of the platform. "But we're not alone. Winter Vale has pledged her resources, her people, her

162

life to stopping this. Crews across the city are joining us. The Bronze Syndicate. The gutter priests. Everyone who's ever been crushed under Parliament's boot is finally ready to stand up."

"And you?" a woman calls out. "Will you fight, prophet? Or just preach?" I close my eyes. Feel the rune burning. Feel my brother's ghost somewhere in the back of my skull, laughing at the boy who used to dream of quiet. "I've already fought," I say. "At the Blood-Market. At the healing grounds. Every time I've used this power, I've been fighting a war I didn't choose. But now..." I open my eyes. "Now I choose it. And I'm asking you to choose it too."

CHAPTER FOURTEEN

ASH CROWNED IN SMOKE

Day Two. Forty-eight hours until the Cathedral ceremony. Forty-eight hours until Parliament reforges the Crown and executes three hundred of our people in front of the entire city. Forty-eight hours to build an army from broken pieces. The abandoned foundry in the Rust Warrens hasn't forged steel in twenty years. The fires went cold when the refineries poisoned the ground, when the workers died or fled, when the district became the kind of place respectable people pretended didn't exist. Tonight, it forges something else. I stand on a catwalk overlooking the main floor, watching crews file in through a dozen hidden entrances. They come in colors and factions that would have been killing each other a week ago. Bronze Syndicate enforcers in their dock-stained leathers. Gutter priests in robes that smell like incense and desperation. Street crews from every corner of the Warrens, armed with whatever they could steal, borrow, or pray into existence. And mixed among them, the believers. The people who've been following me since the first healing, who've built shrines in basements and spread my name through whisper networks. They don't carry weapons. They carry faith. An army of the desperate, the faithful, and the damned. Winter appears beside me, her tattooed arms folded, her expression unreadable. "Three thousand," she says. "Maybe more coming."

"Is it enough?"

"Against Parliament's full force?" She doesn't answer. Doesn't have to. Below us, Moe moves through the crowd, shaking hands, slapping shoulders, doing the work of making enemies into allies. Sable shadows me at a distance, her new sigil pulsing gold whenever Winter gets too close. "They need to hear from you," Winter says. "Not me. Not the crews. You."

"I spoke last night."

"Last night you asked them to fight. Tonight you need to tell them how to win." I look at my hands. The rune has spread past my elbow now, crawling toward my shoulder in lines that look like scripture. Every time I use it, every time I let the power flow, it grows. Takes more territory. Becomes more of me. "And if I don't know how to win?" Winter's smile is thin and sharp. "Then lie. That's what prophets do."

The faction leaders gather in what used to be the foreman's office—a cramped space that smells like rust and old ambition. Krell of the Bronze Syndicate. Mother Vera from the gutter priests. Razor and Ghost representing the street crews. Winter presides. I stand behind her, the prophet on display. "Supply lines," Krell growls. "We need to talk about supply lines. My people can't fight on empty stomachs."

"Your people can't fight at all if Parliament burns the Warrens before we're ready," Razor counters. "Defense first. Then supply."

"Defense with what? Your little knives against Executioners?"

"Better than your boats against fire." Mother Vera raises a hand. Silence falls. Even the half-ghost stops flickering. "Children." Her voice is soft but carries like smoke. "We have forty-eight hours to stop a god from being born. Perhaps we could argue about whose wounds are deepest after we've survived to compare them." Krell's jaw tightens. Razor looks away. "The prophet promised us unity," Mother Vera continues. "I came because I believed him. If I was wrong…" She looks at me. "Tell me now, so I can take my people home to die in peace." The room waits. I step forward. "You weren't wrong."

"Tomorrow night, Parliament holds their ceremony at the Grand Cathedral. They'll have the hostages in the courtyard, displayed like trophies. They'll have Wardens on every entrance, Executioners at the altar, and enough firepower to level a district." I let that sink in. "We

165

can't match them soldier for soldier. Can't match their gold, their weapons, their magic. If we try to fight them on their terms, we lose." Krell leans back. "So what's your plan, prophet? Pray them to death?"

"No. We make them fight on our terms." I move to the table. Spread Winter's maps across the surface. "The Cathedral sits at the center of the Ivory Spires. One main entrance, two side passages, emergency tunnels beneath. Parliament expects an assault from outside—a siege they can crush with superior numbers." My finger traces the streets around the Cathedral. "So we don't give them a siege. We give them chaos."

"Explain," Mother Vera says. "Tomorrow night, while Parliament is focused on their ceremony, we hit every Warden checkpoint in the city. Simultaneously. Not to win—just to occupy. Make them think we're attacking everywhere at once. Pull their reinforcements away from the Cathedral." Razor nods slowly. "Spread them thin."

"Thin enough that a small team can slip through the tunnels beneath the Cathedral. Reach the altar before the ritual completes. Disrupt the reforging."

"And the hostages?"

"A second team hits the courtyard during the chaos. Gets our people out while Parliament is distracted." Krell's brother flickers, whispers something only he can hear. "The dead one wants to know," Krell translates, "what happens when they realize the main assault is a feint. When they pull everything back to the Cathedral." I meet his eyes. "Then I'll be there. At the altar. Giving them something bigger to worry about." Silence blankets the room. "You're going to be the distraction," Winter says flatly. "The bait that keeps their attention while everyone else escapes."

"I'm going to be what I've always been. A symbol." I let the rune flare—just enough for them to see the light through my sleeve. "They want the Crown shard in my arm. They need it for the ritual. If I'm standing at their altar, screaming Relic Tongue at their precious ceremony, they won't be looking anywhere else."

166

"And if they kill you?" I smile. It feels like someone else's face. "Then I die famous. And you finish the job anyway."

Midnight. The foundry has gone quiet, crews catching what sleep they can before the final day begins. Sentries patrol the perimeter. Winter's runners carry messages through the city's veins. I sit alone in the foreman's office, staring at my arm. The rune has spread again. Past my shoulder now. Tendrils of golden scripture crawling across my chest, wrapping around my ribs like a second skeleton. It happened while I was talking to the faction leaders. While I was training the crews. While I was promising things I'm not sure I can deliver. The Crown is growing inside me. I can feel it now—not just as power, but as presence. Something watching from behind my eyes. Something listening to my thoughts. Something that has opinions about what I should do with the body it's sharing. The voice isn't mine. Isn't my brother's either. It's older. Colder.

You could unite them properly. Not through persuasion. Through command.

"I'm not a king," I whisper. "Not a god."

Tomorrow you'll face their ritual. When the Crown calls to itself—you'll have to choose. Break it. Or wear it.

"I'll break it."

Even when you could remake this city? Bring back everyone you've lost?

My brother's face flashes behind my eyes. For just a moment, I want it.

Then I remember what the Crown has done. What it will make me do.

"No. Not for him. Not for anyone."

The presence retreats. But it doesn't leave. It's waiting.

Dawn of the final day. The foundry floor is packed. Three thousand people—maybe more—pressed together in the cavernous space, breath fogging in the cold morning air. They've spent the night preparing, praying, making peace with the possibility of death. Now they need something else. They need faith. I stand on the platform we built from old machinery, looking out at the faces of an army that shouldn't exist. Bronze enforcers shoulder to shoulder with street kids. Gutter priests holding hands with thieves. The faithful and the faithless, united by nothing but desperation and a promise I made in the dark. Winter watches from the shadows. Her expression is calculating—always calculating—but there's something else there too. Concern, maybe. Or fear. Moe stands at the base of the platform, Mercyless sheathed but ready. He gives me a small nod. *Do what you do, prophet.* Sable is somewhere in the crowd, her gold sigil a faint pulse I can feel through the chaos of bodies. She's where she needs to be. Where I need her to be. The room goes quiet. Three thousand pairs of eyes, waiting. The silence is absolute. Three thousand people holding their breath.

I remember what Winter said: *Lie. That's what prophets do.*

But I've never been good at lying. So I tell the truth instead.

"I grew up on these streets." My voice carries further than it should—the rune's doing. "Three blocks from here, there's a gutter where I used to sleep when the weather was warm enough. Four blocks that way, there's a shrine where my mother prayed for miracles that never came. She died anyway. Lung-rot. The kind that eats you slow while the priests tell you it's divine judgment for sins you never committed."

Nobody speaks. The Bronze enforcers are still. The gutter priests have stopped swaying. Even the children have gone quiet.

"My brother Eli used to believe. Used to pray every night, even after Mama was gone. He'd kneel on the floor of whatever squat we were living in, and he'd ask God to watch over us. To keep us safe. To maybe—just maybe—give us something better than what we had."

I feel Eli's ghost stir in the rune. Listening.

"The Wardens killed him when he was fifteen. They held him down and they cut his throat and they laughed while I watched. And you know what his last words were? You know what he said while he was bleeding out in my arms?"

My voice cracks. I let it.

"'Pray for me.'"

The crowd shifts. I can feel their grief echoing mine. Three thousand people who've all lost someone. Who've all watched the Church take and take and take.

"I stopped believing that night. Stopped praying. Stopped thinking there was anything in this world worth having faith in. I was seventeen years old and I was done with hope."

I raise my arm. Let the rune blaze visible through my sleeve.

"Then this happened. Power I didn't ask for, didn't want, didn't understand. The same Church that killed my brother gave me the ability to heal people—the cruel joke of a universe that doesn't care about justice. And I thought about refusing it. Thought about cutting it out of my own flesh rather than becoming something connected to the people who destroyed my family."

I look at them. Really look. The Bronze enforcers who've killed for money. The gutter priests who've sold fake blessings. The street crews who've stolen and cheated and done whatever they had to do to survive.

My people. All of them.

"But then I healed someone. A boy in the Warrens, bleeding out from a Warden's blade, and I put my hands on him and I spoke words I'd never learned and he lived. He *lived*. And his mother looked at me like I was an angel instead of a hustler with a curse."

The crowd murmurs. Recognition. They've seen me heal. They've heard the stories.

"That's when I understood. This power—whatever it is—isn't from the Church. It isn't from Parliament. It isn't from the God they've

169

been selling us our whole lives. It's from something else. Something older. Something that doesn't care about tithes or hierarchies or whether you've got gold in your pocket."

I step to the edge of the platform.

"It's from *us*. From the streets. From every prayer that got ignored, every blessing that got denied, every person who asked for mercy and got nothing but silence. All that faith had to go somewhere. And it went here."

I tap my chest where the rune pulses brightest.

"I'm not special. I'm just the vessel. The place where all your desperate hope collected and became something real. You made me, whether you know it or not. Every time you prayed without expecting an answer, every time you believed in something better even when the evidence said you were wrong—you were building this. Building me."

The crowd is leaning forward now. Hungry for something to believe in.

"Parliament wants to take that away. They want to reforge their Crown, steal back the power that slipped through their fingers, use it to enslave everyone who's ever touched magic in this city. They're going to kill three hundred of our people tomorrow night—sacrifice them to fuel their ritual—and then they're going to come for the rest of us."

I let the words sink in.

"We can't stop them with weapons. Can't match their numbers, their training, their gold. If this is a war of soldiers, we lose."

Krell makes a sound of protest. Razor's hand drifts toward her blade.

"But it's not a war of soldiers." I raise my voice. "It's a war of faith. And faith is the one thing they can't beat."

"They've spent centuries telling us that divine power belongs to them. That the only way to touch the sacred is through their temples,

170

their priests, their laws. They've convinced half the world that the streets are godless—that people like us are too dirty, too poor, too sinful to deserve miracles."

I shake my head.

"They're wrong. They've always been wrong. The streets aren't godless. The streets are where God lives when the churches kick him out. The streets are where prayers get answered because there's nowhere else for them to go. The streets are where faith survives because it has to—because without it, we'd have nothing."

The crowd is swaying now. I can feel their belief pressing against me like a tide.

"Tomorrow night, Parliament is going to try to steal that from us. They're going to take our people, our power, our hope, and they're going to use it to build a throne for themselves."

I let the rune flare bright enough to light the whole foundry.

"Unless we stop them."

A roar goes up. Three thousand voices, raw and hungry and ready.

"I'm not asking you to fight for me." I speak over the noise, let the power carry my words. "I'm asking you to fight for each other. For the gutter monks who pray in abandoned buildings. For the addicts who are still trying to get clean. For the children who haven't learned yet that the world wants them to give up."

The roar grows louder.

"I'm asking you to fight for everyone who's ever been told they don't matter. Who's ever been dismissed, ignored, stepped over, forgotten. I'm asking you to stand up tomorrow night and show Parliament what happens when the people they've been grinding under their boots finally fight back."

I raise both arms. The rune blazes from chest to fingertips, golden light pouring from my skin.

171

"I'm asking you to believe. Not in me. In each other. In the power that we've built together, the faith that we've kept alive when everything told us to let it die. Tomorrow night, we—"

The words stop.

Something else takes over.

I don't remember falling. I remember the light. The sound. The feeling of being used as a channel for something too big to contain. Then darkness. Then Sable's face, streaked with tears and terror, leaning over me. "—can you hear me? Ash? ASH?" I blink. Try to speak. My throat feels like I've been swallowing broken glass. "What... what happened?" She helps me sit up. We're still in the foundry, but it's different now. The ceiling is open to the sky. Glass covers every surface. And the crowd... The crowd is kneeling. Three thousand people, on their knees, staring at me like I'm something they've never seen before. Something they never expected to see. Something holy. "You broke windows across three districts," Sable whispers. "People saw the light from the Ivory Spires. The whole city felt it."

"The sermon..."

"Was more than a sermon." Winter's voice, from somewhere behind me. "That was a demonstration. A declaration. You just announced to everyone—Parliament, the faithful, everyone—exactly what you are." I struggle to my feet. Sable supports me, her arm around my waist, her body warm against my side. "What am I?" Winter steps into view. Her face is pale. Her tattooed arms are crossed tight against her chest. "Something I'm not sure I can control anymore."

Her eyes linger on me a beat too long. Calculating the cost. Calculating the value. I've seen that look before—on merchants pricing cargo. On collectors examining rare acquisitions. The crowd is still kneeling. Still staring. And now, filtering through the broken walls, I can hear sounds from the city beyond. Chanting. From every direction. "SAINT ASH. SAINT ASH. SAINT ASH." It's not just the foundry. It's the whole Warrens. Maybe the whole city. The sermon didn't just rally an army. It created a legend.

172

CHAPTER FIFTEEN

FALL OF THE SILK CRYPT

Sunset of the final day. Six hours until we storm the Cathedral. Six hours until we crash Parliament's ceremony and tear down everything they've built. Six hours until we find out if desperate courage is enough to beat ancient power. The foundry hums with last-minute preparations. Runners carry final messages. Crews check weapons, say prayers, make peace with the possibility that tonight is their last night. The faithful have gathered outside, thousands of them, waiting for their prophet to lead them into battle. I stand at the window, watching the sun bleed red across the rooftops. The rune on my arm pulses with each heartbeat, golden light visible through my shirt. I've stopped trying to hide it. Winter appears beside me. "Teams are in position. Bronze is ready at the checkpoints. The tunnel crew moves in two hours."

"And the Cathedral?"

"Scouts report normal security. They're not expecting us until midnight." I nod. Try to believe that's true. "Ash." Winter's voice drops. "Whatever happens tonight—" She doesn't finish. Because the sky catches fire. The first explosion hits the eastern Warrens. A column of flame erupts three blocks away, bright enough to blind, loud enough to feel in my teeth. Before the sound fades, another explosion. Then another. Then a chain of them, rolling across the city like thunder that won't stop. The window shatters inward. Glass rains across my shoulders. Screams from below.

Ash. Eli's voice, urgent. *Something's wrong. More wrong than the attack. I can feel it—*

I don't have time to ask what he means. The faithful scattering, panicking, dying. "NO." Winter's voice is raw. "No, no, NO—" She's at the door before I can move. "They knew. They KNEW. That's the safehouse on Iron Street. That's the weapons cache in Butcher's Alley. That's—" Another explosion. Closer. The foundry shakes. "—that's everything. They're hitting everything at once."

Moe crashes through the door, Mercyless drawn, blood already streaking his face. "We're compromised. They're hitting every position. Bronze is down. Half the tunnel crew didn't make it out." Sable appears behind him, knives drawn, her face a mask of controlled panic. "The runners—they're being intercepted. Parliament has our frequencies, our routes, our—" "Everything," Winter finishes. Her voice is ice. "Someone talked. Someone gave them everything." She looks at Sable. Sable looks back. "It wasn't me. The sigil would have—" "I know." Winter's jaw tightens. "I know it wasn't you. Which means someone else in our network has been feeding Parliament for months." Another explosion. The building groans. "We need to move," Moe says. "Now."

"Where?" I ask. "If they know everything—" "The Silk Crypt." Winter's voice is quiet. Something passes across her face—loss, yes, but beneath it something harder. Something that looks almost like relief. Like a weight she's been carrying might finally be someone else's problem.

"It's old. Off the books. The only ones who know about it are in this room."

"And if they know about that too?"

"Then we die there instead of here." She's already moving. "At least we'll die on ground I chose."

The Silk Crypt isn't a crypt at all. It's an old theater, buried beneath three collapsed buildings, forgotten by everyone except the Queen of the Underground. The stage is rotted, the seats are rubble, but the walls are thick and the exits are hidden. We gather what's left of the rebellion in the ruins of the auditorium. Street crew survivors, their numbers carved down to handfuls, clutch and bloody weapons. A few gutter priests, their robes torn, their faith tested beyond breaking. Faithful who escaped the slaughter and came to the only place they knew to come. Fifty people. From an army of three thousand. Winter surveys the wreckage of everything she built. "This is it?" someone asks. A young woman, barely old enough to fight. "This is all that's left?"

"This is what survives," Winter says quietly. "This is what we rebuild from."

"Rebuild?" The woman laughs, bitter and broken. "They killed everyone. They burned everything. There's nothing left to rebuild."

"There's us."

"Us?" She gestures at the huddled survivors. "We're dead. We just don't know it yet." I step forward. "Then let's die fighting." Every eye turns to me. "They took our army. They took our plan. They took our hope." I let the rune blaze, golden light filling the ruined hall. "But they didn't take us. Not yet. And as long as we're standing, we're not beaten."

"Pretty words," an old man mutters. "Pretty words from a pretty prophet. What good are words against Executioners?"

"I don't know." I admit it. Can't pretend otherwise. "But I know what happens if we don't fight. They win. Completely. Forever. The Crown gets reforged. Parliament becomes gods. And everyone we lost tonight died for nothing." Silence. Then Moe speaks. His voice is weak, but it carries. "I ain't... dying for nothing." He's propped against a fallen column, his ruined arm wrapped in bloody bandages. "I came too far... fought too hard... to quit now." Sable draws her knives. "I've already betrayed everyone who ever trusted me. Maybe it's time I earned something back." Winter straightens. When she speaks, her voice is steel. "This is where I built my throne. If Parliament wants to take it, they can pry it from my corpse." One by one, the survivors rise. Draw weapons. Find whatever courage they have left. Fifty people.

Against an empire. It's not enough. It was never going to be enough. But we're going to fight anyway.

They come at midnight. Not a squad. Not a company. An army. Wardens ring the Silk Crypt three ranks deep. Executioners take position at every exit, their golden halberds gleaming in the firelight. And floating above them all, a Prelate—the same one from Winter's estate, the one with three vertical scars across its mask. Its voice rolls across the ruins like thunder. "WINTER VALE. ASH MARROW. YOUR REBELLION IS ENDED. YOUR ALLIES ARE DEAD. YOUR CAUSE IS LOST."

Winter doesn't respond. She's positioning the survivors, creating what defensive lines we can manage with rubble and desperation. "SURRENDER THE PROPHET. SURRENDER THE SHARDS. AND WE WILL GRANT QUICK DEATHS TO ALL." I step to the edge of the ruins. Let them see me. Let them see the rune blazing across my chest, visible through my torn shirt like a second skeleton of light. "You want me?" I call out. "Come get me." The Prelate's mask tilts. "SO BE IT." The assault begins. Wardens pour through the gaps in the walls. Executioners follow, their halberds carving paths through anyone in their way. The survivors fight back—street crew blades against holy steel, gutter priest prayers against divine judgment. It's not a battle. It's a slaughter. I cast. Relic Tongue verses ripping through my throat, each one costing something I can't afford to spend. A squad of Wardens flies backward. An Executioner's halberd shatters in his hands. A section of wall collapses onto advancing enemies. But there are always more. More Wardens climbing over their dead. More Executioners stepping through the fire. More death than any verse can stop. Sable fights beside me, her knives dancing, her body a blur of lethal grace. But even she can't be everywhere.

The young woman who questioned me—the one who called my words pretty and demanded to know if we could fight Parliament—goes down three feet from where I'm standing.

I see it happen.

See the Executioner's halberd punch through her chest. See her eyes go wide with surprise more than pain. See her mouth shape a word that might be "mother" or might be nothing at all.

She falls. The Executioner steps over her body like it's rubble.

I scream something—her name, maybe, except I never learned her name—and the rune at my wrist flares hot enough to burn. Verse tears from my throat. The Executioner's halberd shatters in his hands. His mask cracks. He staggers.

Sable finishes him. One knife across the throat, arterial spray painting her face, her silver scars catching the blood like they're drinking it.

"Don't stop!" she shouts at me. "Don't you dare stop!"

But I can't look away from the girl on the ground. She's not dead yet—not quite. Her hand is reaching toward me, fingers twitching, grasping for something she'll never hold again.

Help me, her eyes say. *Saint Ash, help me.*

I try. Drop to my knees beside her, press my hands to the wound, let the healing verse pour out of me. Golden light floods the space between us.

It's not enough. The damage is too deep. The halberd went through her heart—there's nothing to heal, nothing to save, just meat and memory bleeding out on the stones of the Silk Crypt.

"Please," she whispers. Blood bubbles on her lips. "Please, I don't want to—"

She dies mid-sentence. The light fades from her eyes. Her hand falls slack.

I don't know how long I kneel there. Seconds. Hours. Long enough for the battle to shift around me, for more of my people to fall, for the tide to turn irrevocably against us.

Moe can't fight—not really. But he can die. He's positioned himself at the narrowest gap in the walls, Mercyless braced against rubble, forcing enemies to come at him one at a time. His ruined arm hangs useless, but his good arm still swings. Still kills.

Then a Warden's blade catches him across the side. Opens him from hip to ribs. He stumbles. Falls to one knee. Mercyless wavers in his grip.

"MOE!" I'm moving before I think about it, verse pouring from my lips, golden light arcing across the battlefield to slam into the Wardens pressing toward him. They scatter. I reach him in time to catch him before he falls completely.

"I'm fine," he growls, even though he's clearly not. "Get back in the fight."

"You're bleeding out."

"I've been bleeding out for twenty years. Ain't dead yet." He tries to stand. Can't quite manage it. "Help me up, prophet. I didn't come here to die on my knees."

I pour what healing I can spare into his wound—not enough to close it, but enough to slow the bleeding. Enough to buy him time.

Winter is everywhere at once. Her tattoos blaze with blood-magic, contracts activating, debts being called. Enemies who touched her products in the past suddenly find their loyalty twisted, their weapons turning against them.

But it's not enough. It was never going to be enough.

The old man who called my words pretty dies with a Warden's blade in his throat. He doesn't see it coming—he's turning to help a fallen friend when the steel finds him. Quick, at least. Quicker than most.

Mother Vera—I didn't even know she made it here—dies trying to shield a child from an Executioner's blade. She gets the kid behind a fallen column, takes the halberd strike meant for him, goes down with a smile on her face like dying is just another kind of healing.

The child survives. He's maybe eight years old. He looks at me with eyes that have seen too much, and I know—I *know*—that if we don't end this soon, he'll be next.

Fifty becomes forty. Thirty. Twenty. And still they come.

Sable goes down. I don't see the blade that hits her. Just hear her gasp. Just see her stumble. Just watch the blood bloom across her chest like a flower opening to die. "SABLE!" I catch her before she falls. Her eyes find mine, wide with pain and something worse—apology. "Ash... I'm sorry... I couldn't..."

At her collarbone, the binding scars are blazing. Silver fire, brighter than I've ever seen them—bright enough to cast shadows through her torn shirt, bright enough to make her blood look like liquid mercury where it catches the light. "The scars—" she gasps, pressing a bloody hand to her collar. "They're—burning—but not—not painful—" I can feel the heat radiating from her skin. Can feel the echoes in those marks screaming to life, every old contract responding to the terror of her body failing. "Don't. Don't talk. Save your strength." I press my hands to the wound. Try to heal. Try to pour everything I have into keeping her alive. The rune responds. But it's not healing. It's something else. The Crown's voice, cold and patient. Fighting what you are. What you're becoming. But look at them, Ash. Look at everyone you love dying around you. *Moe is down. Still breathing, but barely. Mercyless lies beside him, its hunger finally sated. Winter is cornered, her magic spent, three Executioners closing in. The survivors—what's left of them—are being cut down one by one. You just have to stop fighting.* "No..." But the word has no strength behind it. really looks like. *Sable's hand finds my face. Bloody fingers tracing my cheek. "Ash... don't... don't let them win..." Her scars are still blazing. And somehow, through the pain and the blood and the dying, she's looking at me with something that might be understanding. let them.* Something tears inside me. Not my heart. Not my mind. Something deeper. The last wall between what I am and what the Crown wants me to be. It doesn't ask permission. It just takes.

The world goes gold. I'm not casting. Not speaking. Not choosing. The Crown is using me, and I'm just the vessel. A verse tears from my throat in a voice that isn't mine. Old words. Forbidden words. The kind of language that breaks reality when it's spoken aloud. "BY THE BROKEN HALO AND THE SHATTERED THRONE—" The first Executioner near Winter simply... stops. Every bone in his body snaps simultaneously. He folds like paper. "—BY THE KING WHO FELL AND THE CROWN THAT ROSE—" The second Executioner catches fire. Not normal fire—gold fire. Divine fire. The kind that burns souls, not flesh. "—I JUDGE. I CONDEMN. I UNMAKE." The third Executioner turns and runs. He makes it three steps before the ground opens beneath him and swallows him whole. "—ALL WHO STAND AGAINST THE CROWN SHALL FALL."

I rise. I don't choose to rise. My body lifts from the ground, suspended by power I can't control, surrounded by light that hurts to look at. And below me—still crumpled where she fell—Sable's scars are answering. The silver fire at her collar has spread. Crawling down her arms, across her chest, tracing the hidden network of binding marks that cover her body like a second skin. Where my gold light touches the ruins, her silver light rises to meet it. Two colors. Two powers. Two different kinds of divine energy, resonating like struck bells. She shouldn't be conscious. She's lost too much blood. But her eyes are open, watching me rise, watching the Crown pour through me—and her scars are *reaching* toward the light. The Wardens see me. Some run. Some pray. Some charge. It doesn't matter. The wrath pours out of me in waves. Every wave kills. Every pulse of light is a death sentence. Wardens collapse. Executioners burn. The very stones of the Silk Crypt begin to glow, then crack, then melt. The Prelate floats toward me, scripture spinning around its form, voice booming commands I can't hear over the roaring in my skull. "CONTRA-CROWN. YOU WILL BE CONTAINED." It raises its hand. Divine power gathers. I raise mine. The Prelate shatters. Not kills. Not destroys. Shatters. Like glass. Like a mirror that reflected something it couldn't bear to see. Fragments of mask and scripture and whatever passed for a soul scatter across the burning ruins. And still the power flows. Still the Crown demands more. I watch—trapped inside my own body—as the wrath spreads beyond the Crypt. Beyond the street. Beyond the block. A

181

district begins to die. Buildings collapse. Streets crack open. People— not soldiers, not enemies, just people who lived in the wrong place at the wrong time—burn in the golden fire that pours from my skin. see. They need to understand what they've awakened. *and examples.* I scream. But no sound comes out. The Crown has my voice. Has my body. Has everything except the small spark of Ash that watches, helpless, as his hands reshape the city in blood and fire. When it finally ends—when the Crown finally releases me—I fall. The world goes dark. The last thing I hear is Sable's voice, distant and breaking: "Ash... what did you do...?" I don't have an answer. I don't think I ever will.

I wake in rubble. Dawn light filters through the smoke, painting everything in shades of orange and gray. The air smells like ash and copper and the particular sweetness of burned flesh. I don't move at first. Can't. My body is empty—drained of everything the Crown took when it used me as a weapon. Slowly, sounds filter through. Distant screaming. Closer sobbing. The crackle of fires still burning. I turn my head. The district is gone. Not damaged. Not ruined. Gone. Where buildings stood, there's nothing but foundations and debris. Where streets ran, there's cracked earth and smoldering craters. Where people lived, there's... nothing. Nothing but the remains of lives I ended without meaning to. Without choosing to. The Crown did this. Used my body, my power, my connection to the divine to murder hundreds of people who had nothing to do with Parliament's war. But it was my hands. My voice. My rune. I try to stand. Fall. Try again. Voices nearby. Sable. Winter. Moe—somehow still alive.

CHAPTER SIXTEEN

EXILE IN THE WARRENS

One week since I burned a district. One week since I killed hundreds of people—Wardens and innocents alike—with power I couldn't control and words I didn't choose. One week since I ran from everything I loved because I couldn't bear to see what I'd done reflected in their eyes. The gutter monks found me three days into my exile, curled in an alley, rune blazing so bright it lit up the darkness like a second sun. They didn't ask questions. Didn't demand explanations. Just lifted me between them and carried me into the belly of the Warrens, to a place where even Parliament's hunters won't go. The old refinery sits in the deepest part of the Rust Warrens, where the ghost-ore seeps through cracked foundations and the air tastes like metal and forgotten prayers. Once, it processed ether for half the city. Now it processes souls. The monks—if you can call them that—are addicts who found something holy at the bottom of a vial. They brew ether into prayer, cook gutter shine into communion wine, transform addiction into a kind of faith. Most of them are dying. All of them are damned. None of them care what I've done. "You're awake." Brother Cask stands in the doorway of my small cell—a storage closet converted into sleeping quarters with a thin mat and a bucket. He's sixty years old but looks ninety, skin paper-thin, eyes permanently dilated from decades of shine. "How long was I out this time?"

"Fourteen hours. Your light kept flickering." He sets down a cup of something that smells like rust and roses. "Drink. The Abbott wants to see you." I don't move. "I can't see anyone."

"You can't hide forever either." Cask's voice is gentle. Non-judgmental. "The Abbott helped me when I was in your place. Lost in the dark, certain I'd destroyed everything worth saving."

"Did you?"

"Yes." He smiles. It's an expression that knows too much. "And I'm still here. That's either mercy or punishment, depending on the day." He leaves the cup and closes the door. I stare at the ceiling and try to remember what it felt like to believe in anything.

The refinery-temple is a cathedral of rust and revelation. The main processing floor has been converted into a worship space, vats and pipes repurposed as altars and prayer stations. Ether smoke drifts from censers made of old machinery, filling the air with that sweet-sharp smell that makes your thoughts go sideways. Addicts kneel in rows, murmuring prayers that sound like scripture mixed with street slang. I move through them like a ghost, trying not to be noticed. It doesn't work. "Saint Ash." A woman with track marks like constellations on her arms reaches for my hand. "You saved my daughter. In the Warrens. Before." I pull back. "I'm not a saint."

"You healed her. When nobody else would touch us."

"And then I killed a district." Her eyes are clear despite the ether haze. "You fought for us. That's more than anyone else ever did." She releases me. Returns to her prayers. And I'm left standing in the smoke, wondering how people can still believe in me when I can't believe in myself. The Abbott's chamber is at the back of the refinery, in what used to be the foreman's office. Now it's a cell of deliberate poverty—no furniture except a mat, no decoration except scripture written directly on the walls in what might be blood or might be rust. The Abbott himself is ancient. Not old—ancient. The kind of age that suggests he's been dying for so long that death forgot to finish the job. "Ash Marrow." His voice is a whisper wrapped in gravel. "The prophet who unmade a prophet. Sit." I sit. "You've been hiding in my walls for four days. Eating our food. Breathing our air. Using our silence as a shield against your guilt."

"I can leave—" "You can shut up and listen." The Abbott's eyes pin me in place. "You came here to die. I know the look. I've worn it myself. But death is too easy, boy. Death is escape. And you don't get to escape what you've done."

"Then what do I do?" The Abbott smiles. It transforms his face from corpse to something almost kind. "You learn what you are. And then you decide what to do about it."

I wake to find my brother sitting at the foot of my mat. Not a vision. Not a memory. Not the Crown's manipulation. Eli. Solid enough to cast a shadow. Real enough to smile that crooked smile I remember from every stupid thing we did as kids. "Took you long enough to stop moving," he says. "Hard to have a conversation when you're running from everything, including me." I don't move. Don't breathe. Don't trust my own senses. "You're not real."

"I'm as real as anything else in your head right now." He tilts his head, studying me. "Which, admittedly, isn't saying much. You look like shit, brother."

"You're dead. I watched you die. I felt you die."

"Yeah. That happened." Eli shrugs like we're discussing weather. "But death's not as permanent as people think. Not when the Crown's involved. Not when someone's got a shard of divinity carved into their arm." I look at the rune. It's quiet now—no blazing, no burning. But in the golden lines, I can see something moving. Something that looks like scripture. Something that looks like Eli. "The Blood-Market," I whisper. "Your spirit was there. In chains."

"Until you freed me. Broke the binding. Let me go." Eli's smile fades. "Or let me in. Depends on your perspective."

"In?"

"Where do you think I went when those chains shattered, Ash? Where do you think a spirit bound to the Crown ends up when the Crown's vessel decides to level a district?" The cold in my chest

185

spreads. Understanding arriving like a funeral procession. "You're inside me."

"I'm inside the rune. Which is inside you. So... technically? Yeah." Eli leans back, ghost-weight making no impression on the thin mat. "Welcome to the family business, brother. We're both prisoners of the Crown now. The difference is, you're the one with the body."

"Tell me what's happening to me." Eli sighs. For a ghost, he does a good job of looking tired. "What do you know about the Crown? The real Crown, not the stories Parliament tells."

"It was whole once. Worn by a king. When he fell, it shattered into shards. The shards corrupt whoever holds them."

"Close. But wrong in the important parts." Eli stands, paces the small cell. His feet make no sound. "The Crown wasn't worn by a king. The Crown made kings. It was the original source of divine authority— the thing that allowed mortals to touch the power of gods. When it shattered, the shards didn't just carry power. They carried... potential."

"Potential for what?"

"For the Crown to rebuild itself. To find a new vessel. To make a new king." Eli stops pacing. Looks at me with eyes that hold centuries of sorrow. "Why do you think Parliament wants to reforge it? Why do you think they've been collecting shards for generations? They think they can control it. Use it. Make themselves gods."

"Can they?"

"No. The Crown doesn't serve. It rules. Anyone who tries to wear it without being chosen gets consumed. Burned from the inside out." He crouches beside me. "But you weren't trying to wear it, Ash. You were just trying to survive. And the Crown... recognized something in you."

"What?"

"Sorrow. Guilt. The weight of everyone you've failed." Eli's voice drops. "The Crown feeds on those things. Not because it's evil—

because that's how divine power works. It needs an anchor. A wound deep enough to hold the weight of heaven." I think about everyone I've lost. Everyone I've failed. My brother. My people. The innocents I burned. "The rune isn't just a shard anymore," Eli continues. "It's been growing. Spreading. Every time you use its power, every time you feed it your pain, it becomes more. You're not a vessel anymore, Ash." He touches my chest. His hand passes through, but I feel it anyway—cold and familiar and gone. "You're becoming the Crown itself."

"So what do I do? How do I stop it?" Eli laughs. It's not a happy sound. "Stop it? Little brother, the Crown isn't a disease you cure. It's not a demon you exorcise. It's evolution. You're becoming something that hasn't existed for a thousand years."

"I don't want to become anything. I want to be normal. I want to go back to—" "To what? The streets? The hustle? Pretending you're just another runner in Winter's crew?" Eli shakes his head. "That was never you, Ash. You were always more. You just didn't know it yet."

"I'm a murderer. I killed hundreds of people."

"The Crown killed them. Using your body."

"Same thing."

"No." Eli's voice hardens. "It's not. And that distinction matters. Because right now, you have a choice. The only choice that matters." He sits across from me. Cross-legged. The way we used to sit when we were kids, planning schemes, dreaming of escape. "Option one: you keep running. Keep hiding. Keep fighting the Crown until it breaks through anyway. And when it does—and it will—you won't be there to shape what happens. You'll just be gone, and the Crown will use your body to do whatever it wants."

"And option two?"

"You stop fighting. Stop running. Accept what you're becoming." Eli holds up a hand before I can object. "Not surrender to it. Accept it. There's a difference."

187

"What difference?"

"The difference between a rider and a horse. A king and a crown." His ghost-eyes meet mine. "The power is already yours, Ash. It chose you. Bonded with you. Grew into you. The question isn't whether you'll have that power. The question is whether you'll be destroyed by it or transformed by it."

"And if I choose transformation?"

"Then you might survive. You might even be able to use the Crown instead of being used by it. You could finish what we started. Stop Parliament. Save whoever's left to save."

"Or?" Eli's smile is sad. "Or you become exactly what they're afraid of. A god walking the streets. A king with no kingdom. A crown in the gutter, waiting to burn the world." I close my eyes. Feel the rune pulsing against my skin. Feel everything I've done and everything I might still do. "How do I choose transformation without losing myself?"

"That," Eli says, "is what the monks can teach you. If you're willing to learn."

I sit. The worship floor is hard beneath me. Ether smoke drifts past. The addicts pray their broken prayers. And I close my eyes and do something I've never tried before. I stop fighting. Not surrender. Not giving up. Just… release. Like unclenching a fist you didn't know was clenched. The rune responds immediately. Warmth floods through me. Not burning—warming. Like sunlight. Like being held. The golden light spreads across my skin, visible even through my closed eyelids. The Crown's voice. But different now. Not cold. Not demanding. Almost… relieved. long enough to listen. *I don't respond out loud. Think the words instead. worn. To fulfill my purpose.* mortals. *and the gutter. I was made to connect, Ash. To let power flow between worlds. When I shattered, the connection broke. The divine became distant. Mortals became… this.* I feel something like sadness in the warmth. Something like grief. shards. Hoarding. Controlling. Using divine power to enslave instead of elevate. They want to reforge me so they can rule. But that's not what I was made

188

for. *bridge. Not a crown that rules—a crown that serves.* The warmth intensifies. I feel Eli's presence somewhere in it, watching, waiting. I realize. *Because I've spent my life trying to help people who have nothing.* guilt is deep enough to anchor worlds. Because you've already died a thousand times for people you love, and you'd do it a thousand more. *The Crown's voice drops to something almost tender. work with you. Give me your sorrow, and I'll give you the power to change things. Feed me your guilt, and I'll help you earn forgiveness. We can be what Parliament fears—not a weapon of control, but a revolution of mercy.* together. Fighting until there's nothing left of either of us. *I think about the district I destroyed. The innocents I killed. The weight of everything I've done. And I make a choice. being crushed.* The warmth becomes light. And the light becomes something new.

Three days of sitting with the Crown. Three days of feeding it my sorrow, my guilt, my grief. Learning to let the pain flow through instead of building up. Learning to be a channel instead of a dam. The rune stops spreading. Not because I've contained it—because I've integrated it. The golden script that crawls across my chest, my arms, my back isn't a parasite anymore. It's a partnership. A contract written in shared suffering and mutual purpose. Eli watches. Sometimes he talks. Mostly he just… exists. A presence in the rune, a voice when I need guidance, a connection to everything I've lost. "You're different," he says on the third night. I open my eyes. We're in my cell, the refinery quiet around us. Moonlight filters through cracks in the ceiling. "Different how?"

"Calmer. Steadier." He tilts his head, studying me. "Less afraid."

"I'm terrified."

"Yeah. But you're not running from it anymore." I look at my hands. In the darkness, the rune-lines glow faintly golden. Not blazing. Not threatening. Just… present. "The Abbott says I'm ready."

"Ready for what?"

"To go back. To find the others. To finish what we started." Eli is quiet for a long moment. "Parliament's ceremony already happened," he says finally. "While you were hiding. While you were learning. They

189

reforged the Crown." The words hit like a fist. "Then we lost. They won. It's over."

"Not quite." Eli's ghost-smile returns. "They reforged something. But it wasn't the real Crown. They don't have the most important shard." He reaches out, touches my chest where the rune burns brightest. "You do."

"I don't understand."

"The Crown has seven shards. Seven vices. Each one essential to the whole." Eli sits cross-legged, floating slightly above the mat. "Parliament collected six. Greed, Lust, Wrath, Pride, Envy, Sloth. They've been hoarding them for generations, waiting for the right moment."

"And Hunger?"

"Hunger was different. Hunger didn't want to be collected. It chose its own vessels, generation after generation, passing from one suffering soul to another." His eyes meet mine. "Until it found you."

"Why me?"

"Because Hunger isn't just the vice of addiction. It's the core of the Crown's purpose. The thing that makes it want to connect, to bridge, to give. Without Hunger, the other shards are just power. Raw, directionless, dangerous." I think about Parliament's ceremony. About the Crown they've forged. "So what they have—" "Is a weapon without a heart. A crown without compassion. They can use it, sure. Channel power through it. But it's unstable. Incomplete. It'll burn through anyone who tries to wear it."

"Unless they get Hunger."

"Unless they get you." Eli nods. "They know, Ash. That's why they didn't hunt you harder after the Fall. They're waiting. They know you'll come to them eventually. Because you can't let them keep what they've built."

"And when I do?"

190

"Then everything depends on whether you've learned enough to take their crown and make it yours." I stand. Feel the rune pulse in response, ready, waiting. "Then it's time to find out." Eli's smile is proud. And sad. And something else I can't name. "Go get our people, brother. Show Parliament what a real prophet looks like."

===
=============
===
=========

CHAPTER SEVENTEEN

SABLE'S REBELLION

Ten days since the world burned. Ten days since I watched Ash level a district and vanish into the smoke. Ten days since his power erupted through me and something in my flesh *answered*. I touch the scars at my collarbone. They're different now—have been since that night at the Crypt. Brighter. More defined. Warm to the touch even when the rest of me is cold. And there's the new one. The silver scar tissue that sealed the wound that should have killed me. I remember the blade going in. Remember falling. Remember the scars *spreading* across my chest, covering the injury, stopping the bleeding like something inside me decided I wasn't allowed to die yet. I don't understand what's happening to me. But I know it started with Ash.

The scars are *echoes*—that's what Symeon called them, years ago. When binding magic writes itself into flesh, it leaves traces. Residue. Like ink soaking into paper until the paper becomes part of the word. I've been bound more times than I can count. Velvet's contracts. Symeon's training marks. Client claims that expired but never fully faded. Every scar on my body is a record of someone else's ownership. flesh. Most people can't hold that much magical pressure. It would tear them apart.* But I held it. Somehow. And now it's waking up.

I remember what Mother Vera said at the safehouse, before the Fall. Watching my scars glow while I slept near Ash. that's been sleeping for a long time.* I thought she was speaking metaphorically. The ramblings of a witch who'd seen too much. I was wrong.

The gold sigil on my wrist burns cold. Winter's claim, transferred from Symeon in that brutal ritual that should have freed me. Should have. But Winter's chains are just as tight as Velvet's ever were. Except now there's something fighting back. I feel it constantly—the gold sigil pulling one way, demanding obedience, reporting my emotions to Winter. And the silver scars pushing *back*. Not obeying. Not rebelling. Just... refusing to be owned anymore. Two magics, warring inside me. The leash and the thing that wants to bite through it. Winter doesn't know. She thinks she controls me. Thinks the sigil tells her everything. The scars have been lying to her for days.

I move through the burned streets of the Warrens, stepping over rubble, passing survivors with hollow eyes. They know who I am. Saint Ash's woman. The shadow who couldn't save him. "Anything?" Winter's voice crackles through the communication sigil behind my ear. "Nothing. The gutter monks aren't talking."

"Keep looking." The sigil goes quiet. I don't tell her what I'm really planning. The scars pulse warm at my collar—approving, somehow. Like they know. Tonight I kill Symeon. Tonight I destroy the original binding, the source code that made me Velvet's property. And then I find out what's been waking up inside me. The sun bleeds red across the rooftops. Time to become something new.

The Velvet House hasn't changed. The same carved doors. The same jasmine-and- darkness scent. The same attendants gliding through shadows. But *I've* changed. I feel it as I slip through the service entrance—the scars at my collarbone flickering silver in the darkness, responding to this place where so many contracts were written into my flesh. They're *remembering*. Every mark, every binding, every time I knelt in these halls and let someone else write their name on my soul. The echoes are stirring. to need it.* I move through the passages behind the walls, toward Symeon's chamber. Wait in darkness. Listen. The door opens. Closes. Footsteps I've known for fifteen years. "You can come out," Symeon says. "I know you're there." Of course they know. I step through the hidden panel.

Symeon stands by the window, fox mask set aside, their face bare. Older than I remember. Thinner. The Fall took something from everyone. "Little shadow." Their voice is soft. "I wondered when you'd come." My knives are in my hands. Symeon's eyes flick to my collar. To the faint silver glow visible at the edge of my shirt. "Ah." A breath. Almost wonder. "So that's what's been happening. The echoes are waking up."

"You knew this could happen."

"I suspected. You've been bound more times than anyone I've ever trained. All that power, all that compressed magic—it had to go somewhere eventually." They tilt their head. "But I thought it would tear you apart. Not transform you."

"What changed?"

"The prophet." Symeon smiles. "Love. The one variable I could never factor out of you. When you started caring about something more than survival, the echoes had something to wake up for."

"At the Crypt," I say slowly. "When Ash's power erupted. The scars—they responded. Like they recognized him. Like they were…"

"Answering," Symeon finishes. "Divine power calls to divine power. The Crown in his flesh and the accumulated magic in yours— they're not so different. Both are compressed divinity. Both are waiting to be claimed." I think about the silver fire that erupted when Winter transferred the sigil. The way the scars *fought* the ownership change. The way they looked afterward—brighter, more alive. "They healed me. At the Crypt. The blade went through my chest and they—they sealed the wound."

"Of course they did." Symeon's eyes gleam. "They've been protecting you for weeks. You just couldn't see it because you still thought of them as chains."

"They *were* chains."

"They were power. Stolen power, yes. Power taken from you by people who wanted to own you." Symeon steps closer. "But the echoes remember. Every binding left a trace. And every trace was *you*—your pain, your survival, your refusal to break. When you claim them, you're not claiming someone else's power. You're taking back what was always yours."

"Why are you telling me this?"

"Because I'm tired. And because some debts can only be paid in blood." Symeon moves to a small table, pours wine. Doesn't offer me any. "I'm going to release you. The original binding—the one I etched when you were twelve. When it breaks, the echoes will have nowhere to go except *into* you."

"That sounds dangerous."

"Extremely." Symeon sips their wine. "Most people would be consumed. Burned alive from the inside by power they can't control."

"But not me."

"Not you." They set down the glass. "You've been carrying this weight for fifteen years. You've survived every binding, every betrayal, every attempt to break you. The echoes know you. They've *chosen* you."

"And if you're wrong?"

"Then you die. And I die. And Winter loses her weapon and Parliament wins and none of it matters anyway." Symeon's smile is sad. "But I don't think I'm wrong. I think I succeeded in ways I never intended. I tried to make a weapon. Instead, I made something that could choose to be more." My grip tightens on the knives. "Do it."

Symeon raises their hand. Old words spill from their lips. The kind of words that cost something to speak. I feel the original binding—the one carved into my soul when I was too young to understand what I was signing—begin to unravel. Pain. Bright and huge and everywhere. Fifteen years of ownership tearing loose from my soul like roots being ripped from soil. I bite back a scream. Taste blood. Feel something *shift* at the core of my being—And then the echoes wake up. All of them. At once.

195

Silver fire. Not the faint glow I've been seeing for weeks. Not the flickering warmth that started when I got close to Ash. It erupts from the scars at my collar—the same silver fire that burned during Winter's ritual, the same fire that spread across my body at the Crypt. But this time it doesn't stop. This time it keeps growing. Every mark on my body ignites. The old Velvet sigil. The training scars from Symeon. The burns from the Blood-Market. The cuts from a hundred jobs. The silver tissue that sealed my chest at the Crypt. Every record of someone else's ownership becomes light. Symeon staggers back, shielding their eyes. "Yes—yes, that's it—" I can't hear them. Can't see anything except the fire pouring out of me, filling the room, filling the world. And inside the fire—Voices.

Thousands of them. Every binding, every contract, every chain—each one left a trace, and now those traces are *speaking*. I hear Symeon's voice from fifteen years ago: I hear the Merchant-Lord who bought me for a season: *Smile prettier. They're paying for the whole package.* I hear Winter's voice from the ritual: Every voice that ever tried to own me. Every word that ever told me I wasn't mine. And underneath them all—My mother. Dying. Whispering my true name like it was the only gift she had left to give. The voices crest. Crash. Wait. And I understand, suddenly, what Vera meant. The echoes don't want to own me. They never did. They're *waiting*—waiting for me to claim them, to accept them, to make them All I have to do is say yes.

So I do. Not with words. Words are what other people used to bind me. I claim the echoes with something deeper. I think about every time I survived. Every beating I endured. Every betrayal I committed because I had no choice. Every night I lay awake hating myself for what I'd become. I think about Ash. His stupid, beautiful belief that people could be saved. His hands on my scars, gentle, like they were something to be treasured instead of hidden. I think about the crew. Moe's gruff protection. Winter's ruthless loyalty. The family I found when I thought I didn't deserve one. And I think: *Mine.* power—stolen, hoarded, compressed into my flesh for fifteen years—is MINE.* The fire answers.

196

I cross the room in a blur. I don't remember deciding to move. The power just—responds. Faster than thought. Faster than anything I could do before. My knife finds Symeon's throat. Clean. Like they taught me. But I hold them as they fall. Catch them before they hit the ground. They don't deserve gentleness—but they gave me answers. And maybe, maybe, that counts for something. Symeon's eyes meet mine. They're smiling. "Beautiful," they whisper. "More beautiful than I imagined. Find him. Save him. Become what I couldn't—" The light leaves their eyes. I lay them down gently. Close their eyes. They made me. Owned me. Shaped me into a weapon. And in the end, they gave me the key to becoming something else. I don't know how to feel about that. Maybe I don't have to know yet.

I find the ledger. My name on the third page from the end. Not Sable—the other one. The name my mother gave me. I hold it over a candle. Watch my name turn to ash. The gold sigil at my wrist flickers—Winter's claim weakening as the source record dissolves. It doesn't break. She still has her hooks in me. But the silver scars flare bright around it, containing it, limiting it. The leash is still there. It just doesn't go as deep anymore. That's a problem for later. Right now, I have somewhere to be.

The gutter monks' temple is hidden in the deepest Warrens—a collapsed cathedral buried under rubble and time. I find it by following the warmth in my chest. The Abbott meets me at the entrance. Old man. Kind eyes. Looks at my glowing scars without surprise. "He said you'd come." The Abbott steps aside. "He's in the sanctuary." The temple smells like ether-prayer and ancient stone. I move through shadows that part for me now, past monks who bow their heads as I pass. And there—Ash. He's sitting in a pool of golden light, the rune across his chest blazing bright, his eyes closed in meditation. He looks different. Older. Harder. The guilt of what happened at the Crypt has carved new lines in his face. But he's alive. He's alive. His eyes open. For a moment we just look at each other. Ten days of fear and searching and not knowing if either of us would survive. Then he sees the scars. The silver light. The mark over my heart pulsing in time with the rune on his chest. "Sable." His voice cracks. "What happened to you?"

"I stopped being someone else's weapon." I cross the sanctuary, kneel before him, let him see what I've become. "I claimed myself. The scars—the echoes—they're mine now. All that power they took from me for fifteen years—I took it back." He reaches out. His fingers brush my cheek, trace the silver lines at my collar. Where he touches, the scars blaze warm. "They always responded to you," I whisper. "From the first night. Getting close to you woke them up."

"I know." He pulls me close. "I could feel it. At the Crypt—when my power erupted—I felt them answer. Felt them healing you." His voice breaks. "I thought you were dying. And then you weren't. And I didn't understand—" "Neither did I. Not until tonight." I pull back enough to meet his eyes. "But I understand now. Divine power calls to divine power. Your Crown and my echoes—we're connected. We were always going to be connected." He laughs—a broken, beautiful sound. "What are we becoming?"

"I don't know." I lean my forehead against his. Gold light and silver light mixing, Crown and echoes, prophet and shadow. "But we're becoming it together."

We stay like that for a long moment. Two transformed people. Two impossible things. Holding each other in a ruined temple while the world outside burns. Then Winter's voice crackles through my communication sigil. "Sable. Report. Now." The gold sigil flares at my wrist—her claim demanding obedience. But the silver scars pulse around it, dampening the pull. Ash sees. Understands. "That's going to be a problem."

"Yes." I stand. The power hums through me—ready, waiting, *mine*. "But not today." I send a feeling through the sigil. Calm. Obedience. Routine. The scars help me lie. "Found him," I tell Winter. "He's ready to come back." Silence. Then: "Good. We have work to do." The sigil goes quiet. Ash takes my hand. Where his skin meets mine, gold and silver light merge. "Time to go save the world?"

"Time to go save the world." We walk out together. Two weapons who learned to be more. Two monsters who found something worth protecting. Two people who chose love over chains. Whatever comes next—we'll face it together.

```
======================================
=============
======================================
=========
```

CHAPTER EIGHTEEN

WINTER'S COUP

Three days after the Fall. While Ash hides in the Warrens, drowning in guilt. While Sable searches for him, pretending loyalty. While Parliament celebrates its victory and prepares to use its reforged Crown. I'm doing what I've always done. I'm planning. The safehouse in the old tannery district smells like chemicals and desperation. Fitting. Twenty of my people survived the Fall—twenty out of hundreds. The rest are dead, arrested, or scattered so far that finding them would take weeks I don't have. Twenty people. Against Parliament. Against an empire. It would be hopeless if I were fighting the same war they think I'm fighting. But I'm not. "The envoys," I say to the map spread across the table. "Parliament is sending three delegations to the major districts. Victory tours. Show of force." My lieutenant—Vera, the one with the knife scar across her throat—nods. "Security will be heavy. Wardens at every entrance."

"But the envoys themselves?"

"Low-level. Parliament wouldn't risk anyone important this soon after the Fall. Too much unrest." I smile. It's not a pleasant expression. "That's what they think. But the envoys aren't the real cargo." Vera's eyes narrow. "What are they carrying?" I tap the map. Three locations. Three delegations. Three opportunities. "Shards. Two of them. Greed and Wrath. Parliament used four shards to reforge their Crown—Pride, Lust, Envy, and Sloth. But their artifact is unstable without all seven. They've been moving the remaining pieces, trying to integrate them one at a time."

"How do you know this?"

"Because I've spent fifteen years building an intelligence network they thought they destroyed." I straighten. "Parliament burned my club. Killed my people. Took my docks. They think I'm broken." My tattoos begin to glow. Blood-magic stirring beneath the skin. "They're about to learn the difference between broken and rebuilding."

"We hit all three convoys simultaneously." The room goes quiet. Twenty faces staring at me like I've lost my mind. "We barely have enough people to take one."

"That's why we're not taking them by force." I unroll a second map—this one showing the sewer systems beneath the city. "Parliament expects attacks. They're prepared for armies, for mobs, for desperate last stands." I trace a line through the tunnels. "They're not prepared for ghosts." The plan is elegant in its simplicity. Three teams. Three diversions. Three extractions. Team one hits the eastern convoy with a street riot—loud, visible, exactly what Parliament expects from my broken forces. While Wardens respond to the chaos, team two slips through the sewers and intercepts the western convoy at the crossing where the underground passages come closest to the surface. Team three doesn't exist. Not officially. Team three is me. "The southern convoy carries both shards," I explain. "Separated for transport, reunited for delivery. Parliament thinks I don't know which one has the real cargo. They're using the others as decoys."

"How can you be sure the south is real?" I tap my chest. Where my heart would be, if I hadn't traded it years ago for power and stability. "Because I can feel them. The shards call to each other. And they've been calling to me since the Crown was reforged." Vera's face pales. "Winter... the shards corrupt anyone who holds them. Parliament's prelates have been studying them for centuries. If you try to take two at once—" "Then I'll burn. I know." I roll up the maps. "But Parliament won't see it coming. They think I'm a defeated queen licking her wounds. They think the only shard-bearer they need to worry about is Ash." I move to the door. Pause. "By tomorrow morning, they'll know different."

Midnight. The tunnels beneath Ashvein smell like centuries of secrets. I move through them like I was born in darkness—which, in some ways, I was. The streets raised me. The shadows taught me. Everything soft about me died a long time ago. What's left is steel and hunger. My team follows in silence. Six people. The best of what survived. Each one carrying enough grief to fuel a war and enough training to end one. Above us, the southern convoy rolls through Parliament-controlled streets. Twelve Wardens. Four priests. Two Executioners. And hidden in a lead-lined case in the central carriage, two fragments of divine power that could reshape reality. Greed. Wrath. I can feel them even through the stone and earth between us. Greed hums like distant music, promising everything I've ever wanted. Wrath burns like a fever, whispering that everyone who hurt me deserves to suffer. Both of them are lying. Both of them are true. "Position," Vera murmurs through the communication sigil. "Thirty seconds." I check my weapons. Knives. Vials of blood-magic. The contracts I've been saving for exactly this moment. "Eastern team?"

"Riot started. Wardens responding."

"Western team?"

"In position. Ready to move on your signal." I close my eyes. Feel the shards calling to me. Feel the blood-magic burning under my skin. Feel the weight of everything I've lost and everything I'm about to become. "Now." The street above us explodes.

I come up through the explosion like something born from fire. The convoy is chaos. Wardens scrambling, horses screaming, priests trying to form defensive circles. My blood-magic contracts activate in sequence—debts called in, promises enforced, bodies moving against their will. Three Wardens turn on their companions. Two priests find their voices stolen. An Executioner's golden halberd melts in his hands. I move through the confusion like a blade through silk. The first envoy dies before he sees me. Throat opened by a knife he didn't know I'd thrown. The second manages to scream before Vera silences him. The third—The third is the one carrying the case. He's young. Younger than I expected. A minor noble's son, probably. Given this "honor" because Parliament thought the convoy was safe. "Please," he whispers. "I'm just—I'm just the courier. I don't even know what's in the—" "I do." I take the case from his trembling hands. "For what it's worth, I'm sorry. You should have chosen better masters." My knife finds his heart. Quick. Clean. Merciful, in its way. The case opens with a whisper of divine wind. Inside, nestled in velvet, two shards pulse with hungry light. Greed glitters like golden promises. Wrath burns like caged lightning. I reach for them. Both at once.

The pain is exquisite. I've felt blood-magic before. I've paid prices in flesh and soul for power. But this—This is something else entirely. Greed enters first. It flows through my fingers like liquid gold, spreading through my veins, rewriting my blood. Every cell in my body suddenly wants MORE. More power. More control. More everything. The shard shows me what I could have—the city at my feet, the Crown on my head, every enemy broken and begging. Then Wrath. Wrath hits like a hammer to the soul. Pure rage, refined over centuries, compressed into something that burns. Everyone who ever hurt me flashes through my mind—the men who killed my mother, the nobles who used me, the Parliament that destroyed my empire. Wrath shows me what they deserve. Shows me how to give it to them. Shows me the beautiful, terrible simplicity of vengeance. I scream. Can't help it. The shards are fighting inside me, each one trying to dominate, each one feeding on the other's hunger. My skin splits along the paths of my tattoos. Golden light pours from the wounds. "WINTER!" Vera's voice, distant and frightened. "Winter, let them go! They're killing you!" But I don't let go. I reach deeper. Past the pain. Past the promises and the rage. Down to the core of what makes me Winter Vale. The shards... hesitate. I feel them considering. Calculating. These aren't mindless powers—they're fragments of divinity, each with its own agenda. Greed speaks first. *What do you offer?* hunger that will never be satisfied. *Wrath follows.* And me? *burning. A war that will reshape the world.* Silence. Then, slowly, the pain begins to fade. Not because the power has diminished. Because it's being... organized. Integrated. The shards finding their places in my soul like weapons finding sheaths. I open my eyes. The world looks different now. Sharper. Hungrier. I can see the greed in everyone around me—their desperate need for safety, power, survival. I can feel the anger beneath their fear—the rage at Parliament, at the world, at everything that's hurt them. And beneath it all, I can sense the other shards. Parliament's Crown, incomplete and unstable. Ash's Hunger, pulsing in the distance like a heartbeat. I stand. My skin has changed. Gold traces my veins like living jewelry. My eyes—I can feel them burning with light that doesn't come from any natural source. "Winter?" Vera's voice is a whisper. "What... what are you?" I look at my hands. At the power burning beneath my skin. At everything I've become. "Something new," I answer. "Something Parliament has never faced."

"Something that's going to take back everything they stole."

Dawn. I walk through the safehouse door and watch my people flinch away. I don't blame them. I can see myself reflected in their eyes—the gold in my veins, the light that flickers behind my pupils, the way I move now like gravity is a suggestion rather than a law. "It's done," I say. "Parliament's envoys are dead. The shards are mine." Vera is the first to speak. "We... we heard the reports. They're saying a demon attacked the convoy. A creature made of gold and fire."

"Not a demon. Just me."

"Winter, the things people are describing—" "I know what I am." I move to the center of the room. Let them see me fully. Let them understand. "I told you all, when we started this war, that I would do whatever it takes to win. Did you think I was speaking metaphorically?" Silence. "Parliament has a Crown. Four shards, reforged into an artifact that could enslave every magic user in the city. They planned to use it against us. To make us bow. To make us forget we ever had the right to be free." I raise my hand. Golden light pulses from my palm. "Now I have two more. Greed and Wrath. And when I find Ash—when I take the Hunger shard he carries—I'll have enough to challenge their Crown directly."

"Challenge it?" Someone in the back. Young voice. Scared. "You mean... destroy it?" I smile. It's not a kind expression. "No. I mean replace it. I mean take everything Parliament built and make it mine." The room erupts. Protests. Questions. Fear dressed up as strategy. I let them talk. When the noise dies down, I speak again. "You followed me because I promised you power. Because I promised you a place in a new order. I'm keeping that promise. But the new order isn't going to be Parliament with different faces. It's going to be something better."

"What could be better than Parliament?"

"Me." I let the word hang in the air. "Parliament rules through fear and tradition. They've spent centuries convincing everyone that divine power belongs to the worthy—meaning them. I'm going to prove them wrong. I'm going to show this city that power belongs to whoever's strong enough to take it."

"And then?"

"Then I'll build something worth ruling. A kingdom where the streets matter as much as the spires. Where the people who built this city finally get to own a piece of it." I look at each of them in turn. See the doubt. The fear. The desperate, hungry hope that maybe—maybe—this time will be different. "You can leave if you want. No judgments. No consequences. But if you stay..." I extend my hand. Golden light trails from my fingers like smoke. "...you'll be building something that's never existed before. A crown forged in the gutter. A throne built on the bones of everyone who told us we didn't deserve one." One by one, they kneel. And deep inside me, Greed and Wrath purr with satisfaction.

Moe finds me at dawn. He's healing—slowly, painfully. His arm is gone below the elbow, the wound cauterized and wrapped, but he's already adapted. Already found ways to fight, to move, to be useful. That's Moe. Too stubborn to let something like losing a limb slow him down. "You need to stop." I don't turn from the window. "Good morning to you too."

"I'm serious, Winter. The shards—" "Are under control."

"Are they?" He moves closer. I can feel his anger like heat against my back. "I've known you fifteen years. I've seen you make hard choices, cold choices, choices that kept the rest of us alive. But this isn't strategy. This is... something else."

"It's survival."

"Is it?" His voice drops. "Because from where I'm standing, it looks like you're becoming the thing you swore to destroy." I turn. Let him see what I've become. Let him see the gold in my veins and the fire behind my eyes. "Parliament rules through a Crown. You want me to beat them with knives and street crews? With the broken remnants of an army they already crushed?"

"I want you to beat them without losing yourself."

"I'm not losing myself, Moe. I'm becoming myself. The self I always should have been." I step closer. "This city chewed me up when I was twelve years old. Spit me out into the streets with nothing but hunger and rage. Everything I built, I built from that. From wanting more. From refusing to accept what they told me I deserved." I tap my chest. Where the shards burn. "Greed and Wrath aren't corrupting me. They're completing me." Moe shakes his head. Slowly. Sadly. "That's what they want you to think."

"Maybe. But it doesn't change the math." I move to the door. "Parliament has four shards. Ash has one. I have two. When we add them together—" "When you take Ash's shard, you mean." I pause. "Does he get a choice in this?"

"He'll understand. He knows what's at stake."

"Does he? Or does he just trust you?" Moe's voice hardens. "The boy walked into fire for you, Winter. He gave up years of his life healing your people. He became a symbol for your movement. And now you're planning to—what? Rip the power out of him so you can play god?"

"I'm planning to win."

"At what cost?" I don't answer. I don't have an answer. I just walk out and let the door close behind me.

The runner arrives at midday. "They've been found. Both of them. Together." I set down the maps I've been studying. "Where?"

"The gutter monks' refinery. They stayed there overnight and left at dawn. Heading toward the old Silk Crypt."

"They're looking for me."

"Looks like. But…" The runner hesitates. "There's something else."

"Tell me."

"They're different. Both of them. The prophet—his rune covers half his body now. They say he walks like he owns the ground under his feet. And the woman—" "Sable."

"She's glowing. Scars across her whole body, lit up like silver fire. The people who saw them said it looked like two gods walking through the Warrens." I absorb this information. Process it. Feel Greed calculating opportunities and Wrath measuring threats. Ash has integrated with his shard. Stopped fighting it. Become something more than the broken prophet who ran from the Fall. Sable has freed herself somehow. Gained power of her own. No longer just a shadow but a force in her own right. They're coming to find me. Coming to help, probably. Coming to rejoin the fight against Parliament. But they don't know about the shards I've taken. Don't know about my plans. Don't know that I've stopped fighting to survive and started fighting to rule. "Orders?" the runner asks. I think about Moe's warning. About the boy who walked into fire for me. About the woman who betrayed everyone she loved because I gave her no choice. I think about what I'm becoming. What I might have to do to win. "Find them," I say finally. "Bring them to me. Tell them the queen wants to welcome her lost children home." The runner nods and vanishes. I turn back to my maps. To my plans. To the war I'm building. Three shards against Parliament's four. Soon to be four against three, if Ash agrees to my proposal. And if he doesn't? Wrath whispers suggestions. Greed offers alternatives. I push them down. Not yet. Not until I've tried everything else. But if it comes to it—if Ash stands between me and victory—I'll do what I've always done. Whatever it takes.

```
=========================================
============
=========================================
=========
```

MOE'S LAST GOOD DAY

The cat is fat. That's the first thing I notice when I wake—
Mercyless the Second (can't call her just Mercyless anymore, not with
the sword taking that name) has gotten properly round in the weeks
since we've been back. Someone's been feeding her extra. Probably
Ash. Boy can't resist anything that looks hungry. I scratch behind her
torn ear. She purrs—actually purrs, which she almost never does—and
butts her head against my palm. "Getting soft," I tell her. "Both of us."
She doesn't argue. Outside, the sun's coming up gold and gentle, like it
forgot what city it's shining on. Tomorrow we storm the Cathedral.
Tomorrow everything changes, one way or another. But today? Today
feels like a gift.

I take my time getting dressed. No rush. The planning's done, the
positions are set, and Winter gave everyone the day to rest before the
storm. Rest, she said. Pray. Make peace with whatever needs making
peace with. Smart woman. She knows what tomorrow might cost. I pull
on the coat—same coat, same pockets, same weight—but today it feels
different. Familiar instead of heavy. Like armor I've grown into instead
of armor I'm carrying. In the cracked mirror, I look at myself. Really
look, for the first time in years. Old. Gray at the temples now, lines
carved deep around eyes that have seen too much. Scars like a map of
bad decisions and worse luck. Hands that have done terrible things and
tender things and everything in between. Not a good man. Never
claimed to be. But maybe—maybe—a man who tried. That's
something.

I head out early. Got errands to run. First stop: Mama Ruth's
tenement. She's on her step when I arrive, wrapped in a shawl that's
seen better decades, watching the street wake up like she's been doing it
for a hundred years. Which she probably has. "Moe." Her voice is
gravel and honey. "You look like a man with something on his mind."

"Always do."

"Sit. I'll make tea." I shouldn't. Got things to do, people to see, a war to prepare for. But her step looks warm in the morning light, and the tea she makes is the only thing in this city that tastes like home used to taste. So I sit. She brings out two chipped cups and a pot that's older than I am. The tea smells like mint and memory. "You're going somewhere," she says. Not a question. "Tomorrow."

"Somewhere you might not come back from." I don't lie to her. Never have. "Maybe." She nods. Sips her tea. Doesn't cry or fuss or try to talk me out of it. That's not her way. She's buried three husbands, five sons, and more friends than she can count. She knows what war takes. "I remember when you first came to these streets," she says. "Young. Angry. Blood on your hands and nowhere to wash it off."

"You gave me meat pies."

"You looked hungry." She smiles, and for a moment I can see the woman she was forty years ago—the one who fed stray soldiers and lost boys and anyone else who wandered into her kitchen looking like the world had beaten them. "You've changed since then."

"Have I?"

"The blood's still there. But so is something else now." She reaches over, pats my hand with fingers like warm paper. "You found people worth dying for. That's more than most get." My throat tightens. I cover it by drinking tea I can barely taste. "Thank you," I say. "For the pies. For everything."

"Come back and thank me properly." She squeezes my hand. "I'll make a fresh batch." I don't promise. Can't. But I squeeze back, and that says enough.

Second stop: the shrine of the Broken Saint. The three orphans are there, same as always—two girls and a boy, none of them old enough to remember their parents' faces. They've built a little camp in the rubble behind the offering box, blankets and stolen cushions arranged like a nest. They scatter when they see me coming. Fair enough. Big man in a black coat, sword on his back—I'd run too. "Easy," I call out. "I'm not here to hurt anyone." The oldest girl—maybe ten, with fierce eyes and a scar on her chin—pokes her head out from behind a broken column. "You're the coin man."

"The what?"

"The one who drops coins in the box. Every week. We've been watching." Of course they have. Survivors watch. It's how you stay alive. "Yeah," I admit. "That's me." She studies me like she's trying to figure out the angle. Smart kid. Angles are all she's ever known. "Why?" Good question. I'm not sure I have a good answer. "Because someone should." I shrug. "Because I've got coin and you need it. Because the world's hard enough without kids going hungry." She considers this. Then: "You got any food?" I reach into my coat. Pull out the packet of bread and cheese I grabbed before leaving—told myself it was for the road, but I knew where it was really going. The other two emerge when they see food. The boy is maybe six, missing two front teeth. The younger girl is even smaller, clutching a rag doll that's more patches than original fabric. I divide the food into three portions. Hand them out. They eat like wolves—fast, wary, watching me the whole time in case this is some kind of trap. "What's your name?" the oldest asks around a mouthful of cheese. "Moe."

"That a real name?"

"Real as any." The little girl with the doll tugs on my coat. I crouch down to her level—harder than it used to be, knees protesting—and she holds out the doll. "Her name's Button," she says. "She's brave."

"She looks brave."

"Are you brave?" I think about that. About all the times I've been scared and done the job anyway. About the sword on my back and the blood on my hands and the people I've killed and the people I've failed to save. "I try to be." She considers this with the gravity only small children can muster. "That's good," she decides. "Trying is important." Out of the mouths of babes. I leave more coins than usual in the box. I might not be coming back to leave more.

I find them in Winter's war room—what used to be a wine cellar, now covered with maps and plans and desperate hope stacked high. Winter's at the table, naturally. Sable beside her, the golden sigil at her wrist pulsing slow and steady. Ash across from them, looking less like death than he has in weeks—the time in the Warrens changed him, hardened something that needed hardening. They look up when I enter. "You're late," Winter says. No heat in it. "Had errands."

"Important errands?" I think about Mama Ruth's tea. The orphans' faces. The coin in the offering box. "Yeah. Important." She doesn't ask more. Doesn't need to. Twelve years together means she knows when to push and when to let things be. "We were just going over the entry points," Ash says. "Want to weigh in?"

"In a minute." I grab a chair—the wobbly one that nobody else likes—and settle into it with a groan my body's been earning for decades. "First, I want to say something." They wait. Patient. Wary. Not used to me making speeches. "I'm not good at this." I clear my throat. "Words. Feelings. All that soft stuff." A pause. "But tomorrow we might die. And if I die without saying this, I'll be pissed at myself in whatever hell takes enforcers." Sable's watching me with those careful eyes. Still don't trust her completely. Probably never will. But I don't need to trust her to say what needs saying. "You're my crew." The words come out rough. Unpracticed. "Winter—you saved my life when I didn't want to be saved. Gave me purpose when I thought I was done. Ash—you remind me why we fight. Why any of this matters. And Sable—" I meet her eyes. "You're complicated. But you're ours now. And I protect what's ours." The silence stretches. Then Winter laughs—actually laughs, a sound I've heard maybe three times in twelve years. "Moe." She shakes her head. "That's the most you've said in a month."

"Don't get used to it."

"Wouldn't dream of it." Ash is smiling—that soft, surprised smile he gets when something touches him he wasn't expecting. "Thank you, Moe."

"Don't thank me. Just—" I wave a hand. "Don't die tomorrow. Any of you. Make the speech worth it."

"Same to you," Sable says quietly. And there's something in her voice that might be genuine. Hard to tell with her. Always hard to tell. But I'll take it.

Later, when the others have gone to bed—or to whatever passes for sleep the night before war—I sit alone in the cellar. The wine's gone. The candles are burning low. Tomorrow is coming whether I'm ready or not. I'm ready. Not because I want to die. I don't. There's a cat waiting for me, and orphans who need coins, and Mama Ruth's promise of meat pies. There's a world out there with good things in it, things worth living for. But if dying is what it takes—if my death buys time for the people who matter, if it means Ash gets to the Cathedral, if it means Winter survives to rebuild, if it means Sable gets to become whatever she's becoming—Then I'm ready. I've spent my whole life trying to be enough. Trying to protect the people who needed protecting. Failing. Getting back up. Trying again. Maybe tomorrow I finally will be. Maybe tomorrow, when the killing starts and the darkness comes and everything falls apart, I'll stand where I need to stand and do what I need to do and it'll be enough. That's all I've ever wanted. To be enough. I blow out the last candle. And wait for dawn.

CHAPTER NINETEEN

THE SIEGE OF IVORY SPIRE

• • •

The army gathers in the shadow of the Spire like a wave waiting to crash.

I stand at the front, watching them assemble. Ex-Wardens in battered armor. Street crews with improvised weapons. Gutter priests in robes that smell like incense and desperation. The faithful who've been following me since the first healing, carrying nothing but prayers and belief.

Three hundred against a thousand. Maybe worse odds than that.

Vera finds me as the sun begins to set.

"They're scared," she says quietly. "Not of Parliament. Of letting you down."

"They shouldn't be. I'm the one who might fail them."

"You already haven't. You're here. You stood up. That's more than anyone else has done in a hundred years." She puts her hand on my arm. "Whatever happens tonight, Ash—you gave them hope. Real hope. The kind that doesn't come from cathedrals or coin. Don't take that away from them by doubting yourself."

I want to believe her. Want to trust that whatever comes, I'll be able to face it.

But the Crown whispers in my chest. The rune spreads up my arm. And somewhere in the distance, Parliament's power waits to consume everything I love.

"I'll try," I tell her. "That's all I can promise."

"It's enough." She squeezes my arm. "It's always been enough."

The sun touches the horizon. The Spire's shadow stretches toward us like a reaching hand.

Time to find out if hope is enough.

The Ivory Spire rises against the night sky like a blade waiting for a throat. I've seen it a thousand times. Served in its shadow for fifteen years before I learned what the Church really was. Before I slaughtered my own unit for refusing to execute children. Before I became what the Wardens call a traitor and what the streets call a legend. Now I'm standing at the head of an army, and the Spire is waiting for me to come home. "How many?" asks Vera, Winter's lieutenant, counting heads in the darkness behind us. "Three hundred. Maybe more." I adjust the strap holding Mercyless to my back. The sword hums against my spine, hungry for what's coming. "Ex-Wardens who couldn't stomach the Church's lies anymore. Street saints from the Church of Vice Redeemed. Gutter priests who've been waiting for a chance to die with purpose."

"Against how many Wardens?"

"Thousand. Plus Executioners. Plus whatever Parliament's got guarding their Crown." Vera's face goes pale in the moonlight. "Those aren't odds. Those are a death sentence."

"Yeah." I roll my shoulder, feeling the phantom weight of the arm I lost saving those kids. The bone-steel prosthetic Winter's artificers built is functional, but it doesn't feel like mine. Nothing feels like mine anymore. "But Ash is coming. Winter's moving on her own plan. And someone needs to keep Parliament busy while the real fight happens inside."

"So we're the distraction."

"We're the statement." I turn to face her. "Every person behind us chose to be here. They know what we're facing. They know most of us won't walk away. But they're here anyway, because Parliament burned their homes and killed their families and told them it was divine judgment." I look back at the Spire. At the glowing glyphs that crawl across its walls. At the Warden formations visible on the parapets. "Tonight, we show them what divine judgment really looks like." Vera nods. Draws her blade. Behind us, three hundred voices begin to chant. "Vice redeemed. Vice redeemed. VICE REDEEMED." And I lead the charge.

● ● ●

The assault comes in waves, and we break each one.

First wave: Standard Wardens. Men and women in blessed armor, singing hymns as they charge. They expect to overwhelm us with numbers—a wall of faith against our ragged defenders.

They're wrong.

Moe takes the center, Mercyless singing her hungry song. Each swing cuts two, three bodies. Each step forward pushes the line back. The ex-Wardens know their old comrades' tactics—know the patterns, the weaknesses, the moments when faith wavers and fear takes over.

The street saints fight like animals. No training, no discipline—just rage compressed into fists and blades. They've waited their whole lives for a chance to hurt the people who hurt them. Tonight, they take it.

The gutter priests do something else entirely. They sing.

I've heard the Relic Tongue spoken. I've heard it screamed. But I've never heard it sung—not like this. A dozen voices braided

215

together, each one carrying a different verse, the harmonies creating something greater than any single prayer.

A squad of Wardens finds their blessed blades turned to rust.

An Executioner's armor cracks along seams that weren't there a moment ago.

A Prelate—floating above the battle, preparing some massive working—suddenly drops from the sky, its mask cracked, its power disrupted.

"Push!" I roar. "Push now!"

We push.

• • •

Second wave: Executioners.

They're everything the Wardens aren't—silent, precise, devastating. Their golden halberds cut through our lines like scythes through wheat. Each swing is a death. Each step forward is territory lost.

"Hold!" Moe's voice rises above the chaos. "Hold the damn line!"

We try. God, we try.

Brother Cask—the old monk who found me in the Warrens— takes a halberd through the chest. He was sixty years old. He'd survived addiction, survived withdrawal, survived everything the streets could throw at him. But he couldn't survive this.

He smiles as he falls. Smiles and whispers something I can't hear over the roar of battle.

Sister Mercy follows him. Then Brother Stone. Then a girl whose name I never learned, who joined the gutter priests because she had nowhere else to go.

One by one, the singers fall silent.

One by one, the Relic Tongue loses its harmony.

"We're being slaughtered!" Vera screams at me. "We need to fall back!"

"Fall back to where? They're everywhere!"

"Then we need a miracle!"

I look at my hands. At the rune blazing gold against my skin.

"Working on it."

• • •

The Prelates descend like judgment given form.

Three of them, masks showing those three vertical scars—Parliament's highest order, the ones who speak directly to the Crown they're trying to reforge. Their scripture spirals around them like living things, each word a weapon, each verse a death sentence.

"CONTRA-CROWN SYMPATHIZERS," one intones. "SUBMIT FOR CLEANSING."

I don't submit.

I open my mouth and let the Relic Tongue pour out—not carefully, not precisely, just raw power channeled through syllables I barely understand.

The first Prelate's scripture shatters.

The second catches fire.

The third—The third is fast.

Its power slams into me before I can finish the verse. I fly backward, crash into a wall, feel ribs crack and lungs compress. The world goes white, then red, then nothing.

Ash! Eli's voice, desperate. *Ash, get up!*

217

I can't. I can't move, can't breathe, can't do anything except lie in the rubble and watch the battle continue without me.

The Prelate floats toward me. Its mask tilts, considering.

"YOU SHOULD HAVE SUBMITTED, PROPHET. THE CROWN DOES NOT SHARE POWER."

Behind it, I see Moe still fighting—bleeding from a dozen wounds, his artificial arm sparking, but still standing. Still protecting the line.

I see Vera organizing the survivors, pulling the wounded to safety.

I see the street saints dying, one by one, but taking Wardens with them.

They're not giving up. Even now, even losing, they're not giving up.

Because I told them to fight. Because I made them believe.

Get up, Eli says again. *Get up, Ash. They need you.*

"I can't—"

You can. You've been doing it your whole life. Every time the world knocked you down, you got back up. Every time they told you to stay broken, you stood. This is no different.

The Prelate raises its hand. Scripture coils around its fingers, preparing the killing blow.

Get up, big brother. One more time.

I get up.

The power comes from somewhere deeper than the rune— somewhere deeper than the Crown's shard. It comes from the same place that let me heal when I had nothing left. The same place that let me survive when surviving was impossible.

It comes from love.

Love for Eli. For Sable. For Moe and Winter and everyone who believed in me. Love for the city that raised me and broke me and made me who I am.

Love for the people dying to protect a future I promised them.

The Prelate hesitates. Just for a moment. Just long enough for me to speak.

"THE CROWN DOESN'T SHARE POWER," I say, my voice layered with harmonics that hurt my own ears. "BUT I DO."

I reach out—not with my hands but with everything I am. Everything I've ever been.

And I pull.

The first wave hits the Spire's outer wall like a storm breaking. Wardens pour from the gates, masks gleaming, blades singing hymns. They expected a mob. Disorganized. Desperate. They didn't expect me. Mercyless comes off my back in a single smooth motion, and the first Warden dies before he knows I've moved. The sword drinks his anger—his righteous fury at the heretics attacking his holy ground—and channels it into the next swing, and the next, each strike stronger than the last. "HOLD THE LINE!" I roar over the chaos. "MAKE THEM EARN EVERY INCH!" The ex-Wardens know how to fight together. They form shield walls, create chokepoints, force the Church's soldiers to come at them in numbers they can handle. The street saints don't have training, but they have rage—fifteen years of oppression compressed into blades and fists and teeth. The gutter priests do something else entirely. They sing. Relic Tongue verses pour from their throats, sloppy and untrained but powered by faith that doesn't care about precision. A squad of Wardens finds their armor suddenly too heavy to move. Another group discovers that their blessed blades have turned to rust. One Executioner—massive, golden, terrible—takes three steps toward our line before a chorus of street scripture brings him to his knees. For ten minutes, we're winning. For ten minutes, I let myself believe we might actually survive this. Then

219

the Prelates come. Three of them, floating down from the Spire's upper levels like angels of death. Scripture spirals around their forms. Their masks show three vertical scars each—the same marks I saw on the one that attacked Winter's estate. "CONTRA-CROWN SYMPATHIZERS," one intones. "SUBMIT FOR CLEANSING."

"Make me," I spit. They do. The first Prelate gestures, and twenty of my people simply... stop. Fall. Dead before they hit the ground, their hearts crushed by invisible force. The second Prelate speaks a word, and fire erupts across our left flank. Screams. The smell of burning flesh. The third Prelate looks directly at me. "THE BETRAYER," it says. "WE HAVE WAITED FOR YOUR RETURN." Mercyless screams in my grip, feeding on my fear, my anger, my desperate need to protect what's left of the people behind me. I charge.

I walk through the gates of the Ivory Spire like I own them. Not running. Not charging. Walking. Because the Crown doesn't rush, and I've stopped pretending I'm anything other than what it's making me. The battle parts around me. Wardens who were pressing forward suddenly find themselves thrown backward by invisible force. Executioners turn to face this new threat—and hesitate. They can feel what I am. Can feel the Hunger shard burning in my chest, the divine power that pulses through my veins with every heartbeat. I'm not just Ash anymore. I'm something else. Something Parliament has been afraid of since they first started collecting shards. A crowned king walking among them. "CONTRA-CROWN." The remaining Prelates float toward me, scripture spinning. "YOU HAVE RETURNED."

"I never left." I raise my hand. The rune blazes gold, covering my arm, my chest, my throat. "I just stopped running." The first Prelate attacks. A wave of divine force that should crush me where I stand. I speak a word. One word, in the Relic Tongue, and the attack dissolves. The Prelate recoils, mask cracking. "IMPOSSIBLE. YOUR POWER SHOULD NOT—" "Should not what? Work? Grow? Become something you can't control?" I step toward them. "You spent centuries trying to reforge the Crown. Trying to contain divine power in artifacts and hierarchies and laws. But the Crown wasn't made to be contained." Another step. The Wardens are backing away now. Even the Executioners are hesitant. "It was made to be worn." I reach out. Not with my hand—with my will. With the Hunger that lives in my chest. And I pull. The Prelates scream. Golden light tears from their bodies, from their scripture, from their very souls. Divine power that Parliament hoarded for generations, flowing into me like water finding its level. When it's done, two more piles of ash drift across the battlefield. And I feel the Crown stirring inside me, satisfied. Eli's voice echoes in my mind: *Careful, brother. You're starting to enjoy this.* exactly what we need.* I find Moe in the chaos. He's bleeding from a dozen wounds, his bone-steel arm sparking where something cracked the casing. But he's still standing. Still fighting. Still refusing to die. "Prophet." He almost smiles. "About time."

"Had to make an entrance." I extend my hand. Golden light flows into him, healing wounds, restoring strength. "Where's Winter?" Moe's face darkens. "Inside. She went in through the tunnels while we hit the front. Said she had business with Parliament."

"Business?"

"She's got two shards now, Ash. Greed and Wrath. And she's not planning to share them." The realization hits like cold water. Winter isn't here to help us win. She's here to take everything.

"Keep them busy!" I shout to Moe. "Hold the Spire until I come back!"

"And if you don't?"

"Then burn it down!" I run. Through the shattered gates, past the bodies of Wardens and saints alike, into the Ivory Spire's depths. Sable catches up to me before I reach the first corridor, her silver scars blazing in the darkness. "Winter's ahead of us. I can feel her."

"Her mark?"

"It's changed. The gold in it is… hungry." Sable's face is grim. "She's not the same person we knew, Ash. The shards have done something to her."

"I know." I keep moving. The Spire's interior is a maze of scripture-covered walls and prayer chambers, but I can feel Winter's presence like a beacon. The Crown shard in my chest responds to the shards in hers, calling out across the distance. "But she's still family. Still ours. I have to try."

"And if she won't stop?" I don't answer. Don't have an answer. The Spire shakes. Somewhere above us, the battle continues—Moe's army holding against Parliament's remaining forces. Somewhere below us, Parliament's Crown waits in its chamber, incomplete and unstable without the Hunger shard that I carry. And somewhere ahead of us, Winter is making a choice that will determine everything. We run faster. The corridors give way to grand chambers—throne rooms and council halls where Parliament has ruled for centuries. Bodies litter the floor. Wardens. Priests. Minor nobles who were in the wrong place when Winter came through. She wasn't subtle. Wasn't careful. She was making a statement. "There." Sable points to a staircase descending into darkness. "Below the main chambers. That's where I feel her." We descend. The air grows heavier. Warmer. Charged with divine power that makes my skin prickle and my rune flare in response. At the bottom of the stairs, a massive door stands open. Beyond it: Parliament's Crown Chamber. And standing at its center, surrounded by golden light, Winter Vale waits for us.

The Crown Chamber is everything Parliament claimed it wasn't. Not a place of worship. Not a sanctuary of faith. A vault. A treasury. A place where power is hoarded and counted like gold coins. The walls are covered with scripture, but the words are wrong—twisted variations of the Relic Tongue, designed to bind rather than liberate. Alcoves hold artifacts I can only guess at. And at the center of it all, on an altar of black stone, Parliament's Crown blazes with unstable light. Four shards. Pride, Lust, Envy, Sloth. Reforged into a circlet that pulses with power even incomplete. Winter stands before it, her back to us, gold veins visible through her skin, her silver braids unbound and floating in the divine wind that fills the chamber. "I wondered when you'd come." Her voice is different. Deeper. Resonant with power that isn't entirely hers. "The prodigal prophet, returning to save the day."

"Winter. Step away from the Crown." She turns. And I see what she's become. The gold doesn't just trace her veins anymore. It fills her eyes, replacing the dark irises I remember with pools of molten light. Her tattoos have changed too—the blood-magic sigils now interwoven with Crown scripture, Greed and Wrath burning beneath her skin like twin suns. She's beautiful. Terrible. Inhuman. "You feel it, don't you?" She gestures at the Crown on its altar. "The pull. The need. Your Hunger shard calling to its siblings, desperate to be reunited."

"That's not why I'm here."

"Isn't it?" She takes a step toward me. The chamber shakes. "You're the heart of the Crown, Ash. The piece that makes all the others work. Without you, their artifact is unstable. Dangerous. It'll burn through anyone who tries to wear it."

"I know."

"But with you…" Her smile is sad. Almost loving. "With you, I could complete it. Forge something new. Not Parliament's Crown— ours. A power that could reshape this city, this world, into something better."

"By force."

"By necessity. Look around you, Ash. Look at what faith and diplomacy have built. Oppression. Slavery. The poor grinding themselves to dust so the powerful can live forever." The gold in her eyes blazes brighter. "We could end that. Together. We could become gods who actually care about their people." I feel the Hunger shard respond to her words. Feel it wanting what she's offering. Power. Unity. Purpose. And I feel Eli's ghost, somewhere in the rune, whispering: *Don't. Don't let her take you.* "I've already become something, Winter. And it wasn't by taking more power. It was by learning to use what I have."

"That's not enough."

"It has to be. Because the alternative is becoming exactly what we fought against." Winter's expression hardens. "Then I'll take what I need." She attacks.

Winter moves like lightning wrapped in gold. Her first strike catches me across the chest, hurling me backward into a pillar. Stone cracks. I feel ribs give way. The Hunger shard flares in response, healing the damage even as I crash through the rubble. "You could have ruled with me!" Winter's voice thunders. "You could have been a king!"

"I don't want to rule!" I roll to my feet, raise my hand. Relic Tongue pours from my throat, shaping the Crown's power into a shield. "I want to serve!" Her next attack shatters my defense. I fly again. Hit the wall. Taste blood. stronger. Greed and Wrath combined—they're feeding each other. You can't match her power.* I don't try to block her next strike. I redirect it. Channel the force through my body, through the Hunger shard, transform it into something else. Healing. Not for myself. For her. Golden light flows from my hands into Winter's chest. Not attacking—giving. Pouring energy into the shards she carries, not to empower them but to satisfy them. Winter staggers. Confused. "What are you doing?"

"Feeding them. Giving them what they want." I step toward her, keeping the connection. "Greed wants more. Wrath wants release. But they're not satisfied because you're not giving them the right things."

"You don't understand—" "I do. Better than anyone." Another step. "Hunger is the core of the Crown, Winter. The thing that makes all the other vices work. And I've learned something about hunger. It's not about taking. It's about needing. About wanting so badly that you'd give anything to have it." The gold in her eyes flickers. For a moment, I see the woman underneath—the queenpin who built an empire from nothing, who protected her people, who sacrificed everything for power because she thought it was the only way to save them. "I've lost everything," she whispers. "My club. My people. My throne. All I have left is this."

"That's not true." I reach for her hand. "You have us. Me. Sable. Moe. Whatever's left of the people who believed in you. We're still here."

"But I can't protect you anymore. Not as I was. I need more—" "You need rest. You need to stop fighting. You need to let the hunger be satisfied by something other than power." Tears streak her golden cheeks. The shards in her chest burn brighter—resisting, demanding, refusing to release their hold. "I can't stop," she says. "They won't let me."

"Then let me help." I pull her close. Press my forehead to hers. Let the Hunger shard reach out to Greed and Wrath, not to take them but to calm them. And for one perfect moment, the Crown is whole. Not reforged. Not combined. Just… connected. Seven vices in three bodies, recognizing each other, remembering what they used to be. The chamber fills with light. And then everything goes wrong.

CHAPTER TWENTY

THE LAST GOODBYE

The Silk Crypt is a tomb now. Not metaphorically. Literally.

The walls that used to pulse with music and moonlight are charred black. The dance floor where I first saw Winter hold court is buried under rubble. The private rooms where deals were made and unmade are nothing but ash and memory.

We've come home to die.

"How is she?" I ask Sable, kneeling beside the pallet where Winter lies.

"Stable. The shards are quiet." Sable's silver scars pulse gently as she checks Winter's vitals. "Whatever you did in the chamber—it put them to sleep. But I don't know how long it'll last."

Winter's face is peaceful for the first time since I met her. No calculation. No hunger. Just a woman resting after carrying too much weight for too long.

I wish I could let her sleep forever. But the city won't allow it.

Moe limps in from his post at the ruins' edge, bone-steel arm sparking where the casing cracked during the battle. He's lost more blood than any normal person should survive. He's still walking. Still fighting. Still refusing to die.

"We got a problem," he says.

"Just one?"

"A big one." He jerks his head toward the east. "The Spire rubble is glowing. Not regular fire—gold. Like the shards, but bigger. Spreading."

My stomach drops. "The Crown."

"Whatever's left of it. The thing Parliament reforged." Moe's face is grim. "It didn't get destroyed when the Spire fell. It got… freed."

I move to the edge of our shelter, look toward where the Ivory Spire used to stand.

Moe's right. Golden light pulses from the rubble, rhythmic, like a heartbeat. Like something breathing. Like something waking up.

My brother's ghost stirs in the rune.

The four shards Parliament collected… they're trying to reform. Trying to become whole without the other three.

And if they succeed?

They'll feed on every drop of ether in the city. Every magic user. Every blessed object. They'll become something worse than what Parliament intended—a Crown driven purely by hunger, with no purpose except consumption.

I watch the golden pulse grow stronger. Faster.

It's been hungry for a thousand years. And now it's awake.

"Moe," I say quietly. "Get everyone who can walk ready to move. The Crown's going to pull every piece of ether in Ashvein toward itself. Anyone near it when it reaches critical mass…"

"Understood." He doesn't argue. Doesn't question. Just starts organizing the survivors with the efficiency of a man who's evacuated a hundred positions in his life.

• • •

"This ends tonight." I turn back to where Sable tends Winter. "One way or another."

"You're not seriously considering this." Sable has followed me to the edge of the ruins, her voice sharp with fear she's trying to hide.

"The Crown wants to be whole," I say, watching the golden pulse grow stronger in the distance. "It's reaching for my shard. For Winter's. For anything that will complete it."

"So we run. We take Winter somewhere the Crown can't reach—"

"There is nowhere." I turn to face her. "Eli's right. The Crown isn't just reforming—it's feeding. Every piece of ether in this city is fuel for its hunger. If we run, it follows. If we hide, it finds us. The only way to stop it is to give it what it wants."

"And then what? You become the Crown? You turn into whatever Parliament wanted to create?"

"No." I take her hands. Feel her silver scars pulse against my skin. "I become something else. Something that can contain it without being consumed by it."

"How do you know that's possible?"

"I don't." The honesty hurts. "But I've spent weeks learning to work with the Hunger shard instead of fighting it. Learning that the Crown wasn't meant to rule—it was meant to bridge. To connect. If I can hold that truth while I absorb the rest…"

"You might survive."

"I might become something that can save this city. Or I might burn. But either way, the Crown stops here."

Sable's eyes glisten. She doesn't cry. She never cries. But I can see the tears she's holding back, feel them through whatever connection her transformation created between us.

228

"I just found you again," she whispers. "We just found each other."

"I know."

"And you're going to leave me."

"I'm going to try to come back." I pull her close. Press my forehead to hers. "But if I don't... you need to know. Everything I am, everything I've become—you made it possible. The love you gave me when I didn't deserve it. The faith you had when I'd lost mine. You're the reason I can do this."

"That's not fair."

"No. Nothing about this has been fair." I kiss her. Slow. Deep. The kind of kiss that says everything words can't. "But it's the truth. And I needed you to hear it."

When we break apart, her face is set. Determined. The woman who killed her master and freed herself from chains. The woman who chose me when she could have chosen safety.

"Then go," she says. "Save the city. And then come back to me."

"I will."

"Promise."

"I promise."

She doesn't let go of my hands.

"Do you remember the night we met?" she asks. "Really met, not the formal introduction in Winter's office."

I remember. "The dock warehouse. You were supposed to kill me."

"I was supposed to evaluate you." Her smile is sad. "Symeon wanted to know if you were a threat. If your healing was genuine or just a con. I was supposed to watch you work and report back."

"And instead?"

"Instead I watched you heal a girl who'd been beaten by her father. Seven years old. Broken arm, broken ribs, broken spirit. You knelt in front of her and you talked to her like she was a person instead of a victim. You made her laugh—I don't even know how—before you healed her body."

Her thumb traces circles on my palm.

"That's when I knew the reports were wrong. You weren't a con artist using healing as a cover. You weren't a saint performing miracles for glory. You were just a man who couldn't walk past someone in pain without trying to help."

"Sable—"

"Let me finish." She squeezes my hands. "I reported to Symeon that you were harmless. A genuine healer with no political ambitions. I told them you weren't worth watching."

"You lied for me."

"I lied for myself. Because I'd spent fifteen years being a weapon, and watching you that night... it was the first time I could imagine being something else."

The silver scars at her collar pulse warm.

"When the binding started responding to you, I was terrified. I thought it was a malfunction. Thought the echoes were waking up to drag me back under someone's control. But that's not what was happening."

"What was happening?"

"They were recognizing you. All that compressed magic, all those old contracts and broken promises—they felt your power and they responded. Not because you wanted to own me. Because you wanted to *free* me."

She pulls one hand away, presses it to her chest where the scars run deepest.

"You're the only person who's ever looked at these marks and seen something other than ownership. Everyone else—Symeon, Winter, the clients—they saw chains. Evidence of service. But you looked at them like they were wounds that deserved to heal."

I don't have words. Don't have anything but the ache in my chest.

"So when you walk toward that Crown tonight," Sable says, "when you face whatever's waiting for you—remember that. Remember that you already saved me. Whatever happens next, you already gave me something I never thought I'd have."

"What?"

"A choice." She kisses me again, soft and final. "Now go make the same choice for everyone else."

• • •

Moe is waiting at the edge of the ruins, as I knew he would be.

"Sable told you to let me go?" I ask.

"Sable told me to watch your back until you got clear of the rubble." He falls into step beside me. "After that, you're on your own."

We walk in silence for a while. The golden pulse from the Spire ruins grows stronger with every step.

"Can I ask you something?" I say finally.

"Depends on the question."

"That prayer you whisper. 'This time I'll be enough.' When did you start saying it?"

Moe is quiet for a long moment.

"After Grace. After my unit." His voice is rough. "I woke up in a field hospital with burns across half my body and the knowledge that everyone I cared about was dead because I trusted the wrong person. I wanted to die. Probably should have died."

"But you didn't."

"No. I got up. Put on the uniform. Went back to work." He shrugs. "What else was there? The world doesn't stop because you want to. So I kept going. And every morning, before I did anything else, I told myself: 'This time I'll be enough.' It was a lie at first. A way to make myself get out of bed."

"And now?"

"Now I don't know." He looks at me. "Maybe it was never a lie. Maybe I just needed to keep saying it until I found something worth being enough for."

We've reached the edge of the safe zone. Beyond this point, the ether streams are visible—ribbons of blue-green light flowing toward the golden pulse like rivers to an ocean.

"This is where I leave you," Moe says.

"Moe—"

"Don't." He holds up a hand. "You're going to say something about honor or sacrifice or how much I've meant to you. Save it. I don't need the words."

"Then what do you need?"

He's quiet. Then: "Come back. That's all. Whatever you find in there, whatever you have to become—come back. The world's got enough martyrs. It needs more people who survive."

I want to promise. Want to tell him I'll walk out of this alive.

But we both know I might not. So I just nod.

"Guard them," I say. "Sable. Winter. Everyone who made it out."

"Till my last breath."

"I know."

I turn toward the golden light. Take a step. Then another.

"Ash."

I look back one more time.

"It's been an honor."

I nod. Can't speak. Don't trust my voice.

And then I leave him behind, walking toward the golden light, toward the Crown that's been waiting for me since the night my brother died.

Moe's voice stops me at the edge of the ruins. He's standing in full battle stance, Mercyless drawn, bone-steel arm locked despite the damage.

"No."

"Wasn't asking permission." He falls into step beside me.

"You need someone to protect the others. Parliament's survivors will regroup. They'll come for Winter while she's vulnerable."

"Sable can—"

"Sable needs to be ready to get Winter out if this goes wrong. You're the only one who can hold a defensive position long enough for them to escape."

Moe's jaw tightens. He knows I'm right. He hates that I'm right.

"Besides," I add quietly, "you've already given enough. Your arm. Your blood. Your whole life fighting other people's battles. You don't owe anyone anything else."

"That's not why I fight."

"Then why?"

He's quiet for a long moment. The golden pulse from the Spire ruins reflects in his eyes.

"When I was a Warden, I did terrible things. Killed people who didn't deserve it. Enforced laws that existed to protect the powerful. I told myself it was duty. It was faith. It was just following orders." His voice drops. "Then I saw what the Church really was. What they did to children who couldn't pay their tithes. What they did to anyone who questioned them."

"You killed your own unit."

"I stopped them. And then I ran, because I didn't know how to be anything else." He looks at me. "You showed me something different. That power doesn't have to mean oppression. That strength can protect instead of destroy. That even someone like me could be..."

"Could be what?"

"Good." The word comes out rough. Like it costs him something to say it. "Or at least better. Less of a monster. More of whatever you need me to be."

I put my hand on his shoulder. Feel the solidity of him. The stubbornness that kept him alive through everything.

"Then be what I need you to be right now. Guard our people. Give them time to escape if this goes wrong."

"And if it goes right?"

"Then I'll buy drinks when this is over."

He almost smiles. Almost.

"I'm going to hold you to that, prophet."

"I know."

I start walking again. Get ten steps before his voice catches me one last time.

"Ash."

I turn.

"Whatever happens… it's been an honor."

I nod. Can't speak. Don't trust my voice.

And then I leave him behind, walking toward the golden light, toward the Crown that's been waiting for me since the night my brother died.

The city opens before me.

Guttersea, where I grew up counting coins that would never be enough.

The Warrens, where I learned that prayer was cheaper than medicine.

The docks, where Winter taught me that power always costs something.

All of it—every street, every temple, every desperate corner—leading toward that golden pulse on the horizon.

My home. My battlefield. My grave, maybe.

I keep walking.

The Crown is waiting.

CHAPTER TWENTY-ONE

THE LONG WALK

The city burns gold behind me.

I walk through streets I've walked a thousand times, but they're different now. The ether-glow that used to pulse from every den and corner is streaming—actually streaming, visible ribbons of blue-green light flowing toward the Ivory Spire's ruins like blood returning to a heart that refuses to stop beating.

People stare from doorways. Addicts clutch their arms, feeling their fixes being pulled from their veins. Dealers watch their product evaporate into mist. The whole economy of desperation unraveling in real time.

I should feel something about that. Later, maybe. Right now there's only the walk.

You're going to die.

Eli's voice is quiet in my head. Not arguing anymore. Just stating fact.

"Probably."

The Crown has consumed everyone who ever tried to hold it whole. Saints. Prophets. Emperors. It doesn't matter how strong you are or how pure your intentions—the power eats you from the inside.

"Then why'd you help me get here?"

He's silent for a long moment.

Because you're my brother. And because if anyone could do the impossible, it would be the kid who prayed three nights straight to save Mama.

I stop walking. The golden pulse from the Spire ruins beats against my skin, warm and hungry.

"You remember that?"

I remember everything now. Being dead gives you perspective. His voice softens. *You were eleven. You hadn't slept in three days. You were so exhausted you could barely stand, but you kept praying. Kept bargaining. Kept offering yourself in exchange.*

"It worked."

Did it? I can feel him thinking, sorting through memories that aren't quite memories anymore. *Or did something just notice you? Something old and hungry, looking for a vessel?*

The rune on my wrist—the one that appeared the night Eli died—pulses in response.

"You think the Crown's been watching me since I was eleven?"

I think power recognizes power. I think the part of it you carry—the Hunger—has been calling to the rest for a very long time. And I think you walking toward it right now isn't fate or courage or prophecy. It's just the last move in a game that started before either of us was born.

"That's not comforting."

Wasn't meant to be.

• • •

The streets empty as I get closer. Even the desperate have survival instincts. The golden light ahead pulses brighter, faster—a heartbeat accelerating as its meal approaches.

I pass a shrine to the old gods. The ones Parliament replaced. It's been defaced so many times the original carvings are barely visible, but someone's left fresh flowers on the steps. White lilies. Funeral flowers.

I stop. Pick one up.

My mother used to grow lilies in the window box of our tenement. Said they reminded her of her mother's garden, back before the family lost everything, back when Marrow was still a name that meant something other than poverty.

I tuck the flower into my pocket.

Sentimental.

"Shut up."

I'm not judging. I'm just saying—you're walking to your death and you stopped for a flower.

"I stopped because Mama would've wanted me to."

Eli doesn't respond. But I feel something shift in the space where he lives inside me. Something like grief. Something like love.

• • •

Three blocks from the crater, I find the body.

A Warden. Young—couldn't be more than twenty. His mask is cracked, showing half a face frozen in terror. The golden light has already started to work on him, veins glowing beneath dead skin.

He died running. Toward the ruins or away from them, I can't tell. Doesn't matter. He's gone either way.

I kneel beside him. Close his eyes. Speak the words without thinking:

> *"Rest now, runner, your race complete—*
>
> *May the road rise soft beneath your feet—*

Whatever sins you carried here

Dissolve like shadows, disappear."

The verse costs me. I feel it—years sliding off the back end of my life, the Relic Tongue's price extracted in flesh and time. The Warden's face smoothes. The terror fades.

You just blessed a man who would've killed you on sight.

"He was somebody's son."

He was Parliament's weapon.

"He was twenty years old and scared and probably didn't choose any of this." I stand. "That's the difference between them and us. They see enemies. I see people." The city opens before me like a book I've been reading my whole life.

Every corner holds a memory. Every alley whispers a story. I pass the bakery where Mrs. Chen used to slip me day-old bread when I came in pretending to browse. She's standing in the doorway now, watching the golden light pulse in the sky, her face a mask of fear and wonder.

"Saint Ash." Her voice cracks. "Is it true? Is this the end?"

"I don't know." I stop in front of her. She smells like flour and yeast and all the mornings I woke up hungry. "But whatever happens— thank you. For the bread. For pretending not to notice when I couldn't pay."

Her eyes fill with tears. "I always knew you were special."

"I'm not special. I'm just the one who's still walking."

She presses something into my hand. A roll, still warm. The last one from this morning's batch.

"Then keep walking. And eat something. My mother always said you can't save the world on an empty stomach."

I pocket the bread next to the lily. Symbols of everything I'm fighting for—the small kindnesses that make life bearable. The people who give what they have even when they have nothing.

• • •

The Tanaka house is empty now. Has been since the children went to the workhouses and the parents followed them into graves they couldn't afford. But someone's lit a candle in the window. A vigil, maybe. A hope that the family will come home even though everyone knows they won't.

I stand outside for a long moment.

I could have saved them. If I'd had the power then that I have now. If I'd been faster, stronger, better. If I'd been enough.

You can't save everyone.

"I know."

You've saved more than most.

"Not enough. Never enough."

And that's why you're the one walking toward the Crown right now. Because you'll never stop trying to be enough. Eli's voice is gentle. *That's not a flaw, Ash. That's what makes you different from everyone who's ever held this power before.*

"What do you mean?"

Parliament wanted the Crown to rule. The old emperors wanted it for conquest. Every vessel for a thousand years has reached for divine power because they wanted more—more control, more authority, more of everything.

"And me?"

You want less. Less suffering. Less hunger. Less of everything that makes life hard for people who've never had anything. His laugh is soft, sad. *You're the first vessel in history who wants to give the power away.*

"I'm not sure I want to give it away. I just don't want to keep it for myself."

Same thing. Different words.

I start walking again. The golden light is close now—I can feel it like a physical pressure, like standing at the edge of a fire that wants to pull me in.

• • •

The last street before the crater is empty. No one lives this close to the Spire ruins—the radiation or corruption or whatever leaks from the shattered artifact has made the ground toxic. Plants don't grow here. Animals don't come. Even the rats have fled.

But someone's painted something on the wall.

Graffiti. Fresh, from the look of it. Done in the last few hours while the city held its breath.

SAINT ASH WAS HERE

Underneath, in smaller letters:

AND HE'S COMING BACK

I stare at it for a long moment.

"Who did this?"

Does it matter?

"Yes."

Someone who believes in you. Someone who needed to mark the wall before the world changed. Someone who wanted to make sure history remembers you were here.

I touch the painted words. The letters are rough, hasty—someone working fast before they were caught. But they're clear. Deliberate.

Someone risked coming this close to the ruins just to leave me a message.

"I don't deserve this."

No one deserves faith. That's what makes it faith.

I take a breath. Let it out.

The crater waits.

• • •

The edge of the ruins is where the world ends and something else begins.

Below me, the crater spreads like a wound in the earth—half a mile across, deep enough to swallow temples. At its center, the golden light pulses. The remnants of the Ivory Spire jut from the rubble like broken fingers reaching for heaven.

And floating above it all, orbiting the light like planets around a sun, the remaining shards.

I can feel them. Pride, Lust, Envy, Sloth—the four Parliament collected. Greed and Wrath, taken from Winter's body when she fell. And beneath them all, calling to me like a mother calling a child home, the core of the Crown.

The thing that will either save me or destroy me. There's no third option anymore.

I take out the roll Mrs. Chen gave me. Eat it slowly, standing at the edge of the world. It tastes like morning and kindness and every meal I ever shared with people I loved.

I take out the lily. Hold it to my nose. It smells like Mama's window box. Like the hope she carried even when hope was foolish.

You're stalling.

"I'm saying goodbye."

I look back at the city one last time. The Rust Warrens where I was born. The docks where Winter taught me that power always costs something. The temples and tenements and hidden places where the people I love are waiting to see if I survive.

"Goodbye," I whisper.

And then I step into the light.

And when those people are trying to murder everyone you love?

"Then I stop them." I start walking again. "But I don't have to hate them to do it."

The golden pulse intensifies. The Crown knows I'm close. I can feel it reaching for me—not just the Hunger shard in my chest, but something deeper. Something in my blood. In my bones. In whatever part of me has been marked since childhood.

Ash.

"Yeah?"

I'm scared.

I stop again. In all the months he's been haunting me, Eli has never said that. Never admitted weakness. Not even when he was alive.

"Me too."

You don't seem scared.

"That's because I've had practice." I look toward the golden light—so bright now it hurts, so hungry I can feel it pulling at my organs. "Being scared doesn't mean you stop. It just means you know what you're risking."

What ARE you risking? Specifically?

"Everything." The word comes out simple. True. "My life. My soul. Whatever's left of my sanity. If this goes wrong, I don't just die—I become the thing I'm trying to stop. Another Crown-bearer who lost themselves to the power."

And you're okay with that?

"No." I take a breath. "But I'm less okay with letting the city burn. With letting Sable lose everyone she's ever cared about. With letting Moe die for nothing."

He might die anyway.

"He might." My chest tightens. "But if I do this right, his death buys something. It means something. And if I fail—"

If you fail, we all die, and none of it means anything.

"Then I'd better not fail."

· · ·

The last block is the hardest.

The golden light is everywhere now—not just from the crater but from the air itself, from the stones beneath my feet, from the ruins of buildings that used to house families and businesses and dreams. The Crown's hunger has turned this whole district into a feeding ground.

I pass a temple that's been consumed. The walls still stand, but everything inside is gone—furniture, icons, even the paint on the murals. The Crown ate it all. Converted matter to energy, faith to fuel.

This is what happens if I fail. This spreads. This becomes everything.

There's still time to run.

"No there isn't."

Ash—

"The Hunger shard in my chest is the only thing keeping the Crown from going critical. It's incomplete without me. If I run, it follows. If I hide, it finds me. And every minute I delay, it feeds more, grows stronger, gets harder to contain."

So you're not being brave. You're being practical.

"Why can't it be both?"

The crater opens before me. A wound in the city's flesh, ringed with rubble and ash and the golden light of something ancient trying to be born.

At the center, Parliament's Crown hovers.

It's beautiful. That's the first thing I notice. Whatever else it is— weapon, prison, vessel for seven deadly sins—it's beautiful. Golden light spiraling around a core of pure power. Fragments orbiting like planets around a sun. The shape suggesting a crown, a halo, a corona of divine authority.

Four shards orbit the central mass. Pride. Lust. Envy. Sloth. The ones Parliament collected. The ones they tried to forge into a weapon of control.

They're incomplete. Unstable. Without the other three—without Hunger, Greed, and Wrath—the Crown can't fully form. But it's trying. God, it's trying. Forcing itself into coherence through sheer will, feeding on the city's ether to compensate for what it lacks.

The four are weaker than they should be. Eli's voice is thoughtful now, analytical. *Parliament tried to bind them with scripture and ritual. It's holding, but barely. If you can absorb them before they fully integrate with each other—*

"I can take them one at a time instead of all at once."

Theoretically.

"Better than nothing."

I step into the crater.

The Crown feels me immediately.

The golden light swings toward me like a spotlight, like a predator scenting prey, like a lover recognizing the other half of their soul. The pulse changes—faster, hungrier, more desperate.

And for the first time, I hear it speak.

"SHARD-BEARER."

The voice comes from everywhere. From the light. From the stones. From the hollow space behind my own eyes. It's not words exactly—more like meaning impressed directly onto my brain, translated through whatever connection the Hunger shard creates.

"YOU HAVE COME."

I walk forward. Slow. Steady. Each step sending ripples through the golden light like waves in a still pond.

"I've come to end this."

"THE SAME THING."

The Crown pulses brighter. I can feel it reaching for the Hunger shard in my chest—not violently, not yet. Gently. Seductively. Like a hand extended for a dance.

"YOU CARRY THE HEART OF US. THE HUNGER THAT DRIVES ALL OTHER VICES. WITHOUT YOU, WE STARVE. WITHOUT US, YOU HOLLOW."

"I've been doing fine."

"HAVE YOU?" The voice curls with something like amusement. "WE HAVE WATCHED. WE HAVE FELT. THE ACHE IN YOUR CHEST WHEN YOU HEAL OTHERS—THE NEED FOR MORE, ALWAYS MORE. THE EMPTINESS THAT NEVER FILLS NO MATTER HOW MANY YOU SAVE."

I want to deny it. I can't.

The Hunger shard has been eating at me for months. The compulsion to use my power. The inability to stop even when it's killing me. The void at the center of my being that no amount of blessing can fill.

"That's not me. That's you."

"WE ARE THE SAME. WE HAVE ALWAYS BEEN THE SAME."

"No." I take another step. "You're hunger for the sake of hunger. Taking because taking is all you know. I'm hunger for something else. For justice. For mercy. For people who've never had anyone fight for them."

"PRETTY WORDS. BUT IN THE END, HUNGER IS HUNGER. YOU CANNOT ESCAPE WHAT YOU ARE."

"Watch me."

I reach for the first shard.

• • •

Pride comes at me like a golden avalanche.

Not the shard itself—the essence of it. The accumulated weight of a thousand years of arrogance, of certainty, of knowing you're better than everyone around you. It hits me before I can grab the physical fragment, a wave of absolute conviction that nearly drives me to my knees.

I SEE MYSELF ON A THRONE.

Not metaphorically. Literally. A vision so clear it's almost memory—me, wearing the Crown, sitting in judgment over a city that finally understands its proper place. Below me. Beneath me. Serving me as they should have always served.

I could do it. The power is right here. All I have to do is take it, and no one would ever disrespect me again. No one would ever doubt

247

me. No one would look at the street kid from Guttersea and see anything but the god he was always meant to become.

ASH.

Eli's voice cuts through the golden haze. Faint but present.

THAT'S NOT YOU.

"It could be." My voice comes out strange. Layered. "It should be. I've earned it. I've suffered more, sacrificed more, given more than any of them—"

That's the Pride talking.

"Maybe the Pride is right."

It's not. You know it's not. His voice cracks. *Remember the shrine, Ash. Remember the flower. Remember why you blessed that dead Warden even though he didn't deserve it.*

The vision wavers. The throne flickers.

I see myself at eleven years old. Kneeling by Mama's bed. Praying for hours, days, until my voice gave out and my knees bled through my pants. Not because I deserved anything. Not because I was better than the fever that was killing her.

Because I loved her. Because I would've done anything to save her. Because the prayer wasn't about me at all.

"I'm not better than them."

The words cost me. Pride screams in protest, claws at my thoughts, tries to reassert its vision.

"I'm just someone who got given a gift. And gifts aren't about deserving. They're about what you do with them."

The shard tears into my chest.

I scream. Can't help it. The agony is beyond anything I've felt—not just physical pain but spiritual violation, centuries of accumulated sin trying to make itself at home in my soul.

But I don't let it rule me. I hold onto Mama's face. Eli's voice. Sable's hands in mine.

Pride settles. Quiets. Becomes part of me without consuming me.

One down.

Six to go.

• • •

Lust comes next.

It doesn't wait for me to reach for it—it reaches for me. Golden tendrils of desire wrapping around my limbs, my chest, my throat. Showing me every want I've ever felt, every need I've ever denied, every desperate craving I've buried under duty and sacrifice.

I see Sable.

Not the real Sable—a fantasy version. Compliant. Willing. Offering herself to me completely, holding nothing back, giving me everything I've ever wanted without question or resistance.

I see Winter. I see every woman I've ever found attractive. I see comfort and pleasure and release from the endless weight of responsibility.

All I have to do is take. Take what's offered. Take what I deserve. Take because wanting is enough, because desire justifies itself, because the body's hunger is the truest form of worship.

This one's harder.

Eli's voice is strained. Like he's fighting too.

"I know."

The fantasy-Sable moves closer. Her hands on my face. Her lips on my neck. Her voice whispering everything I've ever wanted to hear.

"You've given so much," she breathes. "You deserve to receive. You deserve pleasure. You deserve—"

"Stop."

"—me. All of me. Without conditions. Without complications. Without—"

"I SAID STOP."

I think of the real Sable. The one who fights back. The one who argues. The one who chose me not because I was powerful or special but because she saw something in me worth choosing.

The one whose love isn't about taking or giving. It's about choosing. Every day. Even when it's hard. Especially when it's hard.

"Love isn't about deserving."

The fantasy flickers. Tries to reassert itself.

"Love is about choosing to give even when giving costs you. It's about wanting someone's good more than you want your own pleasure. It's about—"

I reach into the golden tendrils. Grab the shard at their center.

"It's about Sable freeing herself from chains because love made her stronger, not weaker."

Lust screams as I pull it into me.

The agony is different this time. Deeper. More intimate. Every nerve ending alive with sensation that borders on pain.

But I hold onto the memory. Sable's face when she broke Symeon's binding. The moment she chose herself—and chose me—not because she was compelled but because she was finally free.

That's what love looks like. Not the taking. The choosing.

Lust settles. Two shards down.

• • •

Envy is subtle.

It doesn't hit me with visions or sensations. It just… whispers. Constant. Insidious. Pointing out every injustice, every inequality, every time someone who deserved less got more.

Parliament's towers. The merchants' warehouses. The Church's gold. All that wealth, all that power, all that safety—hoarded by people who never had to watch their mother die because they couldn't afford medicine.

They have everything, the whisper says. You have nothing. And that's not fair. That's not right. They should lose what they have. They should feel what you've felt. They should—*Ash. Don't listen.*

"But it's true." My voice is bitter. I can't help it. "It IS unfair. Parliament DID steal from the poor to feed the rich. The Church DID let people die while they counted their gold."

Yes. And that's real anger, real injustice. But Envy isn't about fixing what's wrong. It's about wanting others to suffer because you suffered.

"What's wrong with that?"

Nothing. Until it consumes you. Eli's voice is gentle. *Moe spent his whole life angry at the system. But he didn't let that anger poison him. He turned it into protection. Into service. He died defending children instead of punishing the people who made those children orphans.*

The whisper fights back. Shows me all the people I could punish. All the vengeance I could take. All the ways I could make them feel what I've felt.

But I see Moe's face in the vision. Calm. Certain. Choosing protection over punishment even at the end.

251

"I don't want them to suffer."

The whisper falters.

"I want them to stop MAKING others suffer. I want to build something better, not just tear down something worse."

I grab Envy before it can recover.

This one hurts like acid—the accumulated resentment of a thousand years of inequality, of comparison, of watching others have what you lack. It burns through my thoughts, trying to turn every memory bitter.

I hold onto Moe. His sacrifice. His choice.

That's what it means to fight injustice. Not matching cruelty with cruelty. Breaking the cycle instead.

Three shards. Four to go.

• • •

Sloth is the quietest poison.

It doesn't attack. It just... drains. The will to move. The desire to fight. The belief that any of this matters.

Why struggle? Why sacrifice? The world will keep turning whether you save it or not. The poor will still suffer. The powerful will still exploit. Nothing you do will change the fundamental nature of things, so why not just... rest?

You've earned it. You've fought so hard, for so long, against so much. Wouldn't it be easier to stop? To let go? To finally, finally lay down the weight?

I feel my legs weaken. My arms drop. The golden light around me pulses slower, matching my breathing, lulling me toward acceptance.

Ash. Don't you dare.

Eli's voice is desperate now. Angry.

Don't you DARE give up. Not after everything. Not after Mama and me and Sable and Moe and everyone who's ever believed in you.

"Believing didn't save any of you."

No. But it gave us something to believe IN. Something worth dying for. His voice cracks. *If you stop now, all those deaths mean nothing. If you give up, Parliament wins. The Crown wins. And everyone who ever loved you dies knowing their faith was wasted on someone who couldn't finish what he started.*

The lethargy fights back. Shows me all the times I've failed. All the people I couldn't save. All the evidence that trying is pointless.

But underneath the despair, I see something else.

The gutter monks, still praying in their temples even though no one listens.

The addicts who keep trying to get clean even though they've failed a hundred times.

The children who keep hoping even though the world has given them nothing but reasons to stop.

"They didn't give up."

Sloth hisses.

"The people with the least reason to keep fighting—they kept fighting anyway. Not because they were sure they'd win. Because stopping was worse than losing."

I reach for the shard.

This one doesn't burn or ache or whisper. It just weighs. Drags at my soul like chains made of exhaustion. Every step I've ever taken, every breath I've ever drawn, every moment I've forced myself to keep going when giving up would have been so much easier—it all piles on top of me.

253

I hold onto the gutter monks. The addicts. The children.

They kept going. So do I.

Four shards. The Crown is half mine.

Three more. The hard ones. The ones I took from Winter.

Greed. Wrath. And Hunger, which has been part of me from the beginning.

You need to rest, Eli says. *Even for a minute. Your body can't—*

"Can't stop. If I stop, I won't start again."

I look at the remaining shards orbiting the Crown's core.

Greed glitters like gold coins. Wrath burns like banked coals. And beneath them both, the Hunger shard in my chest pulses in recognition.

Three sins that have always lived close to my heart. Three pieces of myself I've never fully acknowledged.

This is where I find out if I'm strong enough.

This is where I find out who I really am.

I reach for Greed.

CHAPTER TWENTY-TWO

MOE'S STAND

The wall comes down at third bell. I feel it before I hear it—a shudder through the stone, the groan of ancient masonry deciding it's had enough. Then the sound catches up: thunder without sky, a roar that rattles my teeth and sets Mercyless humming against my back. The secondary corridor. That's my position. Winter chose it because she knew what it meant—the weak point, the place they'd hit hardest once the main assault drew defenders away. The place that needed someone who wouldn't run. She didn't ask me to take it. She knew I'd volunteer. "Moe." Her voice crackles through the speaking-stone at my belt. "Report."

"Wall's breached. Got Wardens pouring through the gap—maybe thirty, more coming." I draw Mercyless. She sings as she clears the scabbard, hungry and ready. "I'll hold them." Silence. Then: "How long?"

"Long as it takes."

"Moe—" "Get Ash to the sanctum. I'll buy you time." I don't wait for her answer. Don't need to. She knows what this is. What I'm choosing. Twelve years of service. Twelve years of standing beside her, killing for her, protecting everything she built. This is what it was all leading to.

The first Wardens come through the breach at a run—young ones, eager, thinking glory waits on the other side of one old man with a

255

sword. They're wrong. Mercyless takes the first one through the throat before he knows he's dead. The second catches steel in the gut, folding around the blade like wet paper. The third manages to raise his weapon—I take his hand off at the wrist and open his chest on the backstroke. Three bodies. Three seconds. The others pause. Reassess. Good. Fear buys time. "Come on then." I settle into my stance, blade ready, breathing steady despite the ache in my knees and the burn in my shoulders. "I've got all night." I don't. But they don't need to know that. The next wave comes smarter—spreading out, trying to flank. I give ground deliberately, drawing them into the narrow part of the corridor where numbers don't matter. Where one man with a good sword can hold back an army. For a while.

Cut. Parry. Thrust. Step back. Cut again. The rhythm of violence is familiar as breathing. I've been doing this for thirty years—more if you count the bad old days before Winter, before purpose, before I learned that killing could be something other than habit. A blade catches my arm—first blood. Not deep, but it stings. I reward the Warden with a slash that opens him from hip to shoulder. Another one down. Another. They're piling up in the corridor now, making their own friends' footing treacherous. Good. But more keep coming. Always more. I think about the cat. Hope someone remembers to feed her. Hope she doesn't wait too long by the window before she figures out I'm not coming back. Stupid thing to think about in a fight. But there it is. I think about Mama Ruth. Her tea. Her hand on mine, warm and papery. "Come back and thank me properly." Sorry, Ruth. Looks like the pies will have to wait. I think about the orphans. The little girl with the doll. "Are you brave?"

Then I hear them. Behind me. Sounds that don't belong in a battle—whimpering, crying, the high thin keening of children too scared to stay quiet. I risk a glance back. The storage chamber. Door half-open. And huddled inside—Children. A dozen of them at least. Cathedral servants' kids, probably, or faithful who brought their families to the siege because they had nowhere else safe to go. Nowhere safe. Like there's any such thing. An older woman—their minder, maybe—sees me looking. Her face is white with terror. "Please," she mouths. "Please." The Wardens see them too. I watch their eyes light up with something uglier than battle rage. Hostages. Leverage. Soft targets. Ice crystallizes in my chest. Not anger. Beyond anger. Certainty. I know, suddenly, exactly how this ends. Know it like I know my own name, like I know the weight of the sword in my hand, like I know the faces of everyone I've ever failed to save. No more. Not today. Not these children.

"Close that door," I call back without looking. "Lock it. Don't open it for anyone but me or the prophet."

"But—" "DO IT." The door slams. I hear the bolt slide home. Good. Now it's just me and the corridor and the army that wants to get past. The speaking-stone crackles. "Moe. Status."

"Got civilians behind me. Children." Silence. Winter knows what that means. "Can you extract them?"

"No exit. Corridor's the only way out."

"Then we'll send—" "No time. You need everyone on Ash." I take a breath. "I've got this."

"Moe—" "Winter." I cut her off. Gentle but firm. "This is what I'm for. This is what I've always been for. Let me do it." The silence stretches. I can hear her breathing through the stone. Twelve years of trust. Twelve years of service. "Hold as long as you can," she says finally. Her voice is steady but I know her well enough to hear what's underneath. "We'll come for you when the sanctum is secure." She won't. We both know she won't. But I appreciate the lie. "Winter."

"Yeah?"

"It was good. Serving you. All of it." A pause. Then, soft: "Yeah, Moe. It was." I drop the stone. Don't need it anymore. Don't need anything but the sword and the corridor and the will to stand.

I'm afraid. That surprises me somehow. Thought I'd be past fear by now, past everything but the mechanical motion of the blade. But no—the fear is right there, cold and bright in my chest, screaming at me to run, to hide, to save myself. I don't. Not because I'm brave.

Because there's something stronger than fear in me right now. Something that looks at those children huddled in the dark and says: *Not them. Not while I'm breathing. Not while I can stand.* Here's the truth about monsters like me. We're good at killing. That's what we're made for, what we're trained for, what we do when there's nothing else left. But sometimes—sometimes—the killing can be turned around. Pointed at the darkness instead of creating it. Sometimes the monster stands between the children and the wolves. And the wolves die instead. Another one down. Another.

My arm is numb below the elbow.

Blood loss, probably. The cut from earlier has opened up again, painting Mercyless's handle slick. I have to focus on my grip, adjust my stance, account for the weakness spreading through my right side.

The Wardens see it. Of course they do. They're trained to spot weakness, to exploit it, to kill the wounded before they can recover.

Three of them come at once. Coordinated. Professional. The kind of assault that would have dropped me five years ago, before Winter's training, before I learned that staying alive is just another form of violence.

I take the first one's blade on Mercyless's edge, turn it, let the force spin me into the second attacker. My sword goes through his neck while I'm still moving. The third hesitates—just a fraction of a second, just long enough for me to yank my blade free and bring it across his chest.

He falls. They all fall.

But there's always more.

My knee gives out on the next parry. Just for a moment—a flash of pain from an old injury that never healed right. I compensate, roll with the fall, turn it into a lunge that catches the Warden off guard. He dies with a surprised expression, like he can't believe an old man with a bad knee just killed him.

Join the club.

The children whimper behind me. I can hear them through the storage room door—small voices trying to be brave, failing, needing someone to protect them.

That's me. I'm all they've got.

"Come on!" I roar at the next wave. "Is this the best Parliament has? Send me someone who can actually fight!"

It's a taunt. A trick. Anger makes people sloppy, and sloppy gets you killed. The Wardens know this—they're trained to stay calm, to fight without emotion.

But training only goes so far.

The youngest one charges. Maybe nineteen. Fresh mask, clean armor, eyes burning with the need to prove himself. He comes in fast, blade singing a hymn I don't recognize.

I step sideways. Let him pass. Open his back from shoulder to hip.

He screams. Falls. Doesn't get up.

"Anyone else?"

The others hesitate. Look at the bodies piling up around me. Look at the old man with the bloody sword who should have died five wounds ago.

"You're already dead," one of them says. The one who looks like a captain. "You just don't know it yet."

"Maybe." I grin. It feels like a skull's smile. "But I'm taking as many of you with me as I can. So ask yourself—is this mission worth dying for?"

The captain doesn't answer. Just gestures his men forward.

They come.

I meet them.

The next minutes blur together. Cut. Parry. Thrust. Block. Take a blade across the thigh—deep, bad, the kind that makes your leg go cold and heavy. Kill the one who gave it to me. Take another blade across the ribs—glancing, mostly armor, but I feel something crack. Kill that one too.

I'm not fighting to win anymore. I'm fighting to buy time. Every second I hold this corridor is a second Ash gets closer to the sanctum. Every Warden I kill is one fewer chasing the prophet.

That's the math. That's the deal.

I think about the prayer I whisper every morning. *This time I'll be enough.*

All those mornings. All those prayers.

Maybe they were all leading to this. Maybe every time I said those words, I was practicing for the moment when being enough would cost me everything.

The Executioner comes through the breach like a golden avalanche.

He's twice my size. His halberd glows with scripture that hurts to look at. His mask shows seven vertical scars—the mark of the highest rank, the Prelates' personal guard.

The Wardens fall back, make room for their champion.

I plant my feet. Raise Mercyless.

"Okay," I say to myself, to the sword, to whatever's listening. "One more."

I've lost count. Lost everything except the rhythm and the pain and the stubborn refusal to fall. one I've been making every morning for years. *This time I'll be enough.* Maybe I finally am.

I don't know how I do what I do next. There's nothing left—no strength, no speed, no reserves. Just an old man with a sword and a promise he made to himself in a hundred dark mornings. But I do it anyway. I catch the next strike on Mercyless's blade—catch it and hold it, locked together, his strength against mine. He's stronger. Of course he is. But strength isn't everything. I step inside his reach. Let his halberd slide past me. And drive Mercyless up through the gap in his gorget, into the soft place where the helmet meets the armor. The Executioner makes a sound like surprise. Then he falls. And his halberd—already committed to the swing I stepped inside of—Takes me through the stomach. Cold. That's what I feel first. Cold steel in places steel should never be. Then the pain comes—bright and huge and impossible—and my legs stop working and I'm falling, falling, the world tilting sideways—I hit the stone. Face down. Can't move. Can't breathe right. Something's very wrong inside me, something that isn't going to fix itself. Mercyless lies beside me. Still humming. Still hungry. But my hand won't close around her anymore. it.*

The remaining Wardens stand over me. I can see their boots through the blood in my eyes. Hear them arguing about whether to finish me or push past to the door. "Leave him," one says. "He's done."

"The children—" "Forget the children. The prophet's the mission. Move." Boots rush past. Over me. Around me. They're not bothering with the storage room. Too focused on Ash. On the real prize. I smile. Or try to. Hard to tell if my face is doing what I want anymore. The children are safe. The children are safe. I held long enough. Killed enough. Bought enough time for them to find another target. I was enough. I was finally enough.

The world is getting dark at the edges. Quiet. The pain is fading— never a good sign, but I can't bring myself to care. I think about Grace. Funny. Haven't thought about her in years. But she's there now, in the darkness, young and lovely and smiling the way she did before everything went wrong. should have done it years ago. But I forgive you.* The cat. Someone will feed her. Ash will remember. He's good about things like that. The orphans. Winter will find them. She takes care of her territory. Always has. Mama Ruth. She'll understand. She's buried enough soldiers to know how this works. Ash. Sable. Winter. My crew. My people. I hope they make it. I hope the prophet does whatever prophets do and the Crown finds its head and something good comes out of all this blood. I won't be there to see it. But maybe that's okay. Maybe that's what enforcers are for—standing in the gap, buying time with our bodies, making sure the people who matter get through to the other side. Maybe that's enough. It's enough for me.

The last thing I see is the door. Still closed. Still locked. Still safe. And then I don't think anything at all.

CHAPTER TWENTY-THREE

CROWN IN THE GUTTER

I pause at the threshold.

The corridor beyond is black—the kind of dark that swallows sound and light and hope. The kind of dark where monsters live.

"You don't have to do this alone," Sable says behind me.

"Yes, I do." I turn to face her one last time. "Whatever's in there—whatever I have to become to stop Parliament—I need to know you'll survive. I need to know someone will remember who I was before."

"Ash—"

"Promise me." I take her hands. Feel the warmth of her, the solidity. "Promise me that if I don't come out, you'll keep fighting. You'll protect our people. You'll build something from whatever's left."

Her eyes are wet. She doesn't cry—she never cries—but I can see the tears she's holding back.

"I promise."

"Then that's enough." I kiss her forehead. Press my lips there for one long moment. "That's everything I need."

I turn. Face the darkness.

And I walk in.

• • •

Greed is different from the others.

It knows me. Knows the hollow place in my chest where poverty carved its home. Knows every night I went to bed hungry so Eli could eat. Every time I counted coins that would never be enough. Every moment I watched people with more take from people with less.

The vision starts small.

A single gold coin in my palm. Warm. Heavy. Real.

Then another. And another. Until I'm standing in a room full of them—gold coins, silver bars, gems that catch the light and scatter it into rainbows. More wealth than I've ever imagined. More than Guttersea has seen in a century.

YOURS, the shard whispers. ALL OF IT. YOU JUST HAVE TO TAKE IT.

"I don't want it."

LIAR.

The coins multiply. The room expands. Now I'm walking through warehouses full of food—grain and fruit and meat, enough to feed every hungry child in the Warrens for a decade.

YOU'VE WATCHED THEM STARVE. YOUR NEIGHBORS. YOUR FRIENDS. YOUR MOTHER, AT THE END, TOO WEAK TO EAT EVEN WHEN YOU FINALLY SCRAPED TOGETHER ENOUGH TO BUY HER BROTH.

"Stop."

THIS COULD FIX IT. ENOUGH MONEY TO BUY MEDICINE. ENOUGH FOOD TO FILL EVERY EMPTY BELLY.

ENOUGH POWER TO MAKE SURE NO ONE YOU LOVE
EVER GOES WITHOUT AGAIN.

The vision shifts. Now I see the people. The ones I couldn't save.
The ones who died because I didn't have enough—enough money,
enough influence, enough of anything that mattered.

Mrs. Delacroix from the third floor, who died of a fever that cost
three silver to cure.

The Tanaka kids, who disappeared into the workhouses because
their parents couldn't pay the rent.

Mama. Always Mama. Coughing blood while I held her hand and
prayed for a miracle I couldn't afford.

ALL OF THEM COULD HAVE BEEN SAVED. ALL OF
THEM WOULD BE ALIVE TODAY IF YOU'D HAD MORE. IF
YOU'D TAKEN MORE. IF YOU'D BEEN WILLING TO DO
WHAT WAS NECESSARY.

"What was necessary?"

WHATEVER IT TOOK.

I feel the truth in that. The cold, hard logic of survival. The part of
me that would have stolen, cheated, killed if it meant keeping the
people I loved alive.

"You're right."

Eli stirs in alarm. *Ash*—

"You're right that I would've done anything. You're right that
poverty killed people I loved. You're right that having more would've
saved them."

The shard pulses with something like triumph.

"But you're wrong about what that means."

I reach into the golden vision. Grab the shard at its center.

"Greed says 'take more so you can have more.' I say 'take less so everyone can have enough.' Greed says 'hoard against the future.' I say 'share because the future isn't promised.' The answer to scarcity isn't acquisition. It's distribution."

The shard fights me. Shows me every person who ever took from me. Every landlord, every tax collector, every merchant who charged more than they should because they knew I couldn't walk away.

WHY SHOULD THEY HAVE WHAT YOU DON'T? WHY SHOULD THEY PROFIT FROM YOUR SUFFERING?

"They shouldn't." I pull the shard closer even as it burns. "But the answer isn't becoming them. The answer is building something where no one has to be them."

I think of the refuge Sable wants to build. The tithe house we'll reclaim. The future where no child has to count coins for their mother's medicine.

Greed screams as I absorb it.

The pain is sharp. Immediate. Every desire I've ever denied, every need I've ever suppressed, every want I've told myself I didn't deserve—all of it flooding through me at once. The shard tries to convince me that wanting is the same as deserving, that hunger justifies any taking.

I hold onto Sable's vision. The house full of people who have enough because everyone shares. The world where scarcity is a problem to solve, not an excuse to exploit.

Greed settles. Quiets. Five shards.

Two to go.

• • •

Wrath has been waiting.

I feel it before I reach for it—a furnace heat radiating from the last orbiting shard, ancient rage that's spent a thousand years with nowhere to go. The anger of every person who was ever hurt by the powerful. The fury of every victim who never got justice.

I know this anger. I've carried it my whole life.

The vision hits like a fist.

I'm in the Cathedral. Parliament's great hall. And lined up before me are everyone who's ever hurt me or the people I love.

The merchant who foreclosed on our apartment when I was seven.

The Warden who broke my arm for begging too close to the temple district.

Cardinal Red, whose policies killed more poor than any plague.

And at the front of the line, smiling that cold smile—Symeon. The man who bound Sable. Who used her. Who treated her like property instead of a person.

THEY DESERVE YOUR WRATH, the shard whispers. And unlike the others, it doesn't feel like temptation. It feels like truth.

"Yes."

THEY HURT PEOPLE. KILLED PEOPLE. DESTROYED LIVES FOR PROFIT AND POWER AND NOTHING MORE THAN BECAUSE THEY COULD.

"Yes."

THEY'VE NEVER BEEN PUNISHED. THEY'VE NEVER BEEN HELD ACCOUNTABLE. JUSTICE HAS NEVER TOUCHED THEM BECAUSE THEY OWN JUSTICE, THEY WRITE THE LAWS, THEY DECIDE WHO'S RIGHTEOUS AND WHO'S CRIMINAL.

"Yes."

Ash. Eli's voice is careful. *This one's different.*

"I know."

The anger is real. The injustice is real. This isn't temptation—it's truth. They DO deserve punishment.

"I know."

So what are you going to do?

I look at the line of enemies. Feel the heat of Wrath's furnace burning through my chest. Every cell in my body wants to hurt them. Wants them to feel what they've made others feel.

Symeon's smile widens. As if he knows I'm going to break. As if he's counting on it.

"What I've always done."

I reach for the shard.

"Choose."

Wrath screams into me. Not like the others—this one doesn't try to seduce or deceive. It just amplifies. Takes the anger I already carry and multiplies it beyond all control.

I see every cruelty I've ever witnessed.

Every child hit by a parent who was hit by their parent who was hit by theirs.

Every cycle of violence perpetuating itself generation after generation.

Every person who was hurt and decided to hurt others because that's all they knew.

THE CYCLE NEVER ENDS. THE ONLY ANSWER IS TO BURN IT ALL DOWN. DESTROY THE DESTROYERS. HURT THE HURTERS. MAKE THEM PAY UNTIL THERE'S NO ONE LEFT TO PAY.

"And then what?"

The shard pauses. Just for a heartbeat.

"When you've burned down the Cathedral—what grows in its place? When you've killed everyone who deserved killing—who decides who's next? When you've made everyone pay—who collects?"

JUSTICE. VENGEANCE. RECKONING.

"No." I pull the shard deeper even as it sears my soul. "That's not justice. That's just more violence. Different direction, same result. More bodies. More pain. More children learning that hurt is all there is."

THEY DESERVE—"They deserve consequences. They deserve to be stopped. But what they DON'T deserve is to turn me into them."

I think of Moe. The Warden who became a protector. The killer who learned to save.

I think of the anger he carried. The rage at everyone who'd made him what he was. And how he chose—every day, every moment—to point that fury at something worth destroying.

"Wrath says 'burn it down.' I say 'build something better.' Wrath says 'make them pay.' I say 'make it so no one else has to.' The answer to violence isn't more violence. It's breaking the cycle. Even when it hurts. Even when they don't deserve the mercy."

The shard fights back. Shows me every person who escaped justice. Every monster who died comfortable in their bed while their victims rotted in unmarked graves.

ISN'T THAT UNFAIR? ISN'T THAT WRONG?

"Yes." The word comes out broken. "It's unfair. It's wrong. And I have to accept it anyway. Because the alternative—becoming just another link in the chain—is worse than injustice. It's surrender."

I think of Moe's final stand. Protecting children instead of punishing the people who made those children orphans.

That's what breaking the cycle looks like. Not revenge. Rescue.

Wrath settles into me like a bed of coals. Still burning. Always burning. But contained now. Directed. A furnace instead of a wildfire.

Six shards.

One to go.

• • •

Hunger has been waiting since I was eleven years old.

I don't have to reach for it. It's already inside me—has been since the night Eli died, since the rune appeared on my wrist, since the first verse came boiling up from somewhere deeper than my throat.

The other shards orbit me now, six vices contained but not destroyed. I can feel them reshaping my soul, trying to find places to settle. My body burns. My mind cracks. Every cell screams that this is too much, that no human vessel was meant to hold this weight.

But there's one more. The heart of the Crown. The hunger that drives all other vices.

You already carry it, Eli says. *You've carried it for years. This isn't about absorbing something new—it's about accepting what you already are.*

"What am I?"

You really don't know?

I feel the Hunger shard pulse in my chest. The void that's been part of me since childhood. The need that's never been satisfied no matter how much I give, how much I heal, how much I sacrifice.

270

"A broken person trying to be less broken."

No. Eli's voice is gentle. *You're a bridge. That's what the Crown was meant to be, Ash. Not a weapon. Not a throne. A bridge between divine and mortal. A way to transform power into service.*

"That's not what I feel. What I feel is hunger."

Because you've been fighting it. The Hunger shard isn't about taking—it's about wanting. About the ache that drives us to become more than we are. It's the reason you heal people even when it costs you. The reason you can't stop giving even when you have nothing left.

I look at the six shards inside me. Pride, Lust, Envy, Sloth, Greed, Wrath. Seven deadly sins—six absorbed, one waiting.

"The wanting never stops."

No. But the wanting can be pointed at something worth wanting. Pride becomes confidence. Lust becomes passion. Envy becomes ambition. Sloth becomes rest. Greed becomes care. Wrath becomes justice.

"And Hunger?"

Hunger becomes love.

The word hits me like a revelation.

Love is hunger, Ash. The need for connection. The ache for someone else. The emptiness that only another person can fill. The Crown wasn't designed to rule—it was designed to yearn. To reach. To bridge the gap between what is and what could be.

I think of Mama, praying over my crib.

I think of Eli, teaching me to read with stolen books.

I think of Sable, choosing me even when I didn't deserve it.

I think of Moe, dying for children he'd never met.

All of them hungry. All of them reaching. All of them bridging gaps that should have been uncrossable.

"I don't want to stop wanting."

Good.

"I want to want better things. Want them more. Want them for everyone, not just myself."

Then accept what you are. Accept the Hunger. Accept that the emptiness isn't a flaw—it's a feature. It's what drives you to fill others because you can never be full yourself.

I close my eyes.

The six shards orbit inside me, each one a weight, each one a wound, each one a truth I've spent my whole life avoiding.

I'm proud. I've always been proud. Convinced I knew better, could do better, was better than the world that tried to crush me.

I'm lustful. I want things. Comfort. Pleasure. Sable's skin against mine. The simple human need to be touched and wanted and loved.

I'm envious. I've spent my life watching others have what I couldn't. Resenting them for it. Using that resentment to fuel my fight even when I knew it was poison.

I'm slothful. Part of me has always wanted to stop. To rest. To let someone else carry the weight for once.

I'm greedy. I want more. More power to protect people. More influence to change things. More time to spend with the people I love.

I'm wrathful. The anger burns in me constantly. At Parliament. At the Church. At everyone who's ever hurt someone weaker than themselves.

And underneath all of it—I'm hungry. I've always been hungry. For connection. For meaning. For something to fill the void that opened when Mama died and Eli followed and I was left alone in a world that didn't care if I lived or died.

"I accept it."

The words come out quiet. Not a proclamation. Just a truth.

"I accept all of it. The sins. The shame. The parts of myself I've tried to hide and failed. I accept that I'm broken and hungry and desperate and proud and wrathful and everything else the Crown holds."

I open my eyes.

"And I accept that none of that makes me unworthy of love. Or incapable of giving it."

The Hunger shard blazes in my chest.

Not fighting me anymore. Resonating.

The other six shards stop orbiting. They align. Click into place like pieces of a puzzle finally finding their pattern.

And the Crown reforms.

• • •

I've been wrong about everything.

The Crown isn't a weapon. It's not a throne or a prison or a tool of control. It's a mirror. A perfect reflection of whoever holds it—every virtue and vice, every strength and weakness, every capacity for love and destruction.

Parliament made it a tyrant because they were tyrants.

I make it something else.

The power floods through me—overwhelming, incomprehensible, divine in the truest sense of the word. I feel myself expanding, becoming more than flesh and bone, perceiving the city not as a place but as a web of connections, a network of needs and hungers and desperate hopes.

I see everything.

The ether still flowing toward me—blue-green light streaming from every den and stash and desperate hand in Ashvein.

The infected thousands, bodies burning with divine contamination, dying slowly from Parliament's weaponized plague.

The survivors huddled in basements and shelters, praying to gods who've never answered.

And Sable. Standing at the edge of the ruins. Watching me become something else. Terrified. Hopeful. Loving me anyway.

ASH. Eli's voice is different now. Part of me. Part of the Crown. *WHAT ARE YOU GOING TO DO?*

The ether is still coming. Rivers of addiction and desperation, feeding into me because I'm the Crown now and the Crown was always meant to consume.

I could take it. All of it. Become something truly divine—a god of hunger and power, fed by the city's pain, unlimited and eternal.

I could rule.

I could destroy.

I could become exactly what Parliament wanted to create.

Or.

"Eli."

YEAH?

"What did Mama always say about power?"

A pause. Then: *"Power isn't for keeping. It's for spending on people who can't spend it themselves."*

I grab the flow of ether.

Not to absorb it. Not to feed my hunger or fuel my power.

To transform it.

The Hunger shard knows how. That's what it was always meant for—not taking, but changing. Not consuming, but converting. The bridge between divine and mortal isn't about bringing heaven down to earth. It's about lifting earth up to heaven.

I don't take the ether. I burn it.

Every drop of the drug in Ashvein. Every vial and powder and dose. Every fix that was ever used to escape pain instead of healing it.

The Crown converts it all. Turns addiction into light. Desperation into hope. The city's suffering transmuted into the city's salvation.

The infected feel it first. The divine contamination in their veins— the poison Parliament planted—ignites. Not to burn them. To transform them. The shard dust that was killing them becomes something else. Not full Conduits—they'll never be that. But… cleansed. Changed. Given a chance to live instead of a sentence to die.

The ether dens empty. Not because I'm taking anything from anyone. Because the hunger I'm feeding into the city is replacing the hunger they've been feeding with poison.

The ether is gone.

And I'm dying.

• • •

I knew I would be. The Crown isn't meant for mortal flesh. Every second I hold it, it burns through me—years consumed, cells destroyed, the fundamental architecture of my body failing under weight it was never designed to bear.

I can feel my hair going gray. My skin going thin. My heart stuttering as organs that should last decades start to fail.

ASH. YOU NEED TO—

"I know."

YOU'RE KILLING YOURSELF.

"I know."

THERE HAS TO BE ANOTHER WAY. THERE HAS TO BE—

"There isn't." I say it gentle. Certain. "The Crown needs a vessel. Without me, it reforms. It finds someone else. Someone who might not make the choices I'm making."

THEN LET IT FIND SOMEONE.

"Let it find someone weaker? Someone Parliament could control? Someone who'd use this power to rule instead of serve?" I shake my head. "This is what I was made for, Eli. The bridge. The vessel. The street prophet who became something more so the streets could become something better."

BUT I JUST GOT YOU BACK. WE JUST—I CAN'T LOSE YOU AGAIN.

"You're not losing me."

I reach inside myself. Find the place where Eli's ghost has lived since the Blood-Market. The anchor the Hunger shard created between us.

"You're going to become part of this. Part of me. Part of what the Crown becomes next."

WHAT DO YOU MEAN?

"The Crown absorbed Parliament's faith. Their accumulated belief. But it's empty now. Just power without purpose, hunger without direction."

I feel him understand.

"I'm going to fill it with something else. With everyone I've ever loved. Everyone who's ever believed in me. Mama. You. Sable. Moe. Every gutter monk who prayed for a miracle and got me instead."

ASH—

"You'll still be here, Eli. Not haunting me. Not fading. Part of the Crown. Part of whatever I become. You, and everyone else who shaped me into someone worth saving."

He doesn't respond. But I feel something shift inside me. Fear becoming acceptance. Grief becoming peace.

I love you, big brother.

"I love you too."

Make it mean something.

The golden light blazes brighter.

I scream—can't help it—as the transformation completes. The Crown settles into my bones. My flesh. My soul. Seven sins becoming seven virtues. Hunger becoming love. A weapon becoming a bridge.

The light explodes outward.

And Ashvein changes forever.

CHAPTER TWENTY-FOUR

THE PRICE OF DIVINITY

Three days since I became something else.

I sit in the ruins of an old shrine, miles from Ashvein, miles from anyone I might hurt. The stones are ancient—older than the city, older than Parliament, maybe older than the Crown itself. Whoever built this place worshipped something that left no name behind.

I haven't slept since the Spire. Every time I close my eyes, I see sins. Not mine—everyone's. The merchant in Ashvein who waters his milk. The priest who touches children. The mother who wishes her daughter had never been born. Even from here, miles away, I can feel them all. Their guilt. Their shame. Their small cruelties and large ones.

I know things I never wanted to know.

The Crown doesn't sleep. The Crown JUDGES. And now I'm part of it—or it's part of me—and I can't stop judging even when I want to.

I look at my hands. They glow faintly in the darkness—gold light bleeding through skin that used to be brown and is now something between. Like candlelight trapped under parchment. I touched a tree yesterday. Just to see. It caught fire. I touched a stream. The water boiled. I touched a bird that landed too close, curious about the strange light. It died before it could scream.

My touch kills now. My touch BURNS.

278

And I think about Sable—her blistered palms, the horror in her eyes—and I want to scream.

• • •

There's a pool in the center of the shrine. Still water, dark as memory.

I lean over it. Force myself to look.

The face staring back isn't mine. Not entirely. The eyes are gold—solid gold, no white, no pupil. They glow even in shadow. The rune on my chest has spread, climbing my neck in delicate tracework, reaching toward my jaw. Gold lines against skin that's lost its warmth.

But it's the age that breaks me.

I was twenty-three. I looked thirty-five before the Crown—the Relic Tongue takes payment in years, and I'd been spending heavily. Now I look fifty. Maybe older. Deep lines carved around eyes that shouldn't exist. Gray hair—not just threads anymore, but thick streaks running through what used to be black. My hands are veined, spotted, the hands of an old man.

The Crown took decades from me in seconds.

I'm dying. I can feel it. Not fast—the Crown won't let me die fast—but steady. Inevitable. The power is burning through my body like fire through paper. I might have years left. I might have months.

Nobody's held the full Crown in a thousand years. There's no instruction manual for becoming a god.

• • •

Pride. Whispering in the back of my skull.

They never stop. Seven voices, seven sins, seven fragments of something that used to be divine whispering constantly in the cathedral of my skull.

279

I press my hands against my temples. "SHUT UP."

The words come out with power behind them. The stones of the shrine crack. The pool ripples outward. Somewhere in the distance, birds startle from their roosts.

The voices quiet. Not gone—just waiting. Biding their time. They know I'll slip eventually. They're patient. They've been waiting a thousand years. What's a few more days?

• • •

Day four.

I try to pray. The words come out wrong—layered, echoing, like seven voices speaking through one mouth. The blessing I try to speak turns into something else. Not a curse exactly. Just... more. More power than I intended. More weight. More consequence.

I try to bless a patch of dead grass. It explodes into growth—then keeps growing. Vines shooting up, flowers blooming and dying in seconds, the whole lifecycle of a garden compressed into a minute.

Too much. I can't calibrate. Can't control the output.

• • •

Day five.

I try to see normally.

There's a settlement a few miles east. Farmers. Shepherds. Simple people living simple lives. I turn my attention toward them—And I see EVERYTHING.

The farmer's affair with his neighbor's wife. The shepherd's stolen lambs. The children's petty cruelties to each other. The grandmother's secret hatred for the family that takes care of her. Sin after sin after sin, piling up like bodies.

These aren't bad people. They're just PEOPLE. Flawed. Imperfect. Human.

But the Crown doesn't see nuance. The Crown sees transgression. Failure. Guilt.

I tear my attention away. Fall to my knees. Vomit nothing—I haven't eaten in days, the Crown doesn't need food—and gasp for breath that tastes like ash.

How am I supposed to live like this? How am I supposed to look at anyone without seeing their worst moments? Their darkest thoughts? The things they hide even from themselves?

• • •

Day six.

I give up.

I sit at the edge of the pool and think about stepping in. The water probably can't kill me—I'm not sure anything can anymore—but maybe I could stay under long enough to forget. Long enough to stop seeing. Long enough to find some kind of peace.

And I do. God help me, I do.

I think about Sable. Her blistered hands. The horror when she touched me. Even if I go back, even if I learn to control this—will she ever be able to look at me the same way? Will anyone?

I'm a monster now. A necessary monster, maybe—the Crown had to go somewhere, and better me than no one—but a monster nonetheless.

I lean forward. The water is cold. Welcoming.

And then I hear him.

Eli. Not a voice exactly—just a presence. A warmth in the cold. A whisper of something that isn't the shards, isn't the sins, isn't the endless judgment.

I promised.

And if there's one thing our mama taught us, it's that promises mean something. Even the ones that hurt to keep. ESPECIALLY the ones that hurt to keep.

I pull back from the water. The shards scream disappointment. I ignore them.

If I'm going to be a monster, I'll be a monster that keeps his word.

• • •

Day twelve.

I'm sitting in meditation when it happens. Not praying—the Crown twists prayers into something else. Just sitting. Breathing. Trying to exist without drowning.

A fox approaches the shrine. Curious. Hungry. Looking for scraps.

I watch it with my new eyes. See its sins—such as they are. A stolen chicken. An abandoned den when the pups were too young. Animal sins. Survival sins.

And underneath that—just a fox. Scared and hungry and trying to live another day.

I don't reach for it. I've learned that lesson. But I do something else.

I LOOK PAST THE SINS.

It takes everything I have. The Crown wants to judge—that's what it's FOR. But underneath the judgment, underneath the power, I'm still

282

me. Still Ash. Still the street prophet who learned that everyone carries weight they didn't choose.

The fox isn't its sins. Neither is the farmer, or the priest, or anyone else. They're people who've made mistakes. People who are trying. People who deserve mercy, not judgment.

The Crown recoils. It doesn't like mercy. Mercy wasn't in its design.

But I am.

I force the vision to soften. Push the sin-sight to the background. It doesn't disappear—I don't think it ever will—but it dims. Becomes something I can live with instead of something that drowns me.

The fox looks at me. I look at the fox.

Neither of us burns.

Progress.

• • •

Day twenty.

A traveler finds the shrine. Lost, thirsty, looking for water.

I hide in the shadows at first. Watch him drink from the pool, refill his canteen. He's a merchant—middle-aged, road-worn, carrying samples of cloth to sell in the eastern villages.

His sins scroll through my mind without my permission. Price gouging. Adultery. A lie to his mother on her deathbed. The usual human weight.

I push it aside. Look at the rest of him.

He misses his children. He's scared of getting old. He gives coins to beggars when no one's watching. He sang to his wife when she was dying, even though he can't carry a tune.

He's a person. Complicated. Contradictory. Neither good nor evil, just… trying.

Like all of us.

He sees me step out of the shadows. His eyes go wide—my face, my golden eyes, the light leaking from my skin.

"Please," he whispers. "Please don't—"

"I'm not going to hurt you." My voice is still layered, but I've learned to speak softer. To make it less terrifying. "Drink. Rest. The road is long."

He stares at me. Trembling. "What are you?"

"Something new." The truth. "But I'm not your enemy. Go home to your children. Tell them you love them. You don't say it enough."

His face goes pale. How do I know about his children? How do I know he doesn't say it enough?

I know everything about him. Everything he's ever done or wanted or feared.

But I don't have to let that define him.

"Go," I say again. "Live well. That's all any of us can do."

He runs. I let him.

• • •

And I realize I'm ready.

Ready to go back. Ready to face Sable and the city and whatever comes next. Ready to live with what I've become, even if it means living with pain.

I start walking toward Ashvein.

Six weeks. That's how long it takes to learn the basics. To dim the sin-sight enough to function. To contain the burning enough to maybe—maybe—touch someone without killing them. Not perfectly. Not safely. Just enough.

I made a promise.

Time to keep it.

CHAPTER TWENTY-FIVE

THE MORNING AFTER

The first light of dawn paints the ruins gold.

Not the false gold of the Crown—something simpler. Something older. Sunlight finding its way through smoke and ash, touching the broken stones like a blessing nobody asked for.

I watch it spread across the battlefield. Watch it find the faces of the living and the dead alike. Watch it turn horror into something almost beautiful.

"The city's waking up," Sable says beside me.

"Is it?"

"Listen."

I listen. Beneath the crackle of dying fires, beneath the groans of the wounded, I hear it—sounds of life. Voices calling to each other. Footsteps moving through rubble. The clatter of tools as people begin to dig out.

Ashvein doesn't know how to stay quiet. Even after a night like this, it keeps talking. Keeps breathing. Keeps refusing to die.

"They're going to need help," I say.

"Yes."

"A lot of help."

"Yes."

I look at my hands one more time. At the gold light that flickers beneath my skin. At the power I never asked for and can't give back.

"Then let's get started."

Six weeks since the world ended.

Six weeks since the sky turned gold and the Ivory Spire collapsed and every drop of ether in Ashvein turned to dust that tasted like forgiveness.

Six weeks since he touched me and I burned.

I run a refuge now. The House of Vice Redeemed, we call it—an old tithe house I claimed when Parliament's power shattered. We take in the addicts, the withdrawing, the desperate. Mother Vera's gutter priests help me run it.

Most days, it's enough to keep me from thinking too much.

Most days.

The scars on my palms have healed. Sort of. The burns from when I touched him—they sealed over with silver scar tissue, same as all my other marks. But they still ache when I think about him. Still warm when I feel him in the distance, alive, somewhere out beyond the city walls.

He's out there. Learning. Becoming.

And I'm here. Waiting. Like I promised.

• • •

The funeral was three weeks ago. Three thousand people came.

Ex-Wardens who'd heard what he did. Street kids who'd seen him share his meals. The parents of children who survived because he stood between them and the Executioner. Even the Bronze Syndicate sent representatives—old enemies who knew a warrior's death when they saw one.

We didn't have a body. The Cathedral rubble was too deep, too dangerous to excavate.

But we had his name. We had the stories.

Mother Vera led the service. She told them about the morning we found out—how I went to tell Mama Ruth, and the old woman just nodded. Like she'd known. Like she'd been preparing for this her whole life.

"He told me," Ruth said, her voice steady. "The last time he visited. He said he'd finally found people worth dying for."

She looked at me with eyes that had seen too much.

"He was right. He died enough."

I didn't understand what she meant. Not then. Now I think I do.

The gutter priests sang him home. Songs I'd never heard, in languages I didn't recognize. The crowd joined in anyway—humming, swaying, letting grief move through them like a river finding its course.

They never found Mercyless. His sword. It vanished with him, buried in the Cathedral rubble or taken by someone who didn't deserve it.

The gutter priests say it's still down there, still waiting. They say someday, when the right person comes along, it'll find its way back to the light.

I think they're telling themselves a story to make the loss hurt less.

But I hope they're right.

I brought the orphans to the funeral. The three kids he used to leave coins for. The fierce girl didn't cry. The boy sobbed the whole time. And the little one—the one with the rag doll named Button—she just held my hand and stared at the memorial stone like she was waiting for him to come back.

"He was brave," she whispered. "Wasn't he?"

"The bravest," I told her. "The bravest man I ever knew."

The cat came too. The gray tabby with the torn ear. She sat at the edge of the crowd, watching, like she was paying respects in her own way.

I've been feeding her since. Someone has to.

• • •

Winter left the day after the funeral.

I found her at the docks at dawn, boarding a ship bound for the northern territories. She looked different—thinner, older, the gold fading from her eyes but not gone entirely.

She'd managed to extract two of the shards before Ash absorbed the rest. Sloth and Envy, sleeping in lead-lined cases, heading north with her.

"You could stay," I said. "Help rebuild. We could use you."

"No." Her voice was flat. Empty. "You couldn't. Not after what I almost did."

"Winter—"

"I was going to take it all, Sable." She finally looked at me. The woman who'd been my queen, my mentor, the closest thing to a mother I'd had since I was twelve—she looked broken. "The Crown. Ash. Everything. The shards showed me what I could become, and I WANTED it. I wanted it so badly I was willing to burn everything we built."

"You stopped."

"Ash stopped me. The difference matters."

She picked up her bag.

"I'm going somewhere I can't hurt anyone. Somewhere these shards can sleep without corrupting what's around them. Somewhere I can learn to be... less."

"Will you come back?"

She didn't answer. Just walked up the gangplank without looking back.

I watched the ship until it disappeared beyond the harbor. Part of me hated her for leaving. Part of me understood why she had to.

Mostly I just felt tired.

Everyone leaves, eventually. Everyone dies or departs or becomes something you can't follow.

I'm starting to think that's just what love costs.

• • •

Six weeks to the day, I feel him coming.

Before I go to meet him, I visit the shrine.

The gutter monks have rebuilt it—not the old cathedral that collapsed, but something new. Something that fits who we are now. A temple made from salvage and hope, rising from the rubble of the Warrens like a prayer made physical.

Mother Vera meets me at the entrance. She's aged ten years in the last six weeks, but her eyes are still sharp, still seeing things the rest of us miss.

"He's coming," she says. Not a question.

"How did you know?"

"The addicts felt it first. They always do." She gestures toward the temple's interior. "Come. See what we've built in his name."

The inside of the shrine is nothing like Parliament's cathedrals. No gold. No jewels. No scripture carved in marble by craftsmen who never knew hunger.

Instead, there are hands.

Hundreds of them. Thousands. Pressed into the clay walls in different sizes—children's hands, workers' hands, elderly hands, hands that have never held anything more precious than a half-portion of bread.

"Everyone who comes here leaves a mark," Vera explains. "A reminder that they existed. That they mattered. That someone saw them."

"Ash would like this."

"Ash inspired this." She leads me deeper into the temple. "The street faith has changed, Sable. It's not just desperate prayers anymore. It's becoming something else. Something organized."

I see what she means. There are rooms here—small, simple, but clearly designed for specific purposes. A kitchen serving food to the hungry. A clinic treating the sick with the last of our ether supplies. A schoolroom where someone is teaching children to read.

"This is what we do now," Vera says. "Not waiting for miracles. Making them ourselves."

"And when the power runs out? When the ether's gone?"

"Then we find other ways." She smiles. "That's what the streets have always done. Survived by adapting. By refusing to die. By finding purpose in the gutter when the spires cast us out."

We reach a back room—smaller than the others, lit by candles. In the center, a simple altar holds a single object: a crystal vial, glowing faintly gold.

"What is that?"

"The last of him. What was left behind when he absorbed the Crown." Vera's voice is reverent. "The monks have been guarding it. Studying it. Trying to understand what he became."

I step closer. The vial pulses when I approach—responding to the silver scars on my body, the echoes that still connect me to Ash's power.

"He's not dead," I say. "He's out there. Learning."

"We know. But having a piece of him here..." Vera touches the altar gently. "It gives people hope. Reminds them that the prophet who saved them is real. That what happened at the Spire wasn't a dream."

"It wasn't a dream. It was a war."

"Wars end. What matters is what we build after."

I look at the vial. At the golden light that reminds me of his eyes—his old eyes, the human ones, before the Crown remade him.

"Do you think he's still him? Still Ash?"

Vera considers the question. "I think he's more Ash than he's ever been. He just has to remember it."

"How do you know?"

"Because the Crown didn't choose a saint." She meets my eyes. "It chose a street kid who couldn't walk past someone in pain. A hustler who gave away more than he kept. A prophet who never wanted to be worshipped—he just wanted to help."

"That's who the Crown chose. That's who it became. And that's who'll come back to us, when he's ready."

I want to believe her. Want to trust that the man I love is still in there, somewhere beneath the power and the judgment and the seven sins whispering in his skull.

I guess I'll find out soon enough.

"Thank you," I tell her. "For keeping this place alive."

"Thank Ash. And everyone who believed in him." She walks me to the temple's exit. "Go. He's almost here. He'll need you."

"What if I can't help him? What if he's too far gone?"

Vera puts her hand on my arm. Warm. Steady.

"You'll know when you see him. Love isn't complicated, child. It just is. Either he's still yours, or he isn't. Either way—you'll know."

I step out of the temple into the afternoon light.

• • •

The mark over my heart—the silver scar that appeared during my transformation—blazes warm. Not painful. Just… aware. Like a compass finding north.

I'm on the roof of the refuge when he arrives. The same roof where I used to sit with Ash before everything went wrong, back when we were just two broken people trying to figure out how to love each other.

He comes up the fire escape. Slow. Deliberate. Giving me time to run if I want to.

I don't run.

He steps onto the roof, and I see what he's become.

The eyes hit me first. Gold. Solid gold, glowing faintly even in the afternoon sun. No iris. No pupil. Just light, contained and constant.

Then the age. He left looking thirty-five, ravaged by the Relic Tongue. He came back looking fifty. Maybe older. Gray streaking through his hair. Lines carved deep around those impossible eyes. Hands that used to be young now veined and spotted like an elder's.

But underneath all that—It's still him.

The set of his shoulders. The way he stands like he's ready to take a blow for someone. The way his face softens when he looks at me.

"Hey," he says.

His voice is layered—multiple tones running underneath, like seven people whispering along with him. But he's learned to make it soft. To make it almost human.

"Hey," I answer. My voice cracks.

He doesn't come closer. Stands at the edge of the roof, ten feet away, hands in his pockets. Same ratty hoodie. Same worn boots. The Crown of the old gods, dressed like a street kid from Guttersea.

"I can—" He stops. Swallows. "I can control it better now. The burning. It's not—I won't kill you if you touch me. Probably."

"Probably?"

"I practiced. On trees. On rocks. On a merchant who wandered too close." A ghost of a smile. "He lived. Mostly unscathed."

"That's reassuring."

"Sable." His voice breaks. The layers scatter for a moment, and underneath them is just Ash—scared and tired and hoping. "I don't know if I can touch you without hurting you. I don't know if I can ever touch anyone again. I see everything now—every sin, every secret, every dark thing people hide. I can dim it, but I can't turn it off. I'm not—"

He stops. The gold eyes close.

"I'm not what you fell in love with. I'm something else now. Something worse. And if you want me to go—"

"Stop."

I cross the roof.

He tenses—preparing to pull back, to protect me from himself—but I don't let him.

I take his hand.

. . .

It burns.

Not like fire—like sunlight concentrated too intensely, like standing too close to a furnace. His skin is hot against mine, almost unbearably hot, and I can feel the power thrumming through him—vast and terrible and barely contained.

I wince. Can't help it.

He tries to pull away.

"Sable, don't—"

I hold on tighter.

"Does it hurt?" he asks. The layers in his voice are trembling.

"Yes."

"Then let go."

I look at him. At the gold eyes that used to be brown. At the aged face that used to be young. At the man who gave up his humanity to save a city that never deserved him.

"No."

His breath catches.

"I've been burned before," I tell him. "I've been broken and remade and owned by people who didn't deserve me. I've got more scars than skin at this point. What's one more?"

"This is different—"

"No, it isn't."

I step closer. Feel the heat radiating off him, the power barely leashed. My silver scars pulse in response, answering his gold light with their own glow.

"You think I don't know what I'm getting into? I knew the moment I saw you walk through that door. You're going to hurt me. Not because you want to—because you can't not. That's what love is. That's what it's always been."

"I can see your sins." His voice is raw. "Every dark thing you've ever done. Every secret you've hidden. I can't turn it off, Sable. I'll always know—"

"Good."

I lift his hand to my face. Press his burning palm against my cheek.

It sears. I let it.

"Then you know everything. No more secrets. No more hiding. You see the worst of me, and I'll learn to live with you seeing it."

His other hand comes up—hesitant, trembling. He cups my face like I'm something fragile, something that might break if he holds too tight.

It burns. Both palms. Heat spreading across my skin, not quite pain but not quite comfort either.

I don't pull away.

"I love you," he says. The layers harmonize for once, all seven voices speaking in unison. "I love you, and I don't know if I can give you a normal life. I don't know if I can give you anything except burns and truth and whatever time I have left."

"How much time?"

"I don't know. Years. Months. The Crown is burning through me faster than a human body should be able to take."

He smiles—sad and beautiful and so very Ash.

"Probably shouldn't have absorbed the whole thing at once. But you know me. Never learned to do anything halfway."

I laugh. It comes out broken.

"Then we better make the most of it."

I pull him close. His arms wrap around me—careful, so careful, trying to minimize the contact, trying to spare me the burn.

I don't let him be careful. I press myself against him, feel the heat sink through my clothes, through my skin, into my bones.

It hurts.

It's going to keep hurting, every time we touch, for however long we have.

Worth it.

We stand there on the roof, the city spread beneath us, the sun setting gold and red and purple over the harbor. Two broken people holding each other. A shadow and a crown. A woman made of scars and a man made of light.

It's not the ending I wanted. Not the happily-ever-after Mama Ruth used to tell stories about.

But it's ours.

And it's enough.

• • •

The next morning, we walk through the city together.

Ash keeps his hood up. The eyes are hard to hide—he wears dark glasses that barely dim the gold—but people are too busy rebuilding to look too closely. They see a tall man with gray hair walking beside a woman with silver scars. Nothing special. Nothing divine.

He stops at a corner where a mother is begging for help. Her child is sick—one of the withdrawal cases that didn't recover right, still fighting the effects of ether even weeks later.

Ash kneels down. Speaks words that don't sound like any language I know—the Relic Tongue, but deeper, richer, layered with the Crown's power.

The child's breathing steadies. Color returns to their cheeks. The fever breaks.

Ash doesn't touch them. Doesn't need to anymore. The power flows through his words alone.

But when he stands, I see him wince. See him age a little more—just a fraction, just a whisper, but I see it.

Every miracle costs him. Every blessing takes a piece of the time he has left.

I want to tell him to stop. To save himself. To let the city fix its own problems.

But that wouldn't be Ash.

So I just take his hand—feel the burn, let it warm me—and walk beside him to the next person who needs help.

That's what we do now. That's who we are.

A prophet who became a god and chose to stay in the gutter anyway.

A shadow who became a force and chose to protect instead of destroy.

Two people who love each other despite the pain it costs.

I don't know how long we have. Months. Years. Maybe less. The Crown is burning through him, and every miracle makes it worse.

But that's true of everyone, isn't it?

We're all dying. We're all running out of time. The only question is what we do with the time we have.

Ash chose to spend his helping people.

I choose to spend mine beside him.

• • •

At the end of the day, we return to the refuge.

Kira meets us at the door with blankets that need washing and supplies that need organizing. The orphans run past, chasing each other through the halls. The cat appears from somewhere, winding around my legs, demanding fish.

Life. Messy and complicated and full of people who need things.

Ash stops in the doorway. Looks out at the city—his city, the gutter kingdom he's been protecting since before he knew what protection cost.

"You know what Eli told me?" he asks. "Right before I absorbed the Crown?"

"What?"

"He said the shards would either destroy me or transform me. That I'd either become what Parliament feared or what the streets needed."

"And which one are you?"

He pulls his hood back down. Shoves his hands in his pockets. Becomes, for all appearances, just another street kid trying to survive another day.

But I can see the light behind his eyes. The power coiled beneath his skin. The Crown that chose to serve instead of rule.

He grins.

"The Crown ain't gone. It's just wearin' a hoodie now."

I roll my eyes. Take his hand. Let it burn.

"Come on, prophet. We've got work to do."

We head inside together.

Two broken people.

One impossible love.

A city that's learning to breathe again.

It's not perfect. It's not painless.

It's just what we have.

And it's enough.

ABOUT THE AUTHOR

Lampert X Griffin Urban Universe writes urban fantasy that explores the spaces where faith meets the streets, where power costs everything, and where even the broken can become something more.

Book Two of The Hood & The Halo Trilogy

Coming Soon

www.ingramcontent.com/pod-product-compliance
Lightning Source LLC
Chambersburg PA
CBHW070849260626
47170CB00007B/2557